# BURN

a Deep 8 novel

---

## KENZIE MACALLAN

**BURN**
**a Deep 8 novel**

Copyright © 2022 Kenzie Macallan

Published by Steel Butterfly Press

ISBN No. 978-1-7378014-3-6

Cover design © 2022 teblackdesigns.com

## Praise for Kenzie Macallan

"Oh man what a story. Couldn't put it down. So much going on that I don't see how Declan gets through it all. Olivia has been through a lot also, but it's going to take a village as the saying goes. Who's next in line to help take down Deep 8?"

**Jnorri64, BookBub, 5 stars**

"This series is getting better with each book, I went into this series reluctantly but have come to love every bit of it. There's action, mystery and romance. I'm already looking forward to the next one in the series which will be Campbell's story."

**Woodatsi, Goodreads, 5 stars**

"This romantic suspense isn't your usual fast paced action story. The story unfolds slowly. As I read, I felt sad for Declan & his pain. I was rooting for him to see what was right in front of him. Liv is strong yet so angry & it's understandable. I kept turning the pages as the action heated up & waited for the HEA they deserved! Good book indeed!"

**Rebecca, BookBub, 5 stars**

"This installment of the Deep 8 series follows Declan and Olivia. And PHEW it is steamy and fast paced. Declan- a scientist who lost his memories in an accident is desperate to remember what happened during that time. What will happen with him an Olivia? You won't want to miss this !!! Read if you love: SPICE!!!!"

**Gabrielle Baker, NetGalley, 5 stars**

Wow! This was the first book I read from this author and it was phenomenal to say the least! I'd rate it 10 stars if I could. Make sure you have tissues nearby. I found tears streaming down my face at times with everything Declan went through. If you like romantic suspense, then this is a must read in my opinion. Highly recommend!

**Shopacz, BookBub, 5 stars**

*"We are products of our past, but we don't have to be prisoners of it."*

*- Rick Warren*

## Chapter One

Declan

Dark Lord.

That's the call sign my new crew at MBK Global Security gave me. They think it's funny. They don't know how close they are to the truth.

Mac, one of my younger brothers, is one of them. He's filled with goodness and shines like a goddamn star. I'm the black hole—the shadow lurking in the periphery, absorbing the darkness others pretend not to see.

Goodness bounces off me like bullets off Kevlar. There is something fundamentally wrong with me. Maybe that's why I was so damn good at MI6. I could predict the moves of men with blackened souls, use their own wickedness against them. But the irony? No matter how many monsters I took down, I never stopped feeling like one myself.

Since my accident, I'm a ghost of the man I was. The scars may have healed, but the fire never left me. Lingering beneath my skin, it flickers in the nightmares I refuse to face. Happiness isn't for men like me. That feeling is a distant memory. I chase shadows instead—pain over peace, longing over love. If there's a God, he should've let me burn to ash.

I have a trail of relationship disasters littering my wake, making sure I don't stay long enough to settle in. Screwing things up seems to be my specialty but it keeps me from truly being seen.

Darkness surrounds me, and I find comfort here, although some of this is a self-induced fortress of protection, keeping people at arm's length.

By a twist of fate, the Dark Lord must go back to the castle that burned down around him. There are some things a man never comes back from. The events that happened here changed me forever.

I've had more than my fair share of bad luck, as life keeps slugging away at me. Coming back was never my intention, but duty supersedes everything else. It has been my purpose in life, the motivation to live.

Lost in dark memories, I amble through the streets of the city. Cologne, Germany, was the city where I lost everything. Where something was taken from me, ripped away in a haze of smoke and blood. Yet I feel like I left something behind here, something I yearn for.

This city makes me edgy. Memories claw at my mind like ghosts reaching from the past. I should remember everything about this place, yet parts of it are missing—fragments of time lost in a black abyss. I don't know if I want them back.

My brothers and teammates think this new assignment is going to be a breakthrough for me, life-changing. What they don't know is, I've already had a life-changing experience, and it sucked, pulling me further into my sad existence.

This is not what I had in mind for my first assignment with the security firm. My brother, Mac, Mr. Good Guy, thought this would be the best transition out of MI6, but I'm having second thoughts. The goal is to get this assignment done and get out. The less time I spend here, the better. My demons live here, and I don't want to visit them.

I pull my coat tighter and flip up my collar. My boots echo against the worn cobblestones as I walk along the Rhine. The bright colors of spring have wilted away as the sun beats down on their beauty.

The heat of summer in this part of Germany is never overbearing, so I can evade the questions about my choice of long-sleeve T-shirts and camouflage jackets.

A smile pulls at my lips when I hear my cell phone ring with "The Imperial March" from *Star Wars*. The song is a perfect fit for the person calling me.

Neil McFadden.

Ex-boss from MI6. The man who sent me here on an off-the-books op riddled with more holes than Swiss cheese. We think a group called Deep 8 is developing a deadly biochemical weapon.

"Neil," I answer, voice flat.

"I see you made it." His voice has a softer tone than usual.

I sit on a bench under a tree, watching an enormous party boat float by while tourists snap photos of the cityscape behind me. I make sure to flip them off. Their gasps and hushed whispers amuse me.

"I always make it in, but I don't always get out unscathed, as we both know so well. What do you have for me, oh wise one?" My reminder to him why I don't want to be here.

Neil exhales. "Declan, I wouldn't send you back there if I had a choice. But you know this city, and your background in biochem makes you the best man for the job."

I don't care about his reasons. "Who's my contact?"

I'm not sure I care about this assignment, but our

teammate, Beck, was poisoned by a drug that came from someone working here.

Poisoning people doesn't sit well with me. A drug that could bring soldiers to their end will not happen on my watch. Once a soldier, always a soldier. We always have each other's backs.

Neil hesitates. That alone sends a warning through my bloodstream."You'll report to Bio2Chem tomorrow as Declan Craig. The receptionist will give you the details."

I sit up. "I'm going in as Declan Craig again? Won't it be odd I'm returning five years later?"

"It's perfect. Given the circumstances last time you worked for them, it makes sense. Your backstory is that you took some time off after the accident and worked for another company close to home. I emailed you the information in your profile. They will suspect even less," Neil explains.

My gut clenches. "Shouldn't I have a full dossier on the person I'm working with? This is unorthodox, even for an off-book op," I question, my voice laced with irritation. Everything about this mission is going against my grain.

"Trust me. This is the only way to get in under the radar. The situation is sensitive. We need to take necessary precautions. The less you know right now, the better. I want you to remember this is for the best."

The line goes dead.

What the fuck does that mean?

Neil has always been straightforward and always watches out for his team. This is not like him. He's hiding something, and I intend to find out what it is. I don't need his cryptic shit right now.

I stuff my phone in my pocket and walk north, up the river. My instinct fires up. Guttural German words surround me, and I easily flip into understanding their meaning.

German is a fluent language for me and helps me blend in, survive, and stay hidden in plain sight.

Languages are like music. Every language has a different beat, inflection, and rhythm. I can feel the culture through speaking the native tongue and slip into my undercover zone. Most people are none the wiser about my Scottish origins. I even embrace the local fare.

The food in Cologne is to die for if you know where to dine, but I'm headed to the cluster of pubs closer to the center of town. During my last stay here, I gave a whole new meaning to the words *pub hopping*. I was the closer, in more ways than one.

Passing by various places brings flashes of memories. The images come to me like a movie trailer in fast forward. I can't make out if the theme is from *Hangover* or *Die Hard* with a splash of *Fifty Shades of Grey*. Many of my memories from my time here are gone, and I consider it a blessing for many reasons.

I stop in front of my favorite place, where I used to hang out after work. The black Guinness umbrellas set up outside are the lure. My brothers and I have Guinness running through our veins. The arched, deep-red, glass-paned door opens too easily as I peer in, knowing I'm headed in the wrong direction, as always. *Why change bad decision-making now?*

The interior reminds me of my homeland. The tables aren't pretty or polished but scuffed, old, and used like people enjoy being here. Red leather stools are scattered around the low tables where people crowd together to share their laughter and woes over a beer.

"Brennan?" I hear a voice from my past behind me. "Brennan, is that you?" he speaks to me in German.

Brennan is the German word for burn. They used to be in

awe of how I could shoot flames out of my mouth with a shot of hard liquor and a match. The nickname makes me flinch. He couldn't possibly know how painful the name is for me now.

I turn around with a well-rehearsed, charming grin pasted on my face.

"Oskar, it's me, in the flesh," I reply in German, cringing at the double meaning of my words. Scarred flesh is evidence of the nightmare that swallowed me whole.

He wraps me in one of his bear hugs as I hug him back with the same familiarity. Oskar is a permanent fixture at this pub. His hugs are notorious.

Sadness rises to the surface as I breathe it in, knowing I will never be a happy-go-lucky guy like Oskar. We stand for a minute too long as I fight the tears of everything I've lost since the last time I was here.

He holds me by the shoulders, away from him.

"It's been too long, my friend. Please sit down. Let me pour you a Guinness." He rushes behind the bar.

I hold up my hands. "Not today. I'm just here for lunch. The flight was long, and I need to stay hydrated. Just water, please."

I'm playing a dangerous game with my sobriety. My weakness for alcohol remains, but the crowd is light, and I can stick to the food. At thirty-seven, it's about time I grow up and commit to fixing the things that can be fixed. I'm the house you buy knowing you're going to have to do a complete gut job and renovate. The outside is bright and shiny, but the interior looks like a wrecking ball went through it.

"You back for a while? Do you need me to hook you up?"

I shrug. "Don't know. I'll see how things go." I wink. He

knows I have a thing for blond-haired, blue-eyed women, but I'm not sure why.

They are abundant here, so getting one into my bed won't be a problem. I crave the company, just not the attachment. There's too much for me to lose and plenty more for them to see. A woman would need a military grade LED flashlight to see her way through my dark crap.

I spend the next hour chatting with Oskar, in between him serving drinks to other customers. The dark ale beckons me, but I resist the urge and focus on my plate of food. The days of one step forward and two steps back are gone. I can't afford to go back. Not drinking alcohol is the one destructive behavior I can change.

We talk about everything and nothing as I navigate the conversation. Fatigue sets in, and I throw a generous tip on the bar and say goodbye, promising to come back soon. The reality is, I probably won't be back. I rub the center of my chest. As much as I hold on to my misery, some pain is too much.

The sweet smell of summer is in the air, and I enjoy the walk back to my flat, which is more like a townhouse. Neil spared no expense on my accommodations in Innenstadt, the section along the Rhine with views for miles.

The keys jingle in my hand. As I approach the bright red entrance to the yellow townhouse, there is an envelope stuck under the door.

I place it in my pocket and turn around. Taking out my phone, I pretend to take a selfie at the front door and smile. I scan the area with my phone but see no one watching me.

Stuffing my phone in my pocket, I unlock the front door. Inside the foyer, I slide my finger under the flap of the envelope and open it carefully.

A paper slips out, typed up and ready to read.

*Welcome back to hell, Declan.*

*I need to finish the job.*

A hand-drawn flame decorates the bottom of the note. Chills run over my bumpy skin, and I swallow the lump in my throat. Not the welcome I was looking for.

Someone already knows I'm here.

They're waiting.

# Chapter Two

## Declan

SOMEONE'S TRACKING ME. Or worse—someone on the inside knows I'm here. My arrival is supposed to be under the radar, but my cover has been blown. My pulse kicks up a notch, and my senses sharpen, which may be to my advantage. They've shown their hand and I might get to kick someone's ass.

The note in my pocket feels heavier than it should. It could be a key to unlocking what happened to me the last time I was here. I exhale sharply. I may not want to be here, but I won't walk away, not now. The intrigue solidifies my resolve to stay and see this to the end, especially if I get answers. I want to know who's pulling the trigger.

Bring it.

I climb the stairs two at a time to the top floor. The sun sinks over the Rhine, painting the sky in streaks of crimson and gold. It looks like the world's on fire—a fitting metaphor. Fire follows me like a curse I can't escape.

My weapon is within arm's reach as I lie in bed, staring at the ceiling. My mind sorts through names, faces, and memories. Who would want me dead? A handful of people were pissed at me, sure, but not enough to arrange an execution. Or so I thought.

Sleep doesn't come easily as I realize my life is in danger and my assignment hasn't even started, but danger is what fuels me. I stride headlong into it, waiting for it to eat me alive.

The pain from my accident claws its way back, a memory surfacing like a ghost from the abyss. The fire. The smoke. The searing agony as my skin blistered. I remember floating in and out of consciousness, the acrid scent of chemicals clinging to me. Someone wanted me dead. They tried to make it look like an accident. They failed.

Images coming into my head seem like a lifetime ago. My friends laughing, drinking beer and my work at the lab were gone in an instant because someone wanted to burn me alive. Their sentiment hasn't changed in the time I've been MIA.

Morning light cuts through the room, but the exhaustion lingers like a weight pressing down on me. Jet lag has never been an issue—I don't sleep enough for it to matter. My body aches, muscles tight as if I've been fighting shadows in my sleep. Maybe I have.

I stand at the window, donning my signature black jeans, a worn band T-shirt, and military-issued boots, looking over the Rhine. The double-shot espresso burns down my throat, bitter and relentless. I've traded one addiction for another. My love for coffee has taken on a life of its own. The bite of coffee beans and caffeine remind me I'm alive.

My journey continues, and for some insane reason, someone upstairs wants me here to slay another dragon. I rub the fire-breathing dragon tattoo over my heart, a reminder to continue the fight and use the fire.

The desire to live a quiet life is thwarted again.

Something is pushing me in a direction I don't want to go in, but if it means finding answers, then I'm all in. Closure to five years of misery would be a welcome relief.

Then there is Olivia.

The one dragon from my past I will never forget. Something pulls at the border of my mind in fragments. We never got along, but I sense something changed along the way when we worked together many years ago. The problem is, I can't remember much about her except I didn't like her, and she didn't like me. We butted heads on a regular basis.

She was smart, driven, popular, and drop-dead gorgeous didn't hurt either. My polar opposite. With us, opposites did not attract, more like repel. Olivia probably doesn't even work at Bio2Chem anymore. Her ambition must have taken her to higher ground and a bigger company. One less hurdle in my way.

I finish the last of my bitter morning cocktail and head to the lab for my introduction to my contact. The bus takes me to the north end of town to a new address.

They've relocated since the last time I worked for them. On the ride, I notice many changes to the outskirts of the city. Modern construction snakes among the old architecture, attempting to modernize a place that thrives on history.

The Bio2Chem building looms ahead, sleek and modern, a stark contrast to the medieval architecture of center city Cologne. The building design tries to reflect the images found in ancient buildings but fails in its approach to blend in or gain attention. The B2C logo lit in blue LED lights screams corporate power. A fortress hiding secrets.

I get off the bus and head to the monstrosity, dressed as the least likely candidate for the job. The huge glass doors open without a sound as I step inside the sterile atmosphere of biotech. One receptionist taps her headset to mute it.

"May I help you?" Her perfect smile covers up her questions about my presence in this building.

"I'm Dr. Declan Craig," I respond to her in German.

Her eyes flicker with recognition. "Ah, yes, Dr. Craig. I'm Helga. I'll show you to your lab." She switches to English, takes off her headset, and nods to the other receptionist.

"Follow me, please." She moves with calculated efficiency.

She opens the door to a room off to the side before the bank of elevators. "We need to get you a company ID card. Please have a seat in front of the screen. The security guard will set you up."

A man with arms the size of cannons stands behind the camera.

"Say cheese."

"Yeah, right," I scowl.

He snaps the picture, and another machine spits out a company card with my photo on it. I turn it over, running a thumb across the smooth plastic. Could be clean. Could be bugged. Either way, I don't trust it.

"The only way to access the building is to use the card. There are different levels of security clearance. Your clearance is a level 1. The badge will get you into the building, your office, and the labs you will work in. Do you have any questions?"

"No." I force a smile. This is an upgrade from the last time I was here. Security was not this extensive.

Helga carries on. "I'll take you up to meet your supervisor. You'll be very happy with your assignment. She's a top scientist in her field and highly revered." She turns out of the room to the bank of elevators.

I follow behind and enjoy the view. "Who would that be,

exactly?"

She looks over her shoulder at me and smiles. "I'll let her introduce herself to you."

suspicion prickles at the back of my neck. The ride up the elevator is silent as I check out the floor numbers on the panel. I count seven floors, yet there are eight buttons. The top button is unlabeled. I tuck my observation away for later.

We stop at the sixth floor and walk down a hallway made of glass. The labs are open, eliminating hiding places. Working in a laboratory setting can be isolating. The new concept and configuration make it feel open and friendly. A smart security tactic.

I'm led to the end of the hall with a set of double doors.

She opens the door. "Welcome to Bio2Chem. Let me know if you require anything."

What I require and what she can give me are two different things. She leaves as the door closes without a sound. I step into a corner office lab with an overlook of the Rhine and the city spread out for miles.

A woman stands with her back to me, working at a table with a microscope. A long blond braid falls down her back. She's wearing a lab coat, but even under the lab coat, she has curves that go on for days. I hope she has blue eyes I can gaze into when I make her come. Things are looking up.

My voice from the past comes shining through. I haven't been with a woman in years. The horror on her face when she sees my deformities would be too much to bear.

"Smart and beautiful," I murmur. "Just my type." I might as well charm her now. Lord knows how long I'm going to be here, and I'll need some company.

She stiffens without turning around.

"I'm Dr. Declan Craig. I assume you're my—."

She turns around slowly. Ice-blue eyes clash with mine, a jolt of recognition slamming into my chest. Olivia.

Shit.

I must have done something horrible in a past life, and punishment is the only recourse. My hopes of having a bed bunny crawl away and hide.

"Hello, Declan." Her voice is smooth, accented, but there's no warmth, no smile. Just cold steel.

The tension crackles between us, something unspoken lurking beneath the surface. Something I should remember but don't.

Underneath her icy mask, there's a look of pain and regret. Whether it's pain because I'm back or something else, I can't determine. Regret? Not a clue.

"Olivia?" Her name feels foreign on my tongue, as if I'm saying it for the first time.

Her appearance is flawless, not a hair out of place, and her suit is nothing short of top designer. The stilettos accent her outfit. Her nails are a French manicure, completing her look. Some things never change.

"Nice of you to show up... five years later." Her crisp English accent gives punch to her words and is coated in frost.

"No great loss for either of us, considering we never got along." Any charm I had has left the room, and we're stuck in a vapor lock.

Her head rears back like I've slapped her, and she frowns, an odd reaction. "Wow. Okay then. Let's move on."

I stand in the middle of the room as if I've entered a movie midway through without knowing the backstory. To say I'm missing something would be an understatement. My memories of us were when we never got along.

She must see the look on my face as we stand in silence,

staring at each other. We're not the same people we were five years ago. I'm broken beyond repair, and she's spread her wings to fly to new heights. We're at opposite ends of life. The nameplate on the door confirms what I already suspect.

Vice President of Pediatric Development.

The Ice Queen has risen.

"I'm sorry, but you disappeared without a trace." Her blue eyes fade to gray and take on a pain I've never seen in her before.

"Yeah. I tend to do that sometimes. Let's just say there was an accident and leave it there." I rub my forearm with my hand, feeling the raised skin underneath.

But there's a question hanging between us, unspoken and heavy. One I don't have the answer to.

What the hell happened between us that I don't remember?

## Chapter Three

Olivia

WHO DOES he think he is? He waltzes back here like nothing ever happened and then disappears without a trace. If he knew how it ended, he would probably vanish into thin air again.

Declan Craig was the last person on earth I expected to see today, much less standing in my lab, looking at me like he belongs here. I had convinced myself that he couldn't handle how we ended, but when he mentioned an accident, there was something in his eyes—something fractured, haunted. A shadow of pain so raw it almost made me forget my own. Almost.

Something tells me I don't have the whole story. He was always a locked box hidden within another sealed box. He never let me in, dodging questions about himself. Curiosity makes me want to hunt for the keys to unlock his history. I have no intention of letting him anywhere near my past.

But if I want to get to the bottom of why he's here, I need to put my pride aside and work with him. That doesn't mean I have to be nice about it. He owes me an explanation, and it better be a damn good one. His assignment has to be over soon so I can get back to my life. He's a distraction I don't need, taking me away from my life's work.

Before I can demand answers about his accident, the door opens, and Lara walks in, her sleek ponytail bouncing with each step.

"Sorry to interrupt, Dr. Marcel, but you're needed in the conference room for departmental updates," she says in English, her voice smooth and professional.

She moves toward Declan with the grace of a ballerina and the appetite of a barracuda.

"Well, hello. I don't believe we've met. I'm Lara, Dr. Marcel's personal assistant." She offers her hand.

He holds her hand between both of his hands like he's meeting royalty. "I'm Dr. Declan Craig. It's nice to meet you," he replies, his voice a mix of warmth and amusement. "Pleasure to meet you." He lays on the charm with his mesmerizing eyes and ruffled auburn hair. I can't go down this road because it always ends badly.

Lara tilts her head, assessing him like he's the next luxury item she's about to acquire. The woman is built like an Amazon and looks like Heidi Klum. Getting men into her bed is a sport. Looks like she's found her next conquest.

Her eyes linger on his lean swimmer's body. "Let me know if you need a tour guide. I know all the best spots in Cologne." She winks before sauntering out, her hips swaying just enough to make sure he's watching.

And of course, he is. A stupid grin tugs at his lips.

The entire scene shouldn't bother me, but it does. The sharp sting of jealousy burns in my chest. I knew him long before she showed up, and he's nothing but trouble, so why do I care?

"Here, I thought I would have to brush up on my German, but everyone here speaks fluent English." He manages to peel his eyes off her butt to look at me.

I force my voice into something neutral. "It is the common language among us. We deal with a lot of pharmaceutical companies in the US, so we're fluent in English. I have a couple of lab coats for you." I walk to the closet, pull one out, and toss it to him.

I toss him one, turning away before I can get caught up in the way his shirt stretches over his chest. Staying in shape was always a priority for him. From the looks of it, he's still in great shape.

Focus.

With every observation, I'm getting in deeper.

I walk past him. "Follow me. I'll introduce you to everyone. It'll be a good way for you to see how things work around here. There have been many changes since you last graced us with your presence," I say briskly.

He grunts in response, but he complies.

As we step into the conference room, conversation halts. Eyes turn to us—some curious, some calculating. The men size up their competition, and the women assess their options. The room is thick with brainpower and unchecked hormones.

I paste on a professional smile. "Hello, everyone. I would like to introduce you to Dr. Declan Craig. He worked with us five years ago and is an exceptional chemist. He'll be assisting me with several projects. Please, have a seat, and we'll get started."

Heads nod as I introduce him to the various scientists in the room. His gaze sweeps the room, sharp and searching.

He's searching for someone.

I take my seat at the head of the table, and Declan sits next to me. Too close. Being this close to him brings back memories I want to stay buried. His aroma of spice drifts to my nose as I close my eyes and breathe in. Conflicting emotions swirl around that have no business being here. I grasp at the anger I had for him when he left, but hormones are fickle company.

"Dr. Marcel?" Someone's voice snaps me out of my recollection.

"I'm sorry. We'll start at the other end with Dr. Rosseau's report and make our way around the table."

I listen to each report with half an ear. Declan's return has me off balance. My present situation can never cross over the things from my past. I need to keep close tabs on him, which means staying near him as much as possible. Not what I had in mind for his time here.

Glancing over at him, he's engaged and interested, a far cry from the party boy he was before. The scoping out he used to do involved who he took home for a ride and then pushed her to the side. His behavior made for a difficult work situation in my department.

The meeting ends with nods and comments about which pub will host the next happy hour. Their reports will be in by the end of the day, and I'll read them to fill in the gaps I missed while sorting out my game plan for Declan. Where they go for happy hour isn't my concern anymore. I haven't been to a happy hour in many years. That thought makes me sad.

Declan and I leave the room to go back to my office. My nerves are tangled up over seeing him again. I wave to people as I pass them in the hall and ask how they are, stopping to listen to their stories about family or other concerns. The trip back to the office takes thirty minutes as my conversations along the way hold us up.

"You're as popular as ever," he says, his tone laced with something I can't quite name.

I place the reports on my desk and turn around to lean on it, ignoring his tone. "Do you want to tell me why you're here? Because I don't—"

He cuts me off with a silent gesture—a finger to his lips. He grabs the clipboard on my desk and writes on it, then hands it to me.

*It may not be safe to talk in your office. There may be bugs and possibly cameras. Can we cut out early today and find somewhere safe to talk?*

"This is absurd," I mumble.

He shakes his head back and forth. The look on his face is dead serious. This is not the same man I knew years ago. The intensity comes off him in waves. He's more mature and grown-up, a man on a mission.

The paper from the clipboard gets put through the shredder.

We spend the rest of the day bringing him up to speed on the projects in development for our department. He listens and pays attention to everything going on without argument or smart-mouthed side comments.

There's a rhythm we fall into easily, a little too easily, reminding me of how things were right before he disappeared. A pang of regret grabs me. I wish he would have stayed. He missed so much.

He shuffles through some of my folders and comes across one marked "Rett Syndrome." I try to grab it before he gets a hold of it, but he pulls it away and leafs through it.

"What's this about? It looks interesting."

My fingers twist together. "Rett Syndrome is a rare genetic neurological disorder that occurs almost exclusively in girls. It leads to severe impairments, affecting nearly every aspect of their lives from their ability to speak, walk, eat, and even breathe. The disorder is caused by mutations on the X chromosome on a gene called MECP2. There are over 900 different mutations found on the gene. Males born with the mutation don't survive."

He looks up at me with deep hazel eyes that are more green than brown. "This seems rather specialized for your company to be handling."

I take the folder from him because the cure would mean everything to me. "My best friend's daughter has Rett Syndrome. She's a beautiful and happy little girl most of the time, but this has been heartbreaking for their family. I became involved about three years ago when her daughter was diagnosed at age two. This is a project close to my heart. I work with other researchers around the world, trying to get this to the biopharma stage, which you and I both know is the 'Valley of Death' for most cures."

In the blink of an eye, I've shared my most precious project with him, reaching for something that doesn't exist between us anymore, and he won't acknowledge.

He looks at me with curious, intense eyes as if he's seeing me for the first time. "You've changed. You're not the woman I remember."

"I could say the same about you." The spark that lit us up years ago attempts to light the wick again, but I push it away.

His eyes never leave mine. "Let's get out of here. You need to know what you're in for with all of this. I'm not sure you're going to like it."

# Chapter Four

Declan

LIV. I used to call her Liv when I wanted to irritate her. She has changed but is still intent on leaving her mark on the scientific community. Her drive, ambition, and intelligence has moved her up the ladder, and it is something I've always admired about her. Her dedication to pediatrics is an interesting switch.

A framed quote is up on the wall: "I don't run away from a challenge because I am afraid. Instead, I run toward it because the only way to escape fear is to trample it beneath your feet." Nadia Comaneci, 1976 Five-time, Olympic gold medalist in gymnastics, achieved the first perfect score of ten. The quote hits me. I'm running toward several challenges, and I'm not sure where I'll end up. Fear of acceptance is one of them.

I nod my head in the direction of the quote. "What are you afraid of?"

Liv looks over at it. "Do you think I'm going to share that with you? You're a ghost from my past, nothing more."

She grabs her coat and heads for the door. We don't speak a word until we get onto the street.

"It's a good quote, and I remember how much you love a challenge. The fear part is intriguing. What are you afraid of? You have the world at your feet and everything you ever wanted."

She doesn't look at me and stops walking. "Looks can be deceiving. I'm still working toward my goal of a cure for those girls."

I step closer to her, casting her in my shadow. "That's not what you fear. It's something else."

She swallows. "Stop analyzing me. Maybe you should spend more time on yourself. Right now, you are my biggest challenge. Let's make this easy and have you get what you need and get out, so I can have my life back." She continues to walk as I follow behind.

"You're a little hostile, considering I just got here. I've been a perfect gentleman," I goad her.

She spins around in front of me, and I almost crash into her. "I don't know what your game is, but I'm not playing. Let's be two adults and get through this with civility. You don't need to deep dive into my psychological profile to find your answers."

My hands shoot up in a gesture of surrender. "I didn't mean to poke the bear."

"Don't you remember? You used to be an expert at poking the bear. I think it was a sport for you," she hisses. "Some things never change."

She whips around and walks toward the nearest pub. I'm left speechless, although it sounds about right. I was a different person back then. Full of myself and a partier.

Those days have been left behind forever, but she doesn't know the new me. She's right. I'll find out what I need and get back to my lonely existence, where I belong. I don't belong in her world.

She heads for a booth in a back corner of the pub. The location will allow me to see everyone who comes in the front door.

"I'm sorry. I—"

"What exactly are you sorry for?" She crosses her arms and leans back.

This is a loaded question. I must have done something more than poke the bear, but I don't know what it is. My past is catching up with me quicker than I can unravel its secrets. Searching my memories, looking for an answer, I come up empty.

"I didn't think it would be this volatile between us. I came here looking for answers about what is going on. Calm down and tell me how much you know."

"I'm starving. I haven't eaten today. Let's order some food and drinks. Then we can talk about all of this." Her hands wave in the air. There's more to this than meets the eye.

She orders schnitzel, and I get Mettbrötchen, two staples in the German diet.

"I see you ordered your favorite." I place my hands on the table, and I refuse to look away as I latch on to the memory.

"Well, at least you remember something." Her words are caustic.

I do remember, but I don't know how. "There are reasons there are holes in my memory, although I don't know what caused it." I drum my fingers together, watching their pattern, my calming technique.

"What happened to you?" Her eyes widen.

I stop and rub my eyes. "I would prefer not to talk about it right now. It's not something I share with anyone."

She nods her head in understanding. "Can I ask what you are doing here?"

Hairs on the back of my neck rise, and I look toward the pub door. Lingering near the doorway are two big guys, who look out of place during a high tourist season in Cologne. They're pumped up as if they stuck their finger in a steroid socket. They have their hands in their pockets, looking around as if they're trying to find someone.

One of them looks in our direction, and I turn my gaze away, putting the menu up in front of me. I don't want them to know I'm on to them yet. Liv follows my gaze to the front of the pub.

"Don't turn around. We need to get our food and go. We'll head back to my place." My voice is low, but she can hear me. "You need to pose for me. It shouldn't be a problem for you. I'm going to take your picture." She frowns but doesn't argue.

I hold up my phone to take a photo of her, moving slightly to my left. I snap a photo of them right before they move farther into the crowd, away from us. The team will be able to identify them if they're in the system.

She rolls her eyes. "Why are we going back to your place?"

I called the waiter over and ask that our food be put in containers so we can leave.

I hate having to explain myself, but I have no choice. "We were followed to the pub. I'm sure it has everything to do with me and not you. It's safer there."

"Yeah, right."

"Don't worry. I won't lay a hand on you." I doubt she has many dates with that attitude.

Her cheeks blush pink, and she gives me a funny look I can't decipher. The waiter comes back with our bag of food. I grab it and head for the street. My gait is slow and casual. I don't want to draw attention to us. I need to know who they are and why they are following me. Liv stays close behind. I look over my shoulder several times to see if they're following us. I scheduled an Uber to pick us up a block from the restaurant to lose them.

I head toward the red door of my townhouse as Liv's hand stops me.

"It's a beautiful day. Can we sit on a bench by the water and enjoy our lunch before things get heavy? Surely, it's safe there." She lays on the sarcasm.

Her face shows exhaustion, probably from not eating and her schedule. I nod my head, and we walk toward the river. She sits on one end of the bench, and I sit on the other, with the food in between us. There always seems to be something in between us, and we're never on the same page, but I need her to work with me.

I watch her while she eats. She enjoys every morsel that goes into her mouth. It's her little piece of escape from her hectic world.

"How many hours a day do you work?" The question is innocent without accusation.

She blows out a breath as she gathers the words she wants to say. "It depends on what I have going on here and at home."

"Home? It was never a priority before. What changed?"

She looks at me, studying my face. There is something she doesn't want to tell me. But she doesn't know how tenacious I can be, and I will find out what it is.

She looks away over the river. The wind blows some of her blond hair out of the tightly woven braid. She doesn't push them back into place. My fingers itch to touch her, but the want confuses me.

"My mom is getting up in years and needs help with the farm. She also has a Belgian Malinois who needs to be taken care of." She doesn't look at me.

"Why do I get the feeling there's more to the story?"

"I could say that about you, too," says the most frustrating woman on the planet.

She goes back to eating her lunch. We're at an impasse, but one of us will break eventually, and it won't be me. I'm already broken.

# Chapter Five

Olivia

HE IS the most infuriating man on the planet. We don't say much when there's so much that must be said, things he needs to know. I'm not sure he's ready or wants to know. I want to make sure he can handle everything I have to tell him. There are other lives at stake. I don't want anyone to get hurt, but I may not have a choice.

He gathers what's left of our lunch, which is not much. He's right. I was starving, and my hours don't allow for lunch much of the time. I hate how observant he is when it comes to me. Maybe he could use some of his insight on himself.

His strong, lithe body moves in a fluid motion toward the trash can. Women walking by on the sidewalk glance and then stare as he exudes an alpha male attractiveness that's hard to find. I've never felt safer than when I'm with him. I wonder if he remembers why.

The lure is the aura of mystery surrounding him. His sexuality is powerful, and its secrecy attracts women far and wide. They want to uncover his secret, among other things.

The bad-boy image works in his favor. He has the *it* factor, but it's darkened over the years as if he's trying to hide. Maybe he always was hiding but in a different way.

I'm curious about what happened to him. The one thing I always admired about him was that he pulled no punches. He always says what's on his mind and gives me his insights whether I want them or not, but he's reluctant to share anything about himself.

My body still pulls toward him while my mind tells me he's trouble. I'm a mind-over-matter kind of person. Besides, my work takes most of my focus, leaving little time for much else. I wouldn't know what to do with his kind of energy.

He smiles at me, oblivious to the female attention, or he's choosing to ignore them. Taking his hand out of his pocket, he waves toward the townhouse.

"Shall we?"

I walk in front of him, wondering if he's enjoying the view. My competitiveness never seems to take a break. He lets us in with his key and ushers me upstairs.

"You've got to see the view from up here."

His high-end townhouse is prime real estate and has a galley kitchen with a sitting area overlooking the river. The bedroom and bathroom are tucked away in the back. He's right, the view is to die for. I stare out the window, trying to recall the last time I enjoyed any view. The sun slips behind the city on the other side of the river as the last of its rays reach out.

My back is to him, but I can feel the heat of his eyes watching me.

"Would you care for something to drink?" he says.

"I would love a glass of red wine. Anything Pinot Noir would be great," I mumble without turning around, afraid to miss the sun's last breath for the day.

There's silence, but I hear him move. The heat of his body rolls off him in waves, letting me know he's close to me. I turn around and look up at his stone-cold face.

"I don't have any wine." There is no apology.

I laugh. "You're kidding, right? The party boy doesn't have every liquor known to man in his bachelor pad?"

"I stopped drinking about a year ago."

This takes me by surprise, and I realize he's not joking. "You're sober? As in you don't drink anymore?"

He shakes his head. "Not a drop. Can I make you a cup of coffee? Maybe decaf? I've become a connoisseur, of sorts, in the world of coffee beans."

He's full of surprises.

"Can you add sugar and two creams, please?"

One side of his mouth curves up. "Sure. At least you're predictable."

I may be predictable, but he gives a new definition to the word unpredictable. We're not a match. He has memories of certain things, little touches, but the big events seem to be lost to him.

He goes to the kitchen and starts operating a very technical coffee machine. I sit at the island and watch as he uses every dial on it to make two cups of coffee. He hits a couple of buttons on his phone, and Kenny Wayne Shepard plays in the background. I don't recall him being into blues music.

This new side of him makes me curious. "Why did you stop drinking?"

He chuckles and hands me a cup of his special brew. "Alcohol ran my life. I couldn't differentiate between days and nights. Things ran together, and my life was out of control. I got in with the wrong people, and my older brother, Mac, had to bail me out of jail in New York City. That was my turning point. Grant me the serenity to accept the things I cannot change, the courage to change the things I can, and the wisdom to know the difference. Accepting the things I cannot change is a hard pill for me to swallow." The steam from his coffee obscures his face.

I remain quiet and don't force him to share why he was in jail. By the time he looks at me, the cheer has left his voice, and his eyes have darkened. I grab my cup of coffee in anticipation. The coffee hits my tongue with the most exquisite flavor I've ever encountered, and I hum.

"You like that? It's my special blend. I drink it at night. There are hints of lavender and passionflower."

He gives me a genuine smile. I haven't been privy to one of those in years. My insides melt a bit. His smile always touched a part of me I hide away from others.

"It's wonderful. I could use a cup of this every night. My schedule takes a toll on me." I reach for the knot in my shoulder, even though it won't do any good to rub it.

His gaze lands on my shoulder, and his fingers curl around his cup. "What do you know about what's going on?"

"Not much. I got a call asking if I could get you into the firm. Of course, I can get you into my department. I have the final decision on who gets hired." I savor every drop of the delicious concoction he's made for me, hoping I'll sleep like a baby.

"I assume you got the call from Neil. How do you know him? It seems like an odd connection. Did you date him at some point, hoping he would be your sugar daddy?" He smirks.

"That would be weird since he is my uncle."

Declan almost spits the coffee out on the counter. "What? How did I not know this? Fucking Neil should have told me. Why didn't you tell me?"

I shrug. "You didn't ask until now." I close my eyes and inhale the scent of my nightcap. "I didn't realize you were undercover last time you were here until my uncle called and asked if you could come back. You showed up out of nowhere last time. MI6, uh? What were you here for back then?"

He peers into an empty cup. "It was highly classified. Even though I don't work for MI6 anymore, I can't share it with you. Is he your mother's brother?"

"No. He's my father's brother." I put my palm up to stop more questions.

He nods his head but doesn't ask about my father. I don't speak about my father with anyone. He's not worth my time.

"You now know everything I know. Why don't you fill me in on why you are here?"

"One of my teammates, Beck McKenzie, was given a memory drug that was poisoning him while he was in Zambia. We think it was supposed to erase all his memories, but it wiped out some and brought back others. The person behind the development of this drug is Dr. Zahara Ugana."

"You must be mistaken." I'm shocked.

"There's no mistake. We tracked her back to this company when she showed up on our radar. What can you tell me about her?"

The air shifts in the room from light and airy to dark and dangerous.

"Dr. Ugana is one of our best scientists. She has a seat on the Board of Directors as the President of International Development. She heads a highly classified group within the company and is extremely elusive." I hadn't considered she could be into unethical practices.

He frowns and drums his fingers together. "What do you mean, elusive? When was the last time you saw her?"

"I can't tell you the last time I saw her. Maybe years. She has nothing to do with my department. The rumor mill says she's been going back and forth between here and Africa for a couple of years." I spin my cup in front of me on the counter. "The few times I have met her, she's always been charming and friendly. She's very popular with the board members and staff when she's around."

His eyes watch me with scrutiny. "You're one better than me. I've never laid eyes on her. I have a dossier on her with a picture."

"Do you think she's the one having you followed?"

"I don't know, but that wouldn't make sense since she doesn't know me."

He moves around the end of the island and stands in front of me. My heart speeds up with his proximity. Damn hormones.

"You need to be extra careful in this situation. She is involved with a group we know little about, but they are extremely dangerous. We need to draw her out so I can get closer to her."

I nod. Sober Declan is intense, not quite as jolly or flippant as drunk Declan.

"We? I'm not the agent here. I got you in. The rest is up to you. I have people who rely on me. I can't get caught up in your spy games." My cheeks warm with anger. Whatever lust was strumming through my veins is gone.

His brows furrow, and he examines me but doesn't say a word for a bit.

"I'm sure your clearance level is higher than mine. What's on the eighth floor?" He holds my stare.

I've always had my suspicions about what goes on up there, but I've never voiced them to anyone. The less said, the better.

"How do you know about the eighth floor? You just got here." I give out a stuttered sigh. "I honestly don't know. My guess is that's where Dr. Ugana does her research. Very few people are allowed up there."

"Who has access?" He's like a dog with a bone.

"Not me. I don't know anyone who has access."

He rubs his chin. "I need to get in. The answers we're looking for may be there."

# Chapter Six

### Declan

THIS MISSION GETS trickier at every turn. I swept my townhouse for bugs the minute I knew someone had eyes on me. None were detected, making the choice simple to bring Liv back here. I would never risk anyone's life while a target is on my back. Staying close to her is my new goal, which she will not be happy about.

I understand her reluctance to want to be involved in this, but I have no choice. I can't do it without her. My years after the accident would've had me blow off being followed as nothing. I view life without alcohol through a different filter and with more intensity.

The sounds coming from her as she drinks my specially brewed coffee almost undoes me. I only remember going head-to-head with her, but my body has other ideas. The island shields the hard-on forming in my pants. The blond hair and those blue eyes are my kryptonite.

I need to get her out of here before I do something stupid.

Even if her icy facade melts, she's not going to want a man as disfigured as me. She's beautiful, well-educated, and poised. She can get any man she wants and probably does.

"I think we should call it a night. I'll ride with you in the Uber back to your car at the parking garage and make sure everything is okay." My fingers curl into fists in my pockets.

She waves her hand away. "I don't need an escort. I know the city like the back of my hand. The parking garage is secure. You need a clearance card for access. I have more work to do at the office tonight."

"Liv, there's more to life than work. Don't burn yourself out." I want to touch her soft, blushed skin but refrain from showing any intimacy or interest. This time, calling her Liv doesn't seem to annoy her.

As if she can read my mind, she says, "You're the only one who ever calls me Liv. I kind of like it." Her finger runs around the rim of the cup. I don't respond for fear she might change her mind. "I want to leave my mark on society and be remembered for finding a cure for children, whether it's Rett Syndrome or something else. Time is fleeting and one of the few things you can never get back."

She has no idea how right she is, as I have missed out on memories of more than a year of my life. The urge to touch her is stronger than ever. I crave a connection I've avoided for years. "We know what we are, but not what we may be."

I throw her a quote to see if she gets it.

"Are you quoting Shakespeare?" She smiles up at me with her eyes half closed. I don't think she means to be seductive, but she makes me want to dive in and never come up. There seems to be a direct line between everything she does and my libido.

"I am. You're very well read." I make a statement, not an observation. Her studies took her through Oxford and then

Cambridge. "What do you say we keep this interesting? I challenge you to a duel of quotes."

She sits up straighter, pushing her breasts front and center. "So, you're prepared to lose."

The energy between us shifts. We cross the line from thinking about being together to wanting to be together. Our minds are unable to make the move, but our bodies are caving. The chemistry is real, maybe because we are older and more mature. The question is, will we ever act on it?

"Not so fast. The only rule is that either of us can quote from anyone on the planet. Are you sure you're up for it?"

"Oh, I'm up for it. Bring it on, big boy." There's a sparkle in her eye, and with every word, I move closer to the edge.

Her smile is genuine, meant for me and no one else, here in our bubble. I bathe in the glow, careful not to get singed by it. Someone scorched me enough to last a lifetime.

"Let's do this. The first one not able to identify the quoter buys dinner at the challenger's choice." I smile.

She holds out her hand so we can shake on the deal. I slip my hand into hers. Her skin is warm, lacking the coolness that sometimes lingers on her words. She's stepped into my territory. I'm a quote nerd. I love finding out what clever people have said. I'll be interested to see if she can keep up. There's an expensive dinner in my future.

I hold her hand longer than necessary as she slips her hand away from mine, aware of the sexual tension between us. She was always cautious and less of a free spirit.

"I got an Uber for you. The app says it will be here in three minutes. Let me walk you to the pickup location. Give me your phone."

She hands it over without question. I punch in my number and send myself a text from her phone.

"There you go. We're a phone call away from each other."

I give her a weak smile. "Send me a text when you get home tonight."

She nods and bites her lower lip. I want to suck on those lips and make her moan. I remind myself it will never happen.

I walk her to the street behind the townhouse where the Uber waits. She slides into the back seat and gives me a look of uncertainty. I'm sure my face is giving her the same look of trepidation because I don't know what this is about or where it's headed. How can two people who are so cautious of one another have this kind of chemistry?

Trudging back to the townhouse, I decide to sleep in the bedroom on the second floor. The position will give me an advantage if someone tries to break in. The decaf coffee with the lavender and passionflower will help me sleep. Right before I close my eyes, I get her text.

**Olivia: I'm home. Thanks for the coffee. Just so we're clear, you are not my keeper.**

**Me: We'll see about that. I'll see you tomorrow. Sweet dreams, Petal.**

Why did I call her Petal? There is a tingling sensation as if I should know the answer. She reminds me of a beautiful flower with thorns.

She can argue all she wants, but I am her new keeper. Something stirs in me that I need to shut down. I fall into a deep sleep without dreams of any kind from the past or present, something I haven't done in years.

I wake up more refreshed than I've been in the last year. The combination of the drink and the company from last night may have made the difference. I feel uneasy about being attracted to someone who used to be a source of aggravation. I can't get involved with her. She won't want a man as damaged as I am, inside and out. The scars on my skin match the charred parts of my soul.

The first order of business is to find an old used car. Something with a powerful engine but looks crappy on the outside. My trust fund allows me to purchase a new top-of-the-line Mercedes-Benz, but I don't want to draw attention. I do a quick search online and find a used car dealer outside the city to the north. I take the bus, and my black card has no limit.

Today is my lucky day, and there aren't many of those. I come across an older Mercedes E63 coupe in black matte with a lot of damage to the body. The salesman said they didn't want to put the money into fixing it. I buy it for a sweet deal. The compact design of the car with the big engine will allow me to get around the city quickly.

The first thing I do is disable the GPS. Rolling the windows down, I take it for a spin around town. The car handles like a dream, and the power is insane.

I park my beat-up ride in the garage for Bio2Chem and head up to the sixth floor, where I am sure Liv is waiting for me. As I walk back to her office, I make a point of introducing myself to a few scientists on the floor. They call their teams pods and are working on pediatric research in one form or another.

I enter her office and close the door.

"Well, thank you for joining us today. It would make a much better impression if you could be on time." She walks toward me on her sky-high stilettos with red soles, which are probably torture chambers for her feet. "When you were here five years ago, we did some brilliant work together. I know you're here for other reasons, but I didn't hire you for show."

"And the honeymoon is over. I'm sorry I'm late. I had to

purchase a set of wheels. It won't happen again." My apology is sincere.

The ice queen is back, and if her change in personality continues, I'm going to end up with whiplash. I like mellow Liv much better, and I need to keep her happy. I've been so selfish over the years; I've never thought about anyone else's happiness.

# Chapter Seven

## Olivia

LAST NIGHT, my hands shook for the entire ride back to the office. He does that to me, and it makes me angry and sad. We could have had so much more.

I hate feeling like someone has control over me. He put me off balance when he called me Petal. I was never sure if it was a term of endearment or his sarcasm working overtime. I'm in a spiral between the past and the present.

This morning, he comes in on his timeframe, just like before. This time, he seems genuinely sorry when I reprimand him. I shouldn't have to reprimand him like he's a rookie. He's a grown man.

I watch him make his way from the elevator around the floor, introducing himself to the various scientists working on projects. He takes an interest in everything they tell him. There are subtle changes about him, and then there are the big changes, like him not drinking anymore, which blew me away.

Over the years, I pictured him as the eternal single party

boy. The way he looks at me, I assume he doesn't have a girlfriend or wife. He was a player, not a cheater.

His accident must have a lot to do with how he has changed. Darkness surrounds him, following him wherever he goes. People don't know what to make of him. I got a glimpse of some of his light last night, and I want more.

He walks to the closet, takes off his jacket, and slips on the lab coat. Grabbing a pen from my desk, he clicks it. He reaches for the same clipboard we used last night, hands it to me when he's done writing, and winks. Cheeky devil.

*Remember, there may be eyes and ears in this office. I can't check for bugs and cameras in here like I can at my townhouse, so we need to be careful. <3*

I nod at him and rip the paper off the clipboard and stuff it in the shredder. If working with him isn't hard enough, I need to worry about being watched and listened to twenty-four seven. I rub my upper arms as if I'm chilled. Maybe they have been spying on me all along. Someone probably took a nap while watching those tapes.

We work through the morning as I bring him up to speed on the various projects being developed in the pediatric department. His attention goes back to the Rett Syndrome research.

"I've always been interested in genetic coding. The proteins involved in the changes that happen during sequencing fascinate me." He flips through my files.

"You're looking at the latest files. There are boxes with years of work to figure out how to reverse the effects of MECP2. I don't know if we will find a cure in our lifetime." My voice sounds defeated to my ears.

He writes me a text. **I think I might have picked the wrong profession. The work I do as a biochemist makes my life feel worthwhile. This is far more industrious**

**than chasing bad guys around the globe. My new job at MBK gives me a little more freedom to not play by the rules. ;)**

He looks up from his file. "But then again, I never played by the rules." He gives me one of his winning smiles, which I ignore and roll my eyes.

I text back. **What's MBK?**

**MBK Global Security is the company I work for, and Neil is working with us. I can't tell you more.**

I nod, understanding his need for secrecy.

I reach for another file at the same time he does. Our hands cross and touch. I allow my fingers to linger on his hand, seeking his warmth from years ago. I can't seem to get that feeling from anyone else. God knows I've tried. The sparks flying between us can't be denied.

His eyes stay on the place where we are joined.

"What happened between us years ago?" His voice is soft, as if he doesn't want to upset the moment.

"The bigger question is, what happened that you don't remember?"

What's clear is there's a chunk of his memory missing, but I don't know why. At this moment, I've found one key, unlocking one box, his lost memories. I don't know what waits for me at the center. Why do I want to pursue what lies at his center? But then I remember what resulted from our night together.

His eyes lock on mine. I've never seen someone look so sad and heartbroken. They are like arrows to my heart, and I'm sorry I asked.

"I'll save that story for another time," he chokes out. "What do you say we go to lunch? I have some things I want to run by you."

I leave my fingers on top of his hand, afraid of losing the

connection. He slips his hand out from under mine as he strokes one of my fingers, sending sparks up my arm.

"I know a pub near here. They have a back room where we can have some privacy." My fingers cool without his touch.

Confusion from last night continues into today and swirls between us, but in order to find out what's going on in this company, we're going to have to push through it. I should never have agreed to this. He could have worked in a different department, and I could have avoided heartbreak 2.0.

"Let's take my car to a place outside the city where no one will know us. Less chance of questions," he says without looking at me.

I'm sure he wouldn't want anyone to see him with me, the uptight lab researcher. Being seen with me will tarnish his wild bachelor image. He'll probably pick up where he left off, looking for a different woman to warm his bed every night. My emotions bounce from one extreme to another. I don't need this.

We take the elevator to the garage and remain silent. I glance at him several times, unsure of who this Declan is, but I'm interested in finding out. He seems to be a dichotomy of many things I've never seen in him before. I follow behind him as we near what looks like a beat-up car.

"Is this the ride that made you late for work?" There's a snarky tone in my voice.

"Yes, she may not be beautiful on the outside, but she's kicking it under the hood."

I slide into the passenger seat. The leather interior is black on black. The seat hugs me in as if we're going to be racing on the Autobahn.

He drives the car out of the parking garage and turns right

into traffic. I notice he is looking in his rearview mirror more often than he should.

"What's wrong?" Being with him always means trouble follows close behind.

"We must have picked up a tail from the garage. The two meatheads from the restaurant are following us in a BMW M5 SUV. Nice ride, but it won't outrun this car."

"How about you let me off at the next corner, and you can have this chase by yourself?" I look out the rear window to see the two men he's going to outrun.

"Too late for that. I need to lose them now. You better tighten up your braid and strap yourself in because we need to lose these idiots. It's about time I let them know I'm on to them."

He maneuvers through the traffic with the agility of a border collie running through an obstacle course. He dodges in and out of traffic as if we're in the Monaco Grand Prix.

On several occasions, my hands reach for the roof or anything else I can get a hold of. He jerks the wheel back and forth, narrowly missing cars and trucks in front of us. There is a trail of honking horns behind us as I remind myself to breathe. He handles the car as if he's driven it his entire life. Impressive.

After several hair-raising turns, the car levels off. I take a chance and turn around to look out the rear window.

"It looks like you lost them, and I've lost my appetite. Why don't you turn it around, go back to the office, and we'll find some food there?" I wipe the sweat from my forehead and hope my antiperspirant is still working.

"We lost them about two turns ago." He stares out the window and continues to drive away from my suggested destination.

I sit back and take a couple of deep breaths, thanking God

I'm still alive. The last time he was here, he upended my life in so many ways. Now he's back for Act Two. He's breaking my routine, my quiet, and my serenity. I need to create space between us before I fall into his dark hole.

We continue to drive until we are well out of the city limits and head into the countryside. There are stretches of farmland with a backdrop of mountains and forests. The scenery is beautiful, and I sit back, allowing myself to enjoy it, but the need to get back to the office strums under the surface. I haven't traveled this far out of the city in years.

He doesn't say a word as he drives in a trance. Maybe some memories are coming back to him. He slows down and takes a turn on a dirt road. His car is ill-equipped for the ruts and rocks in the road, but he doesn't seem to care. His face shows determination to get to wherever this road leads.

In the distance, I can see a small house perched on a hillside. As we get closer, the house gets bigger. He stops in front of a large cabin with a wraparound porch. Someone should showcase it in a magazine.

He turns off the engine. "Welcome to my cabin in the woods."

# Chapter Eight

Declan

I HAD FORGOTTEN about this place until we drove farther out of the city, when my mind went on autopilot. The cabin is a three-story beauty built with logs from the local forest. I bought it six years ago as my sanctuary, not knowing I would use it to recover from my last mission with MI6.

Slipping out of the car, I shut the door and walk toward the cabin. The couple I pay to care for the cabin has done a great job of keeping the lawn short and the fields unattended, as directed by me.

A field of wildflowers and poppies starts at the side, goes around the back, and up toward the woods. The wildflowers are the reason I bought the cabin. They grow everywhere, flying in the wind and anchored to the ground, something I have yet to accomplish.

Somewhere in the drive here, I forgot I had a passenger as I hear Liv shut the car door. Up here, close to the mountains, the air is cooler as the wind whips around us, and she pulls her jacket tighter.

She doesn't say a word but stares at the cabin, the wildflower fields, and the mountains rising behind the forest on a hill. Bringing her here gives her more information than I want her to have about me. This place is loaded with my most guarded secrets.

"I've always loved poppies. They ride the wind, falling apart unapologetically," I say to no one.

"You own this?" Her voice travels on the breeze.

"I bought it years ago, shortly after I started working at Bio2Chem." I don't look at her, too busy taking in the sight of the cabin.

My feelings about everything that happened at this cabin tumble together, out of control, as if I'm on a metal slide trying to grab hold of anything to slow me down. There's a mix of hollowness, filled with pain, sadness, loneliness, and the fight to want to live.

I head for the front door as her footsteps crunch on the driveway behind me. This may be a log cabin, but it has top-of-the-line security. The only way to get in is with the key and a code.

The front door opens easily as I step inside. I have many hidden rooms and other ways to keep the people inside safe. My paranoia got the better of me after the accident, knowing someone wanted me to die.

Light streams through the windows, spotlighting the furniture covered in tarps. A faded quilt lies on top of the couch. We are a quilt of memories, sewn together, making a story with vibrant colors.

My quilt has a hole in it, lacking color and continuity. Being here again may help me capture the memories I lost years ago, but I'm not hanging any hope on it. Nothing seems to jog my memory as jumbled fragments come to me.

"I need to get back. I have a lot of work to do."

I hear her voice, but don't acknowledge her. Ripping the canvas tarps off the leather furniture brings the cabin back to life, a life I don't want to revisit, but I know I need to face my demons. I'm going to face this pain head-on.

The living room opens to a kitchen with two French doors leading to the wraparound deck. I used to sit out there and watch the wildlife in awe of their simple life, wishing my misery would end soon. They would look at me with total disregard, exactly the way I felt about myself.

"Did you hear me? I don't have time for your visit down memory lane." Her voice gets louder.

I make my way into the kitchen, skimming my fingers over the cool moss green granite countertops. Heading for the stairs, I bound up them by twos. Upstairs, there are four bedrooms with full en suite bathrooms. The rooms are untouched, like they have been frozen in time. Most of my time during recovery was spent downstairs.

Liv comes up the stairs to find me in the master bedroom. "How big is this place?"

"There's a third floor with a studio."

"Studio?"

I forgot. She doesn't really know me. She saw what I wanted her to see. I rub the back of my neck, unsure I want to share anymore. I decide to dive in.

"I play guitar, among other things."

Her brows cinch together. "I feel like I didn't know you at all."

"Maybe you didn't." My words are meant to hurt. "Maybe I didn't know myself."

We stare at each other, and what I want to do is strip her out of her clothes and see what she looks like, naked and wild. Her braid, still neat after our wild ride, would be unraveled, with her blond hair kinky and flowing down past her shoulders. Her beauty could breathe life into this haunted place and erase the fog of being here, but I'd be burying myself in another distraction.

I walk toward her, closing the space between us. Her distinct honey scent draws me in as if I recognize it. I can't imagine I would recognize her scent because I was never physically close to her. The light from the window brightens her blue eyes. Before my hand touches the softness of her cheek, she steps back, and the space between us feels like a canyon.

I don't know what possesses me to say the next sentence. "I think we should spend the night here. It might do you some good to get away from work and the city."

She stuffs her hands in the front pockets of her jacket. Her face turns red. "I can't possibly spend the night with you out here in the woods." She takes a step toward me. "Unlike you, I have obligations and people who rely on me. I have to get back to the office and deal with reports. Tonight, I'll drive home where people are waiting for me. I can't up and do whatever I want like you do."

"People? I thought you lived with your mother."

She pulls a hand from her pocket and puts it up in front of me. "It doesn't matter. I'm sure you can find some other female to warm your bed. Since you're my ride out of here, you need to make this a quick visit." Her lips form a taut line as she spins around on her heels and heads for the stairs.

"Those encounters were never about the sex. It was about the company. I hate being alone." I can't stop myself from telling her my truth.

She looks over her shoulder at me as if she's not sure she

heard me correctly and then turns to go downstairs. We can't escape this as much as she would like to.

I check everything upstairs, including the bathrooms, and wander down to join her. Liv is leafing through a large leather-bound notebook, and I realize what it is in an instant. I snatch it out of her hands, tying it with its leather string.

"Did you draw those?" Her eyes are edged with curiosity and wonder.

Sketches of wildflowers fill the notebook. Drawing in pencil and charcoal was my escape and my way of surviving while I was here. I look at her for a moment, trying to decide how much more I want to reveal to her. So much between us is unspoken, undiscovered, and confusing.

"Yes, but I don't share my artwork or music with anyone. It's time to go." I take the leather sketchbook with me.

We follow the dirt road back to the main highway. The tension in the car is brittle. She crosses her arms and huddles next to the window. If I didn't know better, I would say she was vibrating with fury. She speaks her first words as we enter the city limits.

"Next time you want to take a detour, it would be a great idea to let your passenger know where you're going. This little escapade robbed me of valuable time I could've spent at the office getting things done. I don't have a lot of leisure time, but when I do, I will not spend it with you."

Ouch.

"Life is too short to be tethered to an office for the rest of your life."

She responds with, "Umph."

I pull up in front of the office building at the curb and turn toward her. "Look, it's almost dinnertime. Are you sure you don't want to grab a bite to eat? I feel like I owe you a meal, at the very least."

"No," she says through gritted teeth.

"Is that like a hard no, or is it an I'll think about it no?" I say, right before she slams the passenger door shut and hurries toward the glass doors of her prison.

For as many secrets as I have, it would appear she has some of her own. She was intent on getting back to the *people* at home.

# Chapter Nine

Declan

THERE'S a part of me that almost feels bad pushing her out of her comfort zone, but someone needs to do it. She is locked in this place where she only exists within her work.

God knows who or what is at home, but she's intent on keeping them a secret. She reminds me of a tree, tall and proud as she watches the seedlings fly toward the sky. I would love to see what it looks like when she finally breaks free.

Flipping through my sketchbook, I come across drawings of the different flowers, some in pencil and some charcoal. On the next blank page, I can see a portrait of Olivia developing before my eyes. I sit with my back to the window, allowing the early morning light to shine on the page as I grab my charcoal pencil. My hand sketches furiously, as if it can't get out the strokes fast enough.

In a short time, I've created a beautiful sketch of a mysterious woman. Her eyes are intelligent and wide, sitting atop a button nose and full lips. There's no smile, just the seriousness of being committed to her work. I want to bring out her playful side, leading her to want to grin, but it may take time.

I don't know what possessed me to take her out to my place in the woods. I've never taken anyone there. The cabin was my place of refuge to heal and remains as lifeless as it was back then, missing human souls to give it spirit. I remember the endless feeling of loneliness. Memories and emotions attached to my time in Cologne whirl around me.

When Liv stood in the living room in the sunlight, it looked like she belonged there. The cabin is so big and empty, it could do with lots of people to make it a warm, inviting home.

My apology to her will need to be soon and sincere, but not before I get in my laps at the pool. Luckily, there is a swimming pool near the townhouse, Holmes Place Fitness. I talked to the owner, Ivan, and struck a deal, allowing me to exercise before the place opens. I'll be able to swim without glaring looks, pointing fingers, or sneers.

Ivan is there when I arrive.

"Good morning," I greet him in German.

He nods. "Your German is impeccable. If I didn't know better, I would say you were from here."

"Thank you."

I go straight to the pool, change into my swim trunks, and slip into the cool water. I fall to the bottom, where I sit and listen to nothing, one of my favorite sounds. When my lungs burn, I propel myself to the top for air. Stroke after stroke, lap after lap, I find my rhythm, and I'm in my zone.

I swim until I have nothing left. Arms are burning, and legs are twitching. Swimming is my Zen, giving me a calm I can't find anywhere else, making it necessary to do every day.

Being close to an indoor swimming pool was one condition of my assignment.

Taking a quick rinse, I put my clothes back on. As summer heats up, wearing long sleeve shirts is going to get hot, but I don't have a choice. My arms and legs are not ready to be viewed by other people. They require more artwork to cover my skin.

I get back to the townhouse, and there's a ping on my phone. I contacted Antonio Bianchi, our tech guy at MBK, last night to find Liv's address. My apology needs to be in person. He sends me the address on the outskirts of Cologne in Lovenich, which is mostly farmland. I didn't think she lived outside the city.

The ride out to her farm is beautiful as I pass by a vast field of poppies, my favorite. The skyline of the city falls away as rows of plants take over. The windows in the car are down, letting the wind blow through my hair as I enjoy every minute. Liv may not be very amenable to my apology, but I need to give it my best shot.

There's an old stone farmhouse at the end of the driveway. The front door is two huge wood panels put together with wrought iron pieces and hinges. The farm must be from the 1700s, if not older, and has many more stories than my cabin.

I knock on the front door and hear a dog barking as feet slap on the stone floor on the other side. The door opens halfway, but I don't see anyone. The dog, which must be the Belgian, continues to bark.

"Ozzie, stoppen en zitten." I hear the voice of a child speak to the dog in Dutch, telling him to stop and sit.

This is not your average Belgian but a trained guard dog. Most military train their dogs using Dutch commands, which is curious to me. Why do they need a guard dog?

Below me, hanging on to the door handle, is a redheaded little girl with big blue eyes, wearing a tiara in a puffy white dress with bare feet.

Her mouth forms an O, and then she says, "I'm Poppy. Are you the prince who's come to rescue me?" she asks in German.

I'm stunned as I go into rescue mode. Is she in trouble? She smiles. Oh, to be a child again and live in your own world. My experience with children is extremely limited, almost nonexistent. I may have discovered Liv's secret. I guess she and I are even.

I am nobody's prince, but I decide to play along. Being a prince is a vast improvement over being a Dark Lord.

"I'm Prince Declan. Is Olivia here?"

"Are you her friend?" she cocks her head to the side.

"Yes." My strong response as the prince has no effect on her.

During our conversation, Ozzie, the guard dog, inches his way in my direction. He has learned to listen to and protect Poppy. He gets close enough to sniff me. My approval comes as his nose nudges my hand for me to pet his head.

Poppy opens the door wider and invites me in. "Mommy's not here, but you're in time for my tea party." She claps her hands.

I follow the white fluff to the back patio, with Ozzie at my side. He's not letting me out of his sight. The view from the back patio is magnificent. There's a large garden and a barn with horses. I can't see where the property ends beyond the fields.

Set up under the pergola is a small table with two chairs, teacups, and small plates. Let the fantasy begin.

"You can sit down. I'm going to get us muffins." She motions to the chair I should sit in.

Ozzie follows her, looking back at me. I look down at the setup. As lean as I am, my body will not fit into the tiny chair, so I stand and wait.

She comes back with a plate of muffins as Ozzie tries to snag one from the plate.

"What's wrong? Why aren't you sitting?" She pouts.

"I think I'm too big for the chair, and I don't want to break it." I shrug. "Are you here alone?"

"No. Grand-mère is in the barn."

I notice she uses the French word for Grandmother. She hands me the plate and runs away. Ozzie sits in front of me, eyeing the muffins.

"I don't think so," I whisper to him in Dutch. He turns his head to the side and gives me his best puppy dog look.

Poppy comes back, sliding a bigger chair behind her, and wrestles it up to the table. I place the muffins on the table and help her with the chair.

"Sit," she says to me in Dutch and then covers her mouth and giggles. She runs away again and comes back with a plastic crown in her hand.

"I've been waiting forever for my prince to show up so I can give him his crown." Something inside me cracks, wondering if her father is part of her world.

"How old are you?"

"I'm going to be five years old soon." She inspects the crown and then looks at my head. She lifts her arms, signaling me to bend down so she can place the crown on my head.

I've never felt so humbled in my life. This small child, with little effort, has made me feel special. I've never felt special, always an outsider looking in.

She clasps her hands together. "You look so handsome."

She sits across from me as her dress poofs up. Blueberry muffins are piled high on the plate in the middle of the table.

"You must have known I was coming today. You made my favorite kind of muffin."

"Blueberry muffins are your favorite? Grand-mère made them fresh this morning with blueberries from the garden." Splitting the muffin, she puts half on my plate and the other half on hers. She's much better at sharing than I am. I don't share, but I'm sure I would give her anything her heart desired.

I'm a grown man sitting at a child-size table, with a crown on my head, eating muffins, and I couldn't be more content. There is sheer joy on her face, as if she's really found her prince. How great would adult life be if we could pretend more and live in an alternate reality? I'd be on board with living in that world.

The sun beats down, heating this part of the patio as a drop of sweat rolls down my back. Without thinking, I push both sleeves up to my elbows.

"You have colors on your arms. Did you use permanent markers? Mommy tells me to use markers only on paper. Your mommy is not going to be happy with you."

No. My mum wasn't happy with much before she died. She suffered in a world of mental illness that was foreign to me. One of my many unresolved issues. To be young again.

Her tiny hand reaches out to touch my bumpy, scarred arm as I hold my breath. I haven't allowed anyone to touch me in years, afraid of what they might see and what I might feel. Poppy is innocent and touches me without judgment.

"I like how it feels."

"Bumpy?"

"I have bumps, too, on my knees. See?" She lifts her dress and shows me the white scars from healed wounds.

Her eyes grow wide. "Maybe you are my prince. We both have bumpy skin." She smiles.

"Are you cold?" she asks in between bites of muffin. Crumbs litter her plate, but she doesn't clean them up.

"No. Why?" The muffin is delicious.

"You're wearing a winter shirt, and it's hot out." She's not looking at me. Her focus is on the muffin.

"I like to keep my arms covered." I figure honesty is the best policy.

"You're not German," she states as a fact, not a question, disregarding my answer.

"No. I'm from Scotland."

"I speak English," she replies in English. This is one smart, talented, and charming little girl.

I hear the double click of a shotgun behind me. The muffin falls out of my hand onto the plate as I put my arms up in surrender.

"Don't make a stupid move because I will shoot you," the woman says in English with a French accent.

I turn around and face her with my hands in the air. "My name is Declan, and I work with Olivia."

Recognition comes across her face, though I've never met her. She lowers her gun.

"I'm Margot. I'll leave you to your tea party. Olivia should be back soon." She gives me half a smile.

I turn back to the little redhead. "Who was that?"

"Grand-mère." She bites into her muffin.

"Does she always carry a shotgun?"

She nods.

"Good to know."

I hear voices coming from the kitchen. Olivia is arguing with her mother.

"No. I will not allow it," Liv's voice rises.

She storms onto the patio. Her face is red, and her lips are a tight line.

"What are you doing here?" Her hands are in fists at her sides.

Poppy blurts out, "He's Prince Declan, and he's here to have a tea party with me."

## Chapter Ten

Olivia

Damn him to hell and back. It isn't bad enough that I have to deal with him at work, but now he's invading my home, playing tea party with my daughter. He rattles me with little effort and looks handsome in his plastic crown.

"Poppy, go to your room." I point to the house and glare at Declan.

She crosses her arms in front of her. "No, I don't want to go to my room. A princess never leaves her prince."

I take a deep breath and pinch the bridge of my nose, realizing in the space of a few minutes I've lost control in my house. The prince has entered and stolen my daughter's heart without knowing it, just like he stole my heart years ago.

"Mère," I use the French word for mother. "Can you take Poppy to feed Rocky, please?"

Poppy runs to Declan and latches on to his leg. "Will I see you again, Prince Declan? Maybe next time, you can ride with me and Rocky."

His hand rests on the top of her head and brushes away a few wild hairs. A lump forms in my throat, waiting for his answer, praying he doesn't give her false hope that he will be back. He has a habit of disappearing.

"I don't know, but I'll try." He takes the crown off his head and hands it to her. "Will you hold this for me?" She nods. "Who's Rocky?" His eyes look at her with adoration.

"Rocky is my pony. I hope when I see you again, you'll be happier." She shows him her one tooth smile and holds his crown to her chest.

Declan jerks back like someone has slapped him, nods his head, and gives her a faint smile. My daughter is very intuitive and calls it like she sees it.

She blows him a kiss and runs off toward the stable with Ozzie in tow. My mother gives me a weak smile as she passes by.

When they are out of earshot, I turn to him to see a stupid smirk on his face. "What are you smiling at?"

"The apple doesn't fall far from the tree. Looks like you've met your match. She's very smart. How many languages does she speak?" He pushes his hands deep into his front pockets.

I ignore his keen observation. "I want you to leave. Now." I clasp my hands in front of me to keep them from shaking.

"I came to apologize for yesterday. Driving you out to the cabin was a mistake. I wasn't thinking straight. You're dedicated to your work in developing pediatric drugs, and I admire you. At thirty-three, you've accomplished more than most do in a lifetime. After the life I have lived, I realize there's more to life than work. I wanted to take you somewhere away from being inside your head. I'll make sure you're on board with wherever we go next time. Please say you forgive me."

My stomach clenches. This is an about-face from the Declan I knew in his previous life here. His words are considerate and sincere, as if he's thinking about someone else for a change. The party boy has left the party and seems to remember there are other people in the world besides him. I need to pump the brakes on this. Declan 2.0 is more dangerous to my heart than who he was before.

"Let's keep our work relationship to the office. From now on, it's strictly business. There's nothing to forgive. You thought it would be a nice break for me. I get it. Thank you."

He takes a step toward me, closing the distance between us, and I can feel his heat, the heat I want to nude sunbathe in. His hazel-green eyes peer into me, and a strand of auburn hair rests on his forehead. He sees things I've ignored for years. My work keeps me tethered, centered in a crazy world, but if you're tethered, there's nowhere for you to go. There's no freedom, no wild, no fun.

"I didn't know you were married." He tests the waters.

"I'm not married, but I think you know that." I pat the top of my hair with both hands.

"Is Poppy's father part of her life?" He will not let this go.

"No, and that's none of your business. It would be best if you left." I break our gaze.

I pull my braid over my shoulder and play with the ends, a nervous habit. He pulls my fingers away and holds my hand in his. I should pull them back and get away from him, but there's something about him that won't let me leave. I'm bound to him, and like an octopus, he keeps reaching out, grabbing different parts of me.

Sorrow covers his face. "I didn't mean to intrude. Don't lose sight of the fact that you need to stay safe and be aware of things going on around you. We need to stay alert and make sure nothing happens to Poppy or your mum."

I yank my hands away from him. "There is no *we*. There is only *you*. This is your assignment. I'm helping you out by giving you a job at the company. What happens beyond that is up to you. Leave my family out of it." My cheeks feel warm. "I never should have agreed to this."

His eyes take on a darker shade of green, and his lips, those full lips, form a tight line. His alpha side kicks in, and I'm not sure if I'm scared or turned on.

"There are many lives at stake if this drug gets into the wrong hands. I'm not sure it's not already in the wrong hands. It could erase soldiers' memories and put them back into battle over and over again until there is nothing left. It could wipe out the memories of the heads of prominent countries, leaving them impotent and weak enough for someone else to step into power. The implications for this drug are limitless."

My fingers are back playing with the ends of my braid, and my heart is racing, not because of who I'm standing with, but because I understand the ramifications of this drug. I nod, accepting what he's telling me.

"It's a lot to take in and bigger than what I thought." The volume of my voice drops.

"I know, but I can't do this without you. Only those who risk going too far can possibly find out how far one can go," he says above a whisper.

He's playing the game. "T. S. Eliot," I reply and point to the door.

He grins and walks toward the front of the house. The heavy wooden doors close with a thud, and he revs the engine before he leaves.

I search for Poppy and my mother in the barn. My daughter sits on the floor with a tabby kitten in her lap. I bend down to inspect the kitten and notice it has something wrong with its eye.

"It doesn't look like this little guy is going to make it."

Poppy grabs the kitten from me and cradles him in her arms. "Of course, he's going to make it. He needs to go to the doctor."

"Poppy, we'll leave him here with his mother. She'll take care of him." I try to grab the kitten back from her.

"No, I'll take care of him just like Prince Declan would do. He has bumps on his skin like I do. Someone took care of him like you take care of me."

"Bumps?"

"He has bumps on his arms, and he colored them with marker. I want to cover mine in marker, too." She turns and walks away, cradling the kitten in her arms.

I have no idea what she's talking about, but it occurs to me I've seen nothing more than Declan's neck, head, and hands. She describes his skin as bumpy, which could result from a burn. I assume the markers she described are tattoos.

"Olivia," my mother pleads.

I hold up my hand. "Not now. I don't want to discuss it. We need to keep her safe."

"From Declan?"

"From everyone. He filled me in on exactly why he's here, and it's not good. Like it or not, I'm in this with him, even if I don't want to be."

I'm exhausted from my emotions playing ping-pong inside my heart. We take Poppy and her kitten to the vet. The vet says the kitten will be blind in one eye, but he will survive. Poppy doesn't seem disturbed by this. We leave the kitten at the clinic, and she hops in the back of the car.

"I'm going to name him Prince," she proclaims from the back seat.

My mother laughs and gives me a sideways look. "You

better strap yourself in, girl. It's going to be a bumpy ride," she says so only I can hear.

Twice in the space of forty-eight hours, someone has warned me about a rough ride.

# Chapter Eleven

### Declan

Liv drew her line in the sand, and I have to respect the need to keep her family safe. She never answered my question about Poppy's father, which bothers me, but it shouldn't. Who would leave behind the smartest, most adorable child on the planet?

I never thought about children until my brother Mac had Dalia, who's a baby. I'm not sure what to do with her, but Poppy is older and a conversationalist.

I brew coffee for both of us and take it to work. Making amends is my top priority so we can work together smoothly. I step out of the elevator and walk toward her office. Part of her office is behind glass. The dark circles under her eyes are a sign of exhaustion and stress. She prides herself on being put together and looking polished. I'm sure I have something to do with her new unwanted look. Somehow, I don't think the coffee is going to be enough of a peace offering.

"I brought you some of my special blend coffee. I'm

calling a truce." I hand her the coffee, making it the way she likes it, strong with a touch of sweet and cream. She takes it from me and wraps both her hands around the cup.

"I'm sorry for yesterday. Poppy and my mother are my world, and I'm very protective of them. I shouldn't have been so hard on you. After what you told me about the drug, I realize we have to work together, so I'm waving my white flag."

She doesn't look at me as she pops the lid off, inhales the steam coming off the hot liquid, and closes her eyes to take a sip. Her lips seal the rim of the cup as the liquid slips through them. Many erotic scenes are going through my mind, but I need to pull it together.

"This is incredible. I like this addiction better than your last one." She smiles, and her eyes perk up for a moment, but the tiredness is still there.

"I prefer this addiction to my last one, too. Alcohol was ruining my life, and I'm too old to be stumbling around drunk. I missed a lot during that time. My party days are over, despite what you might think."

For some inexplicable reason, I need her to believe me. She needs to understand I'm not the same person I was the last time she saw me. I'm a more broken version of what I was before, with various character flaws for much different reasons. My flaws make me want to hide in the shadows, away from people, but not from her. I want to steal her light, and I can't figure out why.

"I believe you." She's still focused on the coffee. Maybe my special blend wasn't such a good idea. I need her to focus on what I'm saying.

She continues to close her eyes before every sip of my coffee. A warmth fills my chest, knowing she's enjoying something created by me. It's also a huge turn-on. If everything she does speaks to my libido, my restraint won't last long.

"Poppy is a wonderful little girl. She's smart and funny, and her red hair reminds me of my sister, Kendall. Her appetite for languages is interesting. She's more than any one person should try to handle." I laugh.

"My mother, Margot, is French and spoke French to Poppy from the time she was a baby. Since my mom and I are both fluent in German and English as well, we speak to her in those two languages, too. She seems to be a natural when learning other languages. You're right. It takes two of us to wrangle her in. She's almost five. I'm bracing for the teenage years." Laughter flows from her as she talks about the light in her life.

"I don't have a lot of experience with children, but she already has me wrapped around her little finger."

She's the only one on the planet who sees me as a prince and not the Dark Lord, but she could also sense my sadness. I couldn't get away with much around her. There's a tinge of regret at my failure to have a permanent relationship that could have led to something more. I realize how much I've missed in life.

Liv winces at my comment and turns away from me, a puzzling reaction. For me, she continues to be the flower with many colored petals, revealing something new about herself or her life I don't think she knows she's exposing.

"You have a cat named after you." She looks at me over the rim of her cup.

I give her a questioning look.

"She found a kitten in the barn and named it Prince. We had to take it to the vet. One of his eyes has something wrong with it. She was determined we save him."

I smile, touched by the gesture. "By the way, why is your dog named Ozzie? It's an unusual name."

She gives me one of her thousand-watt smiles. "When he was a puppy, he found a bat on the ground and brought it to us. He didn't hurt it. He had a look on his face like he wanted us to help it. My mom named him after Ozzie Osborn."

I laugh. "He's trained in Dutch commands."

"My mother thought it would be a good idea to have a guard dog and give Poppy some responsibility. Poppy is very good with him, and they've bonded."

"Margot seems like she has a wild side, especially toting around a shotgun."

"Trust me. Don't get in her way. She will shoot you."

"That's the impression I got right away."

We belly laugh, which is a welcome relief after the intensity of the last two days. The air in the room lightens as we find common ground. I'm hoping we stay on the same page for many things to come.

We finish our coffee and get down to business. She hands me new files to study and see if I can add anything to them. I suggest running some tests she may not have thought about, and she takes my recommendations under advisement.

Standing or sitting for too long makes me tired, so I take a break and wander around the building. I ride the elevator to each floor, looking for avenues that might lead me to the eighth floor.

As a shot in the dark, I push the elevator button for the eighth floor, but nothing happens. There seems to be a slot next to the button where a card would be inserted. Any stairwell leading to the top floor is only accessible by a key card and a code for a keypad. I've hit a dead end.

When I make my way back to Liv's office, she's checking

email at her standing desk. I look over her shoulder to discover some threatening emails.

"What are those emails about?"

She jumps, startled I'm standing behind her.

"Don't sneak up on me." She opens one of the emails. "I don't pay attention to these. I get them every so often. They come from someone at another company who doesn't want us to pursue a certain type of drug or research. Lately, I've got a couple of them in a row." She shrugs it off.

I read the email and examine a couple of others. Most of them say the same thing. Something about discontinuing research or stopping the production of a drug or else. None of them say what will happen if she doesn't stop. They are threatening up to a point.

"Did you take these to security?"

"Yes, they told me to ignore them."

I open the most recent one, and it threatens her and her family. The email says she needs to stop what she's doing in her department concerning a breakthrough drug for a type of childhood cancer. Antonio needs to get on this and take a deep dive into where these emails are coming from.

"I need you to forward me these emails. I'm going to send them to my tech guy at MBK. I'm questioning whether the two guys who have been following us are for me or you."

Her brows come together, and worry sets in her eyes. "Do I need to be concerned?"

"They didn't get specific about knowing who your family is or where you live, but I will be on the lookout. I can't take any chances."

I hold her by the shoulders and tilt her chin so she's looking at me. "Petal, if anything happens or you feel threatened, I want you to drive Poppy and your mum to my cabin. You will be safe there. Promise me."

She nods. "I never thought about it before, but I guess I need to take the threats seriously."

Under my thumb, her skin feels soft and warm with a blush of pink like a rose. I haven't touched another human in years. Her raspberry-colored lips call to me. We stare into each other's eyes, knowing we're on the precipice of something we may not return from. Like a DNA helix, we seem to wrap around each other, and yet we manage to keep our distance. Every time I try to reach out to her, she cuts me off, breaking the chemistry that we know is between us.

My lips brush hers with the most tenderness I've ever kissed anyone. Then I remember. I'm not good enough for her. Disfigured beyond recognition on most parts of my body does not make me a good fit for her.

She moans in my mouth, which rips through me. Half of me wants to spear her with my tongue and let her know what she's missing. The other half of me wants to run and hide, ashamed of what I've become, a monster hiding in the darkness.

A switch flips for her at the realization she's kissing her arch nemesis from the past. She pushes me away and shakes her head.

"We can't do this. We need to stay focused on what's going on around us. Between my threatening emails and your investigation into a dangerous drug, we can't get distracted. This can't happen again. Promise me."

She uses my words against me. I nod. "I promise." Then, she throws me the unexpected.

"You have to learn the rules of the game. And then you have to play better than anyone else." Her lips curl into a smirk.

"Albert Einstein. Looks like we're even."

She takes a step toward me. "We will never be even."

Something changes in her eyes I can't make out, as if she's bitter or angry toward me, like I've done something to her.

This woman is going to challenge me in every way possible. I hope she's ready for the new me. The one who will not give up on her and keep his promises.

# Chapter Twelve

### Declan

AFTER AN EXHAUSTING DAY, I make it home as the sun sets, lighting up the front of my townhouse in a magnificent shade of orange. I didn't invite Liv to dinner. She made it clear she needed her space. Something gnaws at me, at the edge of my mind, like I should know where her anger comes from. The harder I try to remember, the more frustrated I get.

The memories I lost long ago are frozen in time. My accident may have been so traumatic that I've blocked out memories of everything before it. Nothing I do seems to jog my memory or bring anything back. I've stalled out.

I thought returning here would bring back events and I would remember my forgotten time, but nothing seems to be helping me. The thought occurs to me that my subconscious is trying to protect me, a form of retrograde amnesia.

My first phone call of the evening is to Neil on my secure line. He picks up after the fourth ring.

"Am I interrupting a hot date? I can call back when you're done." I know nothing about his personal life.

"Going without a date seems to be an occupational hazard. What's going on at your end?" His tone is tired and lonely.

"Someone left me a lovely note letting me know they know I'm here, including what happened to me last time I visited."

I read him the note.

"Interesting. There's more to this than I realized," he responds. "Do you have any leads?"

"No. But I have to thank you for letting me know I'm working with Olivia, and she's your niece. Your great-niece, Poppy, is quite the whirlwind." I smile.

Neil is unusually quiet on the other end of the line. I can't even hear him breathe. I wait for him to respond.

"Yes, she is. I thought it would be better if you didn't know you would be working with Olivia. You might not have come. I know things were tense between the two of you last time. Hopefully, you both have grown up since then."

I pick up the cup she drank from the other night. "It would seem she and I have some unfinished business. Although, I'm not sure what it is. We're playing tug-of-war. I can't figure her out," I say, forgetting I'm talking to my boss for this op and her uncle. What a weird combination.

I hear a laugh on the other end. "You're in good company. She must like you. She only goes to war with people she finds challenging."

"Well, she didn't like me last time I was here. We weren't even friends."

He clears his throat. "Remember, people change. You've changed since that time, too. Is there anything else I should know?" He switches gears.

"I need Antonio to trace some threatening emails aimed at Olivia."

The sound of an office chair bumping into a desk comes through the phone. "What are you talking about?"

"Liv has been getting threatening emails. She claims they're coming from a competitor who wants her to shut down and stop developing a drug that could cure a type of childhood cancer. I have two goons tailing me, but I'm not sure if they're following me or her."

"I feel safer knowing you're there." His voice shakes, which no one would pick up on unless they have worked with him as long as I have.

"I have a cabin in the woods, a safe house. I'm going to text you the coordinates. If things go south here, that's where you'll find us, or at least them."

"And here I thought I knew everything about you. You're a man of mystery. Safe house, eh?"

"I've got to have some secrets. Things didn't sit well with me after the accident, which you and I know was not an accident." Frustration rears its head.

He avoids the topic. "I'll contact Sean and have Antonio trace those emails. The less contact you have with MBK, the better. Keep me updated." He clicks off.

Antonio Bianchi has an IQ that is off the charts. While attending MIT, he got in with the wrong group and almost got busted for hacking into the NSA. A couple of his friends went to jail, but he got off with a warning.

They released Antonio under Sean's care, and he works for him at MBK. Sean Knight is one of my bosses at MBK and a helluva warrior as an ex-Navy SEAL. We came to find out that Antonio was the brains behind the hacking operation. We keep that nugget a secret, otherwise every governmental agency would be up his ass.

If I need backup, I know who to call. The team Sean put together, including my brothers, Mac and Campbell, are the best bar none. They are some of the most elite soldiers in the world. Brothers in arms. Under Sean's company, we can do things other military soldiers can't, giving us more possibilities. We break and bend the rules to meet our needs.

I spend the rest of the evening drawing portraits of Liv and Poppy. Even working in charcoal, Liv's eyes are bright, and her cheeks are flush. I draw her with her hair loose and free, giving her an untamed look. Poppy's hair is wild around her head, not acquiring the uptight gene from her mother. My second drawing of her is with the kitten in her arms. I title it "Prince and Poppy."

A blanket of contentment comes over me I haven't felt in years. Drawing always puts me in my zone, but this feels different. The faces I draw bring me warmth and comfort as if they are somehow a part of me. None of what has happened so far has made sense. Emotions are shifting in me; I can't explain.

The kiss I shared with Liv seared itself into my cold, tattered heart. Her kiss felt right and familiar, even though I know there's no way in hell I've ever kissed her before. I've avoided being with anyone for years, avoided feeling, touching, or enjoying the simple pleasure of a kiss.

Living a celibate life has its advantages and forces you to examine yourself closely. You stop getting lost in the pleasure of a woman's body, so you don't have to think about how you're going to screw it up again.

My fingers skim my lips, knowing I want to feel her mouth again and devour it. I was stunned she let me kiss her, lost in her cup of coffee like an aphrodisiac. She broke away, reminding me we needed to stay on course. My scars reminded me I'm not fit for anyone to see. Each of us has an imaginary line keeping us apart. I want to throw paint on those lines so I can see them and get rid of them.

I fix myself a cup of chamomile tea and look out over the river. The night sky is dark with a million twinkling stars and a crescent moon. I relate to the crescent moon, looking at the stars from afar. I've lived as a nomad, trying to see where I fit in, but nothing sticks. I'm a bystander, watching the world go by, but Liv and Poppy make me feel different. Poppy made me feel like I belonged with her.

I'm restless after being on my own for so long. The reality is, I don't like to be alone, even with my artwork or writing my music. Being creative helps me reset, but I crave human contact. The tea does its job as I get drowsy, falling into a deep sleep, temporarily letting go of thoughts of being by myself.

THE MORNING SKY has dark clouds on the horizon. A storm is coming in fast from the west. Drops of rain are small at first and then pelt the window. I grab my swim bag and head out the door. As I open the front door, an envelope sits on my front steps. The paper is soaked as I peel open the flap.

The ink on the note has run down the page, making it hard to read. The words are a warning I should leave because I'm not welcome here. As I read further down the note, it refers to Olivia, Margot, and Poppy. Something about teaching me a lesson and those around me. Why are they threatening me with Liv and her family? As if I have a connection to them.

Before I can finish deciphering the note, I drop it and my swim bag in the foyer and head for my car. My weapon is on me because I never leave home without it. The two goons were tailing me and not Liv, but it looks like they've changed course.

The rain pours down in cold sheets, drenching me from head to toe, not the way I was hoping to get wet today. I feel under the wheel wells of the tires and come across a tracker. I crush it under the soul of my heel, but there may be more, and I don't have time to run the detector.

I jump in the driver's seat and dial Liv's number, knowing she's already at work. She answers on the first ring.

"Calling to tell me you'll be late again?" Her tone is playful.

"I need you to listen carefully and not look alarmed. Look pensive. That shouldn't be hard for you. Stop rolling your eyes at me."

"Okay." Her playful tone turns serious.

"I'm on the way to your house. I need you to leave the office now and tell them you're going to a doctor's appointment. Meet me at Volksgarten and head for the beer garden. Don't take your car."

She cuts me off. "Of course."

"Try to stay close to a group of people. Buy something to eat as if you're going to be there a while. I'll meet up with you there. Please trust me on this. I need you to say this back to me out loud, in case you're being recorded in your office. Repeat this, I must have forgotten my appointment."

She repeats the last sentence, and I end the call. For once in her life, she listened to me and followed through. Miracles do happen, but I don't know what waits for me at the farm.

# Chapter Thirteen

### Declan

THE STORM INTENSIFIES as I dodge and weave through the streets of Cologne, desperate to make my way to Liv's farm. Lightning bolts flash in front of me as thunder cracks, shaking the car.

This is something out of a psycho thriller movie. *Will I make it there in time?* But I may be too late. I white knuckle the steering wheel and say a prayer. I'm not the praying kind, but I'll take anything at this point.

The car powers up the gravel driveway as wet rocks ping off the wheel wells. I slow down as I near the farmhouse to see the same BMW M5 that was tailing me parked in front of the house. I pull my car into one of the smaller barns to keep it out of sight.

My weapon is ready, and my nerves are like steel. This feels personal, knowing Margot and Poppy are in the house, probably with two gunmen. The saving grace is I got to Liv before they got to her. The need to keep them safe overwhelms me. I slow down my breathing and focus.

Opening the side door, I creep down the hallway. Ozzie is barking, and a man is responding in German, telling someone to shut the dog up.

"I will not tell him to shut up," Poppy responds to him in German. "If you don't leave, I will give him the command to attack you." She's fierce, but I don't think she understands what's happening.

I peer around the corner and see the gunman. He tells the other man to go look for the old woman. I don't hear Margot's voice, and I don't know where she is.

The gunman responds, "Go ahead. Then I'll shoot your dog, and he will be dead."

Asshole, I don't fucking think so. I'm close enough to see the scene unfolding in the kitchen. I take in a breath and hold it to steady my hands. My shots are spot-on when I'm in my center.

Poppy cries, and it guts me. Seconds before I'm ready to enter the kitchen and put a stop to the gunman, Margot shows up with her shotgun. She fires a shot, throwing the gunman off-balance.

Poppy gives Ozzie the command to attack in Dutch. "Aanval!"

Ozzie doesn't hesitate, jumping for the gunman's hand holding the gun. He knocks him to the ground as the man tries to get his wrist free from the dog's mouth.

I turn to Poppy. "Go to the small barn and get in the car. Stay there," I say to her in French, hoping they only speak German.

She gives me a curious look.

"Run, now!"

She bolts out of the room, holding her kitten in her arms. I turn around to see Ozzie distracted because Poppy has left, allowing the gunman to jerk his hand free.

He sits up and aims at Ozzie, and I take my shot. The bullet hits him right between the eyes as Ozzie runs after Poppy. I have zero tolerance for anyone who threatens children or animals. I turn around, and Margot is nowhere to be found.

A shot rings out from the large barn at the back of the property. The sound is from a shotgun, which means Margot has taken aim at the other gunman. I sprint toward the barn in time to see Margot standing over the gunman, who's holding his shoulder. Blood oozes up through his fingers.

He looks up at me and says, "That crazy bitch shot me." His weapon sits on a haystack on the other side of the stall.

Without taking my eyes off him, I speak to Margot in her native language, "Go find Poppy in the small barn. I'll take care of this."

She leaves without a word, taking her shotgun with her.

I stand over him. "Who sent you, and why are you after this family?"

"Ha, like I would tell you anything." He smiles, exposing brown-stained teeth from one too many cigarettes.

A shot to the knee might help jog his memory. He screams out in pain.

"I don't think you know who you're dealing with. Now, answer the question, or I'll take out the other knee."

His face turns crimson, and sweat pours down his forehead. "I know exactly who I'm dealing with. You're ex-MI6. There's a hit out on you that's not going away until you're dead."

I don't let my surprise show as I squat down in front of him. Blood seeps into the straw on the barn floor. "Who ordered it?"

He shakes his finger back and forth in front of me and

82

smiles. "You will not find out from me. They are bigger than both of us," he whispers.

The barrel of my gun sits flush with a spot between his eyes. "You're willing to die for them? Although, I doubt you have much upstairs."

He frowns. "Yes, let me show you."

He digs into the front pocket of his pants and throws something into his mouth before I have a chance to stop him. His eyes roll into the back of his head, and foam leaks from his mouth as he collapses.

"Shit!"

I stand up and push one number on my phone. "I need a cleaner."

"Where?" Neil replies.

"At Liv's farm in the house and in the big barn. Poppy and Margot are safe. I'm going to get Liv. I'll give you an update when we're secure." I click off before he responds.

Out of the many ops I've been on, none felt personal until this one, but I'm not sure why. I've hit another roadblock to answers about the hit out on me, and I'm running out of patience. My steel nerves have been scratched, leaving me less polished than usual.

I make my way back to the small barn to look for Poppy, the kitten, Margot, and Ozzie. Margot is sitting in the front passenger seat with her shotgun. Stuffed into the back seat is Poppy with the kitten on her lap as Ozzie sits in the seat next to her. His paws are over her lap in a sign of protection. Poppy's tears have dried, and she seems remarkably calm.

I open the driver's side door and slide into the seat. "Is everyone okay?" I say in French. After Liv told me Poppy's first language was French, I know that's her comfort language.

Poppy pops up. "You saved Ozzie's life."

I look over my shoulder to see her sitting on the edge of the back seat. "You weren't supposed to see that." My head hits the headrest as I close my eyes.

Her hand finds its way into mine, laying on the console between the two front seats. I look down to see her precious tiny hand sitting in the center of my large, open palm. Her fingers slip between mine as she squeezes my hand.

"Prince Declan, you saved our lives. I always knew you would save me."

I almost laugh at the fact that I can barely save myself. Turning in the seat, I touch the tip of her nose with my finger. "You need to listen when I tell you to do something. You shouldn't have seen that."

"I didn't see anything. Ozzie ran to me, and I heard the shot."

"Good."

I squeeze her hand. "You need to sit back and put your seat belt on."

She grabs her kitten, sitting between Ozzie's legs, and clicks in her seat belt. "I'm ready."

I'm sure she is ready. The question is, am I ready? She is one special and tough little girl who takes after her mum. I gently lift the shotgun from Margot's grip.

"Let's put this in the trunk."

Margot hasn't said a word. She simply nods with a grateful smile.

Less than twenty-four hours ago, I was worried about being alone. My car is filled with a grandmother, a child, a dog, and a cat. Lonely went out the window as soon as I met this crew.

The car bolts out of the barn, and I don't take my time getting back to the Cologne city limits. The skies have cleared from the angry storm that rolled through, but things seem more muddled than ever. A fitting backdrop for the day. The last piece of this puzzle is picking up Liv.

Poppy breaks the quiet in the car. "Are we going to get Mommy?"

Her question spears my heart. I don't want anything to happen to Liv for many reasons. I glance at Poppy through the rearview mirror. "Yes. We're going to the Volksgarten where Mommy is having lunch."

"Oh, I like it there. They have a fun playground. Grand-mère, remember when we went there?"

"I do. We had a lot of fun." Her voice is strong and reassuring.

"This time might be less fun, depending on what is waiting for us there," I murmur so only Margot can hear me and stare straight ahead.

Margot pats my arm. "I'm glad you're finally here."

Before I have a chance to ask her what she means, we enter the city. I scan the area for a getaway car, one with more room, considering the number of passengers on board.

# Chapter Fourteen

Olivia

AFTER THE PHONE call from Declan, I don't know what to think. He might have found out who has been harassing me in emails or figured out who's been following us. Either way, I need to listen to his directions.

If I learned anything over the years with my uncle working for MI6, it's that they have a keen sense of danger, better than anyone else. Their lives revolve around precision; one wrong move can lead to a domino effect.

I don't know what's happened in the space of twelve hours, but he feels my entire family is in danger. This almost feels like trust. I don't think he would ever let Poppy get hurt, even though he barely knows her.

I walk to the corner on shaky legs and take the city bus, looking around for anyone unusual. I get off at the stop for the Volksgarten. This is one of my favorite places to take Poppy. The extensive park sits in the middle of Cologne, filled with bike trails, playgrounds, fountains, and, of course, a beer garden.

The path is wet from the storm as I walk around the puddles toward the beer garden. I stay close to the crowd of people heading in the same direction.

Lunchtime is fast approaching, and everyone wants to get their spot at a table on the patio. I glance over my shoulder without looking obvious, but I don't know who I'm looking for.

Servers dry off the tables to get people seated quickly. I pick a spot near a group of people at the same table, facing the park, and order chicken salad with a bottle of water.

When it comes, the lettuce is wilted, but at least the chicken salad looks fresh. My nerves get the better of me, and my appetite is gone as my eyes search the park to find them. I'm anxious to see Poppy and my mother. My guess is Declan left Prince and Ozzie at the house.

A man sits down next to me, close enough we're touching shoulder to knee. I don't move because I'm familiar with his energy and scent.

"When I say eat something that looks like you'll be here a while, I didn't mean a salad and a bottle of water." His deep voice vibrates through my skin and straight between my legs.

I don't look at him. "I have to keep my curves intact for men who want to date a sexy, successful scientist," I quip.

A growl comes from low in his throat. "Maybe you should save those curves for a man who wants to be with who you are, not what you are. Navigating those curves takes skill. Look across the park."

I look up to see my mother, Poppy, holding the kitten, and Ozzie, running around in a game of tag.

"What happened?" I ask as my voice cracks.

"I'll tell you later. We need to get out of here. Look casual."

He helps me up, and I reach for my salad. His hand lands

on my wrist, and I freeze. I already know he's skilled enough to navigate my curves, but I'll keep that to myself.

"Leave it there. It doesn't look fit to eat. We'll get food later."

We exit the beer garden, and Poppy comes running toward me with the kitten bouncing up and down in her arms. My mom holds us together in a big bear hug. Ozzie jumps on us, wanting to get in on the action. Declan stands on the side by the path with his hands on his hips.

"We need to go." He motions for us to follow him.

He holds out his hand. "Give me your cell phone."

I hold it to my chest. "I need it in case the office tries to call me."

"We'll get you a new one. Hand it over. Margot, I need yours too."

I haven't seen this side of him. He's in operative mode and five steps ahead. The way he's giving orders lets me know he has a plan, and he's ticking off the things on his list. His eyes never stop moving and evaluating the situation, although no one would know by looking at him. He has me on edge, and my nerves are spent. His arrival has come with one surprise after another.

We stop at his beat-up car, and he opens the door, throws our cell phones in, and locks it. He presses a button on his cell phone.

"How come you get to keep your cell phone?" I stop walking and put my hands on my hips.

He moves his mouth away from the phone. "Because it's a secure line." He presses his finger to his lips.

"Sean, I need Antonio to call me back on a secure line." He ends the call.

He takes a photo of an SUV across the street and answers his ringing phone.

"I'm sending you a picture of a vehicle now. You need to get me in."

"Why aren't we taking your car?" I ask with frustration.

"I found a tracker on it before I went to the farm. There could be more than one, and we don't have time to find them."

We follow him without a word as he makes his way across the street toward a silver SUV. The doors unlock without Declan having to do anything as he waits silently on the phone.

"Get in. Ozzie, come," he orders in Dutch.

My mom and Poppy pile into the back seat, clicking in their seat belts. I slide into the passenger's seat. Declan opens the back for Ozzie, who takes directions from him. I give my mom a sideways glance. She returns the look and shrugs her shoulders.

He climbs in the driver's seat and pushes a button on his phone, which starts the car.

"How did you do that?"

"Software is amazing, ain't it?" he says with an American twang and wiggles his brows.

"Antonio, I need you to contact Neil to get this car back to the owner. Tell him we're going to the cabin." He pauses. "You need to pick up my beater car and dump it. Grab the cell phones. I have a vehicle at the house. Thanks."

He ends the call and pulls out of the parking spot, gliding into traffic. I don't question why we're going to the cabin, except I know he's taking us to safety.

"Mommy, I have to go to the bathroom, and Prince peed on me."

I look over at Declan to get his reaction. He doesn't react with annoyance.

"We'll stop at a shop on the way out of town, get her some clothes, and she can go to the restroom."

"See, Prince Declan can solve anything," she states with her chin lifted in the air. If this keeps up, she'll be all about Team Declan, and Team Mommy can go fly a kite.

"He can also bring a world of shit with him," I mutter under my breath.

"Petal, I don't think I've ever heard you swear." He turns and smiles.

"Welcome to the new me." I turn in my seat to face him. "The me who's been pushed to her limit, thanks to you."

"There will be clothes for you at the cabin. Neil will make sure of it. I promise it'll get better. Trust me, you haven't been pushed to your limit yet."

"Why don't I believe you?"

Declan pulls into the parking lot of a secondhand shop, and I hand Prince to my mother. Poppy runs ahead of me into the shop. I grab a pair of pants and a top I know will fit Poppy and make quick work of changing her out of her clothes in the bathroom, dumping her wet clothes in the garbage.

Declan makes sure Ozzie takes care of business as my mom sits in the back seat with the kitten in her lap. We buckle up for our ride to the cabin. City pavement and skyscrapers turn into farmland and dirt roads. The city trails behind us as relaxation comes over me. Amid chaos, it's amazing I can find any sense of relief. My sense of peace might have something to do with the man sitting next to me.

His focus is on the road, but I can see where he's sifting through things in his head. Pertinent information he wants me to know and dangerous scenarios he wants to keep from me.

MI6 operatives live in a space where decisions must be minutely navigated to get the best outcome, but they can't account for everything in this world. I'm painfully aware of that as I think about my father, a man who was never around and a victim of circumstance.

Declan's cabin comes into view like it did the last time I was here. This time, his place feels familiar and welcoming. My mom gasps at the sight of the cabin.

"It's beautiful. Declan, is this yours?" she asks.

"It's mine. We need to get inside so I can show you around."

"Prince Declan, this is awesome!" Poppy yells and jumps out of the car, running toward the cabin.

I roll down the window and yell. "You can stop calling him Prince. His name is Declan." My frustration shows.

"He's a prince because he saved us from bad men!" Poppy yells back as the wind carries her small voice away.

I hold my head in my hands and breathe.

Declan leans over and whispers, "Little does she know, I'm a king." He uses his British aristocratic voice.

"Ha, that'll be the day."

"That which does not kill us makes us stronger." He gives me the grin of a Cheshire cat.

"Nietzsche, and let's hope it doesn't kill us." We're even.

"What I want to know is why they are using you to get to me. What's the connection?"

I shrug without looking at him. "Maybe because you work with me." I might know the reason why, but I'm not a hundred-percent sure.

I get out of the car and slam the door shut, heading for my new reality.

# Chapter Fifteen

Olivia

DECLAN CATCHES up to me as we walk side by side. Ozzie chases Poppy to the front porch, and my mom tags along with the kitten in her arms. The last time we were here, the cabin was void of anything emotional or personal items. I'm coming with every piece of my baggage, wondering what the next steps will be.

"You listened to every word I said and followed my orders. Kind of unusual for you, from what I remember, you were the bossy one," he smirks.

He turns to watch Poppy and Ozzie run around on the front porch. There's a smile on his face that comes from the honest joy of watching my daughter play with her dog. He seems fascinated by them. He hasn't mentioned a wife or children, so I imagine he doesn't have any, even if he claims not to be a player anymore.

"Neil is my surrogate father. I know about some of his missions, and I know how well-trained MI6 agents are, so I would be a fool not to listen to your advice, especially when my loved ones' lives hang in the balance. Don't worry, I'm still bossy."

We stand and face each other as I pull my coat closer. A spring wind comes down off the mountain as cool air whips around my bare legs. He's trying to calculate what to say next. He used to be flippant, but now his words are measured.

"Let's get everyone settled in, and then you and I need to talk."

He unlocks the front door the same way he did before, with the key and a code. Poppy runs in and jumps on the couch, giggling, with Ozzie close behind, barking at her and pushing his nose into her.

"Margot, I need you, Poppy, Ozzie, and Prince to stay here for a couple of days until things cool off. I have got to find out what's going on before you can go back to the farm," Declan announces.

My mother puts the kitten on the floor. "I have animals that need tending, especially the horses, goats, and the barn cats."

"Leave it to me. I have a couple who take care of my place, and they can take care of yours, too. I'll call them." He's in control and confident, which is incredibly sexy.

He turns to leave, going out the sliders onto the back deck to make his call.

"Poppy, why don't you go upstairs and pick a room?"

"Okay." She jumps off the couch, and Ozzie follows her upstairs.

I turn to my mother. "What happened at the house?"

"It was the most excitement I've had in years." She rounds the couch to stand in front of me. "He's a good man, Olivia. You can trust him. He shot the gunman, who was going to kill Ozzie. I don't know what happened with the other man, but he saved me in the barn. They were there to kidnap us; at least, that's what I think. I just don't know why."

Declan comes back in from making his phone call. "Frederick and Henri are on their way here with groceries. They want to talk to Margot about how they should handle the animals. You don't need to worry. They are highly trained ex-military and have a farm of their own."

He sweeps his hand toward the stairs. "Let's get everyone settled in. Your clothes should be here soon."

We each pick a room to stay in. The lavender gray room fascinates Poppy.

"Prince Declan, did you know purple is my favorite color?" She stands at his feet, peering up at him. My heart breaks. This is what she would look like with her father.

"No, I didn't. It must be fate." He glances at me sideways with half a smile.

There's a knock at the front door, and Declan goes to answer it. Two men lug our luggage up the stairs and deliver it to our rooms. Neil did well. They packed each suitcase with our clothes and toiletries.

Declan leans against the doorframe, watching me unpack my bag.

"How long do you think we need to stay here?" I continue to move things around the room.

"Your mum, Poppy, and the pets will be here for at least a week. But you and I are going to go back to work. There are things there I need to investigate. Don't worry, I won't keep you from work."

He shuts the bedroom door and tells me everything, including the note, the shooting at the house, and the guy who took the kill pill. I sit on the end of the bed, unable to keep my hands from shaking. He sits next to me and takes my hands in his.

I jerk my hands away and stand up. "When I agreed to have someone come work for me so they can figure out what was going on at the company, I didn't think it would be you. I also thought it would be a straightforward job. You would find what you were looking for and leave. But no, things are never easy where you are concerned. They're always complicated, and now my family is in danger, thanks to you."

The door bangs against the wall as I fling it open and rush down the stairs. I run out the front door and into the wildflower fields. There is a small path separating the fields. My arms pump harder and harder as pricker plants cut my legs, but I keep going. The footsteps behind me pound the earth, and I know who they belong to.

"Leave me alone!" I yell at the top of my lungs.

His hand grabs my upper arm from behind and stops me. I wrestle out of his grasp. I can't even run away from him. We're both panting, me more than him. I need to work out more.

"I had no idea what waited for me here. Someone from my past knows I'm here, and apparently, I'm a threat to them. Running away isn't the answer. We must move toward them, not away. I've got to anticipate their next move," he pleads with me.

"This coming from you. You run away from everything." He frowns. I put my hands up in front of him and walk backwards. "I need some space, please."

He nods, turns around, and walks away.

I'm alone, surrounded by beautiful wildflowers that don't have a care in the world. There are days when I wish I didn't have a care in the world, but my days always get the better of me. They take more than they give. Between work and my daughter, I'm pulled in every direction.

As I look over my shoulder, the sun sets in a blaze to the

west. The last streak of light sneaks behind the horizon, waving goodbye to a day full of the unexpected.

The tether to my mother and daughter keeps me in place, preventing me from running anywhere or any farther into the woods. Guilt crashes over me for running away from them. My struggle lies between work and my daughter. I love both, but finding the balance pulls me in both directions. The familial rope tugs at me, pulling me closer to the house and back inside where I belong and need to be.

I enter through the front door and arrive to chaos. Poppy is running around the living room, screaming because Declan is chasing her as Ozzie chases him. I've never seen this side of him, but I may know more about him than he even knows about himself.

The bewitching hour of five o'clock is upon us. The time when children take their stored energy from the day and release it right around dinnertime. This curse is put upon parents from birth. I secretly hope it exhausts her so she sleeps well tonight.

I move past them into the kitchen, where two gorgeous men are unpacking groceries. They are familiar with each other and seem to know their way around the kitchen.

"Hi, I'm Olivia Marcel." I reach out my hand.

The man with sandy blond hair introduces himself as Henri. His partner, Frederick, is his exact opposite, with jet-black hair and blue eyes.

"Thank you for bringing us food tonight and for taking care of our farm. We can't take care of our animals from this distance."

"It's no problem," Henri says in English with a thick French accent. "We'll take care of everything. We spoke to Margot and know something about farms. Frederick is an excellent cook and is going to make us dinner tonight. We also have a phone for you. I understand you had to ditch your last one."

He hands me the phone, and it's an exact match to the one I had to leave behind. This is my lifeline to the office so they can call me twenty-four seven.

Henri throws his arm around Frederick's shoulder and kisses him on the cheek. They light up around one another. There's only one time I've ever felt that kind of light, and he's chasing my daughter around in the other room.

# Chapter Sixteen

### Declan

MY CABIN HAS NEVER SEEN this much life. In the short time I have been in Germany, I've managed to pack in five adults, one child, a big dog, and a kitten. I've gone from being alone to having no privacy, and it warms something deep inside of me.

A house full of people reminds me of my childhood on the farm in Scotland. Maybe it's why I don't like to be alone.

Poppy's giggle sends me back to when we used to chase Kendall around the barn, playing hide-and-seek. Once my brothers and I found her, she would pop out of her hiding place and squeal while running away.

Those bittersweet memories have a firm grasp on me. I tend to hold on to the past for various reasons, some good, some not-so-good.

I haven't been back to Edinburgh since losing my mother and my sister. There's nothing there for me since my father left the farm to Mac. My anger at Mac simmered for a long time, but we've mended our fences. This cabin was supposed to be my piece of heaven, but it turned into purgatory as I recovered after the accident.

Poppy takes a breather on the couch with Ozzie, and I meander into the kitchen. Liv watches Frederick and Henri flirt with each other with keen interest. She has an odd look on her face. I'm not sure if she's forlorn or sad. My Petal pops with secrets at every turn. *My Petal?* She's hardly mine. We still need to talk about the elephant in the room, the kiss.

I briefed Neil about what happened and the need for our current location. He seemed edgy. I question whether it has to do with the fact I have to protect his niece and grand-niece. Showing any personal investment is not his style.

I enter the kitchen and speak French with Henri, asking what they're making for dinner. He wags his finger back and forth and tsks.

"Frederick has a surprise for us, and I'm not allowed to tell you what it is. Olivia, why don't you introduce me to that wild redhead of yours?" He winks at me as he passes by, like I have a secret he's caught on to.

We sit in the living room with Henri and catch up since the last time I talked to him. Margot sits quietly, keeping an eye on Poppy and her furry friends.

Frederick is busy in the kitchen making a gourmet meal with mystery ingredients. He announces dinner is ready, and we move to the dining room with a view overlooking the mountains.

I sit next to Liv and across from Henri and Frederick. Poppy sits on Liv's other side, and Margot is next to Poppy. Down the middle of the table are dinner rolls and salad as Frederick plates up a quail dish. Quiet veils the room at first, and then Liv starts with her *ums* and *ahs*.

"How long have you known Declan?" she asks in between bites, speaking English. The ding of her phone keeps going off, indicating she has text messages, probably from work, but she doesn't answer them.

Frederick speaks up. "We met Declan in a bar in Paris near the Moulin Rouge. It's not the nicest or the safest part of town, and he was trashed. We took him back to our place and tucked him in."

He gazes over at Henri with adoration in his eyes. "Henri and I were getting to know each other and falling in love, but our military careers would end if we were open about our relationship. We left the military behind so we could be together. The German countryside seemed to be the best place to settle down."

Henri grabs his hand and squeezes. Poppy is so involved in her meal that she's oblivious to the conversation. Ozzie sits at her feet and waits for scraps as Prince sleeps in Margot's lap.

Frederick continues the story. "We bought a farm down the road. Then Declan bought this cabin, and we helped him recover from …"

I shake my head subtly to let him know Liv isn't aware of my story.

"… his accident, but I'm sure he can tell you more."

Liv has silenced her phone and doesn't take the opportunity to ask more questions, which means one of two things. Either she is enjoying the food way too much, or she's exhausted. She nods. The conversation continues with things about the countryside she knew nothing about.

Poppy finally looks up from her food and asked if we can go for a walk in the woods tomorrow. I promised her we'll go for a walk soon.

We end dinner with Frederick's surprise chocolate lava cake. Poppy is mesmerized by the flowing liquid inside the cake. She eats every bite.

When dinner is over, Frederick and Henri say good night, and I help clean up with Liv. She avoids my gaze as we rinse the dishes and load the dishwasher. Margot takes Poppy, Ozzie, and the kitten upstairs to get ready for bed.

I'm walking on eggshells with Liv. I don't want to upset her anymore today, so I make a peace offering.

"Would you like some of my special decaf or some chamomile tea before bed?"

Her face is pale. "I think I'll pass and turn in for the night. I enjoyed talking to Frederick and Henri. They're an interesting couple. I hope to see them again." Her face glows from the blue light of the phone as she catches up on messages.

"I'm sure we will. They'll be in and out to check on Margot and Poppy."

She looks up and tries for a smile but fails. "Good night. I'll see you tomorrow."

As she heads up to bed, I'm left with the quiet of the cabin. Even with everyone in bed asleep, the cabin has an energy it's never had before. There's the hum of leftover laughter, conversation, cooking aromas, and animals. My heart sings, happy not to be alone, but I know it's temporary. Somehow, I need to wean Liv off her phone so she can enjoy some of what this area has to offer.

I head up to bed after a long day. Stripping out of my clothes, I slip in between the cold sheets. Sleep should come easily to me after getting everyone here safely, but it doesn't. I'm restless and want to resolve things with Liv. We need to work together if we're going to figure out the players in this game and how to get to the drug.

After a few hours of tossing and turning, I give up, grab my phone, and tiptoe downstairs. There's a single light on in the kitchen, and Liv is perched on a stool at the island.

"I should've taken you up on your sleep cocktail. My mind is running a mile a minute," she mumbles without looking at me. She spins a coffee cup in her hand. I notice that her phone is missing.

"I can't sleep either. What bothers me more than anything else is that we didn't resolve things between us. I'll make us chamomile tea." I tap my phone and put on another one of my favorite artists, Chris Stapleton, as he sings "Broken Halos."

I heat the kettle with water and sit next to her at the island. "I'm sorry you're involved with things you shouldn't be exposed to. This was not my intention. Neil never told me who my contact was at Bio2Chem. I thought your ambition would've led you to work for a bigger firm." I stop talking long enough to hear what she might have to say.

"I want to make a difference. I know I can make a difference. Life should not amount to nothing." Her voice sounds small as she peels back a layer.

"How can you think your life would amount to nothing? Poppy is your legacy. She's a product of you, and you need to enjoy her while you can because life is fleeting. It can turn on a dime when you least expect it." I swallowed that pill a long time ago and know it all too well.

She laughs. "I am the poster child for how life can turn on a dime. Poppy was unexpected."

"Sometimes accidents are the best things that could ever happen to you. Poppy is a blessing."

"Is that how you feel about your accident?" Her eyes bore into mine.

The whistle from the teakettle breaks the moment. I pour the hot water over the tea bags and carry them to the island.

"I'm not sure I would put my accident in the best things category."

"Poppy told me you put marker on your bumpy skin. She

wants to cover up her scarred knees with marker." She wears a tired smile. "From her description, it sounds like you were in an accident where you were burned."

"They called me Brennen at the bar when I was here before. Brennen is exactly what I did."

## Chapter Seventeen

Declan

THE TIME HAS COME. I've avoided telling anyone the brutal details of my accident for years. The burden has become too heavy to carry, and it weighs on me. Saying it out loud might give me the closure I need to move forward. I'm choosing to walk through the fire again.

She stares down at the teacup as her robe falls open enough for me to see the curves of her breasts. If I ever want to get to the heart of Petal beneath her creamy white skin, I'm going to have to tell my truth. Once she hears my story, she'll understand why I had no choice but to change.

"Some of the details I'm about to tell you are what I've been told because I have almost no memory before the incident. I was working in the lab with aluminum borohydride after hours. We were doing testing on an antidepressant formula, and I had put on a hazmat outfit. I guess I was careless and forgot to check it for tears and holes."

My chest tightens, and my breathing is shallow as I try to

keep my hands from shaking. Saying the words brings me back to that moment in time I've avoided for years. Liv says nothing and watches me with curiosity and empathy.

"Sam left right after I got suited up and entered the lab. Before I knew what was happening, my skin was on fire from the combination of chemicals. Someone must have come back into the lab and saw me on fire. They put me out with a fire extinguisher, tackled me to the ground, and ripped off my hazmat suit."

I can't control my shaking hands, and the tea spills over the edge of the cup. Liv grabs a hold of my hands to steady them. Water crests in her eyes and falls down her rose-colored cheeks.

"My God. I can't imagine how terrifying that was for you." Her tears drop onto the granite countertop, mixing with the tea and disappearing.

"What happened months before the accident, which I don't think was an accident, and the next year are a blur. They took me by ambulance to the nearest burn unit in Aachen. I had no sense of time, but they tell me I was there for six months, in and out of consciousness. MI6 didn't want to move me because of my fragile condition but oversaw my treatment. They had to keep me sedated because of the pain."

She stands up, squeezes her hips between my legs, and holds me to her like a mother would hold a child. I grab her around the waist and bury my face in her shoulder.

Five years of hiding, pain, and uncertainty break loose. I weep into her shoulder as sobs rack my body. With every cry that breaks free, she holds me tighter and rubs my back. I need her to understand why I'm so confused about myself and my past.

What she doesn't do is tell me it's going to be okay or try to shush me. She is there, absorbing my pain. I don't know why I chose her to reveal my darkness to, but it gives me a sense of relief I've never experienced before.

Even in this cathartic moment, my hope that I would retrieve some memories I lost doesn't come to the surface. They stay buried, maybe for my own good.

I let go of my life raft and rest my eyes in my palms. Liv leaves the kitchen and comes back with a box of tissues. I grab a few from the box and dry my eyes. This is as raw and open as I've been with anyone in my life, but I can't think of a better person to share my pain with than Liv. I'm tied to her in a way I don't understand.

"I'm sorry. I very much doubt seeing someone fall apart was on your top ten list," I mumble.

She shakes her head. "You have nothing to be sorry for. I had no idea what happened to you. No one said there was ever an accident at the lab. After that day, I never saw you again. It was weird. I assumed you had taken off. I was wrong."

She didn't know I was on an op to find a cancer-causing drug more elusive than the memory drug. She thought she had hired a regular scientist.

Her hands rest on mine, and she has a frown on her face. "Come to think of it, I never saw Sam after that day, either." She looks at me with questions in her eyes I can't answer.

"After the warnings I received since I've gotten here, there's no doubt in my mind it was no accident. Maybe Sam was the one who put holes in the hazmat suit. I never got a chance to come back and investigate. I was hoping to get those answers while I was here."

"You've been to hell and back." Her hands make their way up my forearms as she rubs them.

"Literally. I might be the devil himself." I try to force a smile, but it doesn't come.

"Where did you get burned?" she asks.

"Mostly my arms and legs where the holes were in the suit. My hands, face, and feet were spared because someone got to me and the design of the suit. Over the years, I've covered most of them in tattoos. The last of my tattoos I want to get here in Germany. There is an artist I have in mind."

"Would you be willing to show them to me?"

I nod. She pulls up the sleeve of my left arm. Her warm hand caresses the bumps on my arm, and I flinch. She pulls her hand back.

"I'm sorry. I didn't mean to hurt you."

"You didn't hurt me. It's been years since I let anyone touch me. Parts of my skin have a lot of sensation, and other sections are numb. After a lot of alone time, I haven't gotten used to the feeling. You might say I've been lost, unable to find an anchor anywhere. This cabin is where I spent much of my time recovering. There were many skin grafts, and I went through a lot of bandages. The inside of these walls felt like purgatory, a place with no past and no future. I traveled around Europe for a couple of years and finally made my way to New York City, where I came face-to-face with some of the ghosts from my past and a lot of anger. That's when I realized I needed to be in recovery."

She rolls up the sleeve of my right arm and runs her fingertips over the bumps, scars, and tattoos. I close my eyes and take in the sensation of her touch. My nervous system is on overload, trying to navigate the oversensitive areas of my skin to the numb ones. I pull my arms out from under her hands. She looks up at me.

"This is a lot to handle. I want to feel you under my fingertips." I wiggle my brows.

Her eyes get wide. My fingers start at the nape of her neck as my thumb strokes her jaw. Her eyes close, and she leans into my hand. My fingers follow the curve of her collarbone, down her chest, and across the swell of her breasts. She doesn't move, but her breath becomes rapid as her mouth opens, and her eyes remain closed.

I take advantage of the moment and finish what we started, hoping this is not an end but a new beginning. I suck on her plump lips, licking them as if they are covered in forbidden Oban, my favorite single malt scotch after a five-star dinner.

My tongue finds hers in the gentlest of play, feeling each other out without dominance. I'll save that for later. She moans in my mouth, and it's all I can do not to lay her out on the island and peel away her clothes to reveal the most beautiful curves I've ever seen. She is a genius, bold, confident, beautiful, and a leader. Everything I'm not and everything I want in a woman.

Holding her forehead to mine, I stop kissing her. "We need to stop before I won't be able to control myself. Besides, it seems like Poppy is everywhere."

"You can't keep a good woman down. She's a very curious little girl and pops up everywhere. Be sure to lock the bathroom door." She laughs.

"Did you throw me a quote? Alice Walker, perhaps?"

She shakes her head.

"Let me be a gentleman and walk you to your room." With perfect timing, the Chris Stapleton song "You Should Probably Leave" plays from my phone.

I hold out my hand to her, and she takes it. I never thought a single touch would change my life.

# Chapter Eighteen

### Olivia

MY HAND FITS PERFECTLY in his as his thumb strokes my knuckles. We stop in front of my bedroom door and turn toward each other. He cradles my face in his hands and kisses my forehead.

"Thank you for listening to me tonight. I've never told anyone what happened to me, not even my family. I banished myself to the dark without hope of relief from the pain. Telling you my story was a relief I didn't expect. I hope I didn't burden you with it."

His hazel eyes are intense, begging me to understand the significance of the evening. The depth of his secret is not lost on me. Perhaps tomorrow I can fill in some of the gaps for him without giving everything away.

"You don't have to thank me. What happened to you is a scientist's worst nightmare. Besides, I love the permanent marker you put on your skin." I smile up at him.

"I'll make sure to hide the permanent markers from Poppy. Washables only. Tomorrow, I thought we could spend some time hiking. There are also things I need to show everyone about the house to keep them safe. I won't let anything happen to them or you. You need to believe me."

He flips into secret agent mode with ease. Some things about his personality are more evident as I see him in a new light. Another one of his boxes opens for me.

"I believe you. You've shown me how much they mean to you, although I don't know why."

"I swear it's the red hair. She has me wrapped in her charm. Good night, and sleep well. I'll see you in the morning."

I was hoping he would tell me we give him a sense of family, somehow filling his hollow places. Lord knows, I know something about family dynamics. I didn't exactly grow up in a perfect family. My father was never part of the picture for me, leaving my uncle to raise his only child.

The hollow feeling is a constant companion. I've always put my feelings in a box, stuffed them away, unwilling to deal with the abandonment of my father. When Declan left without a word, my past came roaring back. I'd like to think I don't overcompensate at work, but it's a lie.

Being this far away from the office cuts the tight rubber band always stretched to the max when I'm at work. Declan gave me some insight into my life. Poppy is my legacy and my love. She's a smart, tenacious, and inquisitive little girl.

Her father should have been part of the picture from the beginning, but I couldn't trust him. Absentee fathers are a running theme for the women in my family. I was hoping to break the trend, but it doesn't look like I'm any closer than I was the day I came into this world.

I slip back into bed and float away, dreaming about tomorrow's hike. My head is usually filled with formulas and research data, but not tonight. Right now, I'm here, away from my rigorous life, trying to prove to myself that I can live without work. There is a new proposal I should consider when I get back. I fight the urge to focus on it and squeeze my eyes closed, thinking of mountainsides and flowers.

THE SUN'S rays stretch into the room as I lie cocooned in the warm comforter. I wake up refreshed, as though I have slept for years. The clock says ten a.m., long past the time when I usually get up. There are hundreds of unanswered texts that came in during the night, but I'll answer them later. The smell of coffee and cooking wafts under the door, making me smile and calling me to get ready for the day.

I head downstairs and follow the giggles of my redheaded girl. Now and then, Ozzie barks and whines. Peeking into the kitchen, I see Declan standing at the stove flipping pancakes. His smile stretches from ear to ear.

"Mommy, look what Prince Declan made. They're Mickey Mouse pancakes. The blueberries are his eyes." She picks the blueberries off and pops them in her mouth.

A shift happens inside me when I see my daughter happy. A special warmth blooms in the center of a mother's heart when she sees their child filled with innocence and fun. In this moment, I don't want her to grow up feeling pain, loss, or regret. I want to protect her from anything having to do with adult lives and lies. The adult world can be so cruel and should be put off as long as possible.

Her face lights up, and she looks down at the large pancake in the shape of Mickey Mouse's head. She kneels on the stool at the island where Declan shared his deepest secret with me. There's a lightness to him I haven't seen until today. Why does life unfold in kitchens?

I wonder if he knows how special he is and how much joy

he brings to my daughter's life. These are the small moments I try to hold on to, the moments sear themselves into my memory so I don't forget.

I clutch the front of my shirt, realizing these are the memories Declan doesn't have, those pieces have crumbled away, and he's not able to retrieve them from some unknown darkness.

"I didn't know you could cook." I pull Poppy into a hug and kiss the top of her head.

"Would you like a Mickey or Minnie Mouse pancake this morning?" He smiles while flipping the pancake in the pan.

"I would like a Winnie-the-Pooh pancake, please." I sit down next to Poppy, placing a napkin on my lap from the place setting.

"Are you challenging me? Because I can definitely make you a Winnie-the-Pooh pancake." We would always compete with one another before we found our common ground.

"Give it your best shot. I would also like a cup of your extra-special coffee, please," I say as I answer questions at a rapid pace on my phone. Responding to the text messages will take top priority today.

"Coming right up."

He pours a cup of coffee and brings it around to the opposite side of Poppy.

"It's hot when you make demands. It's even hotter when you melt under my touch," he whispers in my ear. "Your challenge, should you choose to accept it, will be to live without your phone for a day." He snatches it out of my hand. I try to grab it from him, but he holds it above his head.

I shiver in anticipation of what it will be like when we are together, and I have no doubt we will be together. His touch unravels the tightly wound twine inside of me. I've never been able to figure out what it is about him that keeps me calm. I'm not too sure about the phone challenge, but maybe I'll give it a shot.

The coffee, made to perfection, passes through my lips and touches my tongue, giving a burst of heaven to my mouth. I look over to where he is focusing on the pancake. He looks like an artist creating a masterpiece. He places a plate in front of me with a blob of pancake in the center. Winnie-the-Pooh has chocolate chips for eyes and a shirt slathered with raspberry jam.

"Voilà." He steps back and crosses his arms in front of him, waiting for my evaluation.

"Not bad. I can almost make out Winnie-the-Pooh." I laugh.

"That is clearly Winnie-the-Pooh with his red shirt. You better eat up. We have a long day of hiking ahead of us." His eyes darken.

He sits across from Poppy and me with a short stack of pancakes and a cup of coffee. Poppy ends up feeding half of her pancake to Ozzie, who wolfs it down. She hops off the stool and races out to the back deck, where I see my mom sitting on a lounger with a cup of coffee.

She smiles as the sun warms her face. "Why is my mom out there by herself?"

"I don't know. She asked for coffee and went outside." He shrugs. "She was talking on the phone with someone who makes her smile."

I grab the ends of my hair and put them over my shoulder.

"What are you nervous about?" He sits back and watches my reaction.

"What makes you think I'm nervous?"

He smiles. "You always play with the ends of your hair when you're nervous."

"At some point, you and I need to find time to talk. I can fill in some of those missing gaps for you."

He sits up straight in his chair, then leans forward. "Why didn't you say something last night?" His eyes narrow.

"Last night was intense. The moment was solely yours. I wanted to digest everything first before I told you. I can imagine this is a lot for you to handle, among everything else going on."

We get cut off as Poppy, Ozzie, and Prince bound through the sliding door and take over the kitchen.

# Chapter Nineteen

### Declan

I'M anxious to hear what she has to say. There is an inexplicable pull toward her, which doesn't match the memories I have of the two of us together. We were always at each other's throats and extremely competitive. There wasn't a time when I would ever call us friends, but she's a beautiful woman who is incredibly smart, which makes her irresistible.

She piques my curiosity, but other things need to be tended to first. My past has waited this long, it can wait a bit longer.

I call Margot in from the deck and wave for her to join us inside. She comes in and pulls the slider shut. I get down on one knee in front of Poppy. Ozzie takes the opportunity to lick my face.

"Thank you." I wipe the side of my face with my hand. "Zitten," I tell him to sit in Dutch, and he obeys.

"Poppy, I know you're almost five years old, but there are some things I need to show you, and you need to remember. Do you think you can do that for me?" She is smart as a whip, and I'm willing to bet she takes after her mum in the challenge department.

She nods and gives me a big grin. "Yep."

"I need everyone to know how this cabin works to become a real safe house." I offer Poppy my hand, which she takes and squeezes. Her father is missing out on the only person who matters in this world.

We take a tour of the cabin, and I show them the places where they can press the panic button. They are located throughout the house in various hiding places, but with easy access.

"When you press this button, metal shields come down over the windows. There are small slits in the fireproof shields big enough for a gun. The button will also send messages to my cell phone, my car, and Frederick and Henri, letting us know the defense shields have been activated. I want you to use it if you feel threatened in any situation. If there is someone at the door you don't know or a car you don't recognize, press the button."

The three of them get quiet as Margot and Liv exchange looks. Liv pulls Poppy toward her, crossing her hands over the front of her daughter's chest, a natural reaction.

"I know this sounds scary, but I don't want it to be. You need to feel safe while you are here." I get down on one knee again. "Poppy, will you feel safe living here for the next week?"

She throws her arms around my neck and gives me the most precious hug. The past twenty-four hours is the most I've been touched in five years, and it feels like heaven. I fold her into my arms, relishing the moment. I don't want to let go, even when this op is over.

"Of course, Prince Declan. I always feel safe when I'm with you." Her innocence shines through.

I swallow hard, knowing her life is in my hands. I can't afford to fumble this one. Not this time.

"What do you say we go for a hike?" I pick her up and set her on my hip.

She throws her hands up to the ceiling and yells, "Let's go!"

Liv goes back to the kitchen to pack a lunch and stuffs it in the backpack. Everyone wears hiking boots, lightweight pants, T-shirts, and a light jacket. We take Ozzie but leave Prince at home.

We head out through the wildflower fields, up the path to the mountainside. I packed bear mace and other weapons in case we come face-to-face with any wildlife. The hike starts off cool but warms up as the bright sun has no cloud cover.

Halfway into the hike, Poppy complains of being tired. I hand the backpack to Liv and hoist her up onto my shoulders so she can get a better view. Her fingers grip under my chin as she holds on to my face.

I grab her ankles. "I've got you. You won't fall."

We continue, coming to a fork in the path.

"We're going to take the fork to the right. I have something to show you."

Not far up the path appears a small wooden cabin. I let Poppy down off my shoulders. As soon as her feet hit the ground, she runs toward the cabin. She pushes the door open to reveal a small cot in the corner and a fireplace. In the opposite corner is a sink without running water. The outhouse and well are outside, around the back of the cabin.

"Not exactly luxury accommodations," Liv says.

"I don't know how old this cabin is, but it came with the property. It might have been an original structure to whoever owned the land. I wanted you to know this is here in case something happens at the house and you can't get to the panic button. You can come up here and be safe." I look over to Margot, and she nods as she crosses her arms in front of her.

Ozzie's nose has not left the floor since he got inside the cabin. God knows how many animals or humans have come and gone from this cabin. If the wooden walls could talk, they would have years of tales to tell.

I close the door of the cabin. "There is a clearing on the way back where we can sit and have lunch."

Liv has been unusually quiet during our hike but has stayed off her phone. There's hope yet. Poppy and Ozzie run ahead of us as Margot trails behind them, Liv and I bring up the rear.

"Is everything okay?"

"Yeah, I have a lot on my mind."

"Like filling in my memory gaps. Based on the chemistry between us, I would say we were friends before my accident. Am I wrong?"

"We had mended our fences and found common ground. I'll tell you more when we get back to the house, where we can be alone." She puts her hand up to shield her eyes from the sun, looking for Poppy.

I see Poppy drop out of sight, and I run for her at top speed while yelling her name. Ozzie is barking and whining. When I get to her, she's fallen and landed in a pile of rocks. My hands fly over her arms, legs, and ribs, checking for broken bones.

"Mommy," she cries.

Liv is right behind me and lifts her, cradling her on her shoulder. She is an awesome mum. I think she struggles between work and being a mum, but Poppy wouldn't be so well adjusted if Liv wasn't so attentive.

"I have a first aid kit in the backpack." She nods to it.

I wipe the wounds on her cheek with a sterile gauze and

hydrogen peroxide. I put some salve on it and cover it with a bandage. Her tears dry, and she looks up at me from Liv's arms and smiles.

I tap her nose with my finger. "How about we have a nice lunch so your wounds can heal with some good food?"

"Can I ride on your shoulders again?" she asks. Little daredevil.

"Absolutely, Princess Poppy."

"You've got to stop with the princess stuff. You're going to give her a big head," Liv mumbles under her breath.

"Let her live the fantasy. Life can be a real downer," I reply.

"Good point," she answers.

We soak up the sun, eating a lunch full of greens, meats, cheeses, crackers, wine, and a peanut butter and jelly sandwich for Poppy. Ozzie has his fair share of a little of everything, except for the wine.

Margot comments on the view and says she could spend the rest of her life here. I don't disagree. Staying here was part of my plan until I got restless and lonely.

As we head down the mountain and walk along the path by the wildflower fields, I notice a familiar SUV in the driveway. Frederick and Henri are back to report on anything they found at Liv's farm. By the look on their faces, I would say it's not good news.

Guilt shreds me at the thought of this being my fault. Had I not come back, everyone would be safe, but my life has never been about playing it safe. I didn't want to involve anyone else.

## Chapter Twenty

Olivia

FREDERICK AND HENRI meet us at the front of the house with a look of dread on their faces. Poppy has had enough of her innocence taken away during the last couple of days, and I don't want her to be a part of this discussion.

"Poppy, you need to go in the house with Ozzie and find Prince. I'm sure he misses you." I pull her down off Declan's shoulders as he follows her to the front door.

He opens the door and leaves it open, returning to the conversation. "What happened?"

"I am sorry, Madame Marcel. They set your small barn on fire. We got there in time to stop it from spreading to the house," Henri says in French with a long face and looks at Frederick. "We think they were going to burn it all to the ground. No animals were harmed."

"We spent the day getting the animals transferred over to our farm. Your horses, goats, chickens, and barn cats are safe at our farm," Frederick continues.

We turn to look at my mother, afraid of her reaction. Her

farm means everything to her, giving her purpose and is a source of pride.

"The good news is my animals are safe and just down the road if I want to visit with them." She turns to Declan. "I don't know exactly what's going on or why you're here, but I want you to get these bastards and take them out." She stretches up, takes his face in her hands, and kisses him on both cheeks, then walks past him into the house. "Viva le Declan!" She pumps her fist in the air.

"She is one strong, resilient woman. Now I know where you get it from." Declan turns back to the conversation. "Frederick and Henri, I can't thank you enough for everything you've done. I'll take care of you."

"It's nothing, no worries. We are huge animal lovers, so we do it from our hearts," Henri responds.

"Liv and I are going to work tomorrow. I would appreciate it if you kept an eye on Margot and Poppy."

"Not a problem. We'll pick them up to see their animals. Margot will want to know everyone is okay." Frederick and Henri wave goodbye as they head back to their vehicle.

Declan turns to me and holds my upper arms. "I'm sorry this is happening. It's not what I expected. This mission was supposed to be an easy in and out. They are trying to get to me through you. Believe me when I tell you, I will find them, and they will pay for this." He stands up straight. "Unless you think I should go in order to divert them away from you."

I nod. His apology is sincere, which I register for a nanosecond. The heat of his hands on my arms as his thumbs rub back and forth has my attention. My body recognizes his electricity as if it were its own. Then I snap out of it long enough to realize what he's suggesting.

"No! I mean, no. I think you should stay and see this through; if you don't, they will continue to search for you."

The conflict within me is raging. I want to know who this man is in front of me, but I don't want the man I knew from the past to return.

"Your mum has been quiet today. Is she okay, or is she putting on a good front?"

"She's made of sturdy stuff and has been in situations worse than this. I think she's trying to give us some space."

He frowns. "Why would she be trying to give us space?"

I pull my arms away, breaking the spell he seems to have me under every time he touches me. Some secrets are better left unsaid, and this is one of them.

"Let's make dinner and get Poppy to bed. Then we can talk."

Declan decides he's going to make dinner. He putters around the kitchen, gathering ingredients. He doesn't engage with anyone except minor small talk with Poppy. She gives up and goes into the living room with my mother.

I've seen this before. He goes inside himself, trying to figure things out. Sometimes, I think he's the most sensitive man on earth. His walls are hard to break down when he's in this mode, but he always comes out the other side with some epiphany about his life or someone else's.

I admire his ability to be self-reflective. He's always known himself so well, but the man I see before me is not one I recognize. Time and maturity, along with his accident, have made him more of a man and less of a frat boy, and it's sexy as hell. I have a hard time turning him down. The attraction from long ago has picked up where it left off and burns hotter than ever.

Tonight, I'll fill him in on some of the pieces, just not the entire picture. I'm not ready yet. I'm hoping for some divine intervention to tell me when the right time will be.

Declan makes a simple dinner of green beans and chicken. He offers me a wonderful French Pinot Grigio.

I wave off the glass he puts down in front of me. "I don't need to have wine, but thank you."

He shrugs. "Wine was never my weakness. Scotch, on the other hand, was an expensive habit I soaked in. The wine is a nice way for you to end the day."

I accept the wine which compliments the meal and mellows me out. We discuss the sights on the hike, and Poppy is excited to revisit the small cabin in the woods.

She eats half the food on her plate and gives some of the green beans to Ozzie. He's allergic to chicken, so she knows not to give him any. Her eyes close as she props her head on her hands. A day of sunshine and fresh air has finally taken their toll, and she succumbs to sleep.

I gather her in my arms and carry her upstairs. She's a limp rag. I lay her on the bed and peel her out of her clothes, slipping her into pajamas. Her red hair fans out on the pillow, and her cheeks are rosy from a touch of sun.

Without her, my life would be so different, but it wouldn't be richer. I would've been more obsessed with my job than I already am. She gives me the break I need, a relief from the internal mechanism driving me to make the world a better place. In the long run, I'm committed to my work for her generation. They deserve a life of improvement, maybe one without pain, cancer, and disability.

The day catches up with me as I yawn and make my way downstairs. The sun falls behind the horizon, and the cabinet lights on are in the kitchen giving it a soft glow. Declan sits at the island with his hands wrapped around a coffee mug.

"Hey, do you have one of those for me?" I speak softly, not to disrupt his moment.

"Sure." He turns back to the stove without looking at me.

He places a coffee mug in front of me and returns to his stool on the other side of the island. We sit in silence for a while, sipping our drinks.

He looks up at me with intense eyes. "We need to talk. I need you to fill in some of those missing pieces because I'm confused."

I nod. "How about we talk on the deck?"

"Grab a coat. It's cool outside. I'll light the firepit."

The old Declan wouldn't have cared if I brought a coat or if I froze to death. This man attends to every detail. I grab a light jacket and head out to the deck, taking a deep breath to ready myself for the words I want to say.

The firepit blazes, and Declan reclines in an oversize lounger made for two. When I come out, he looks up at me and pats the place next to him on the lounger. Being this close to him while telling him some of his past is probably not the best idea, but my body trumps my head.

## Chapter Twenty-One

### Declan

SHE STOPS WALKING as if thinking about her choice to lie with me on the lounger. I watch her with anticipation to see which side of her wins the war to come sit with me. She slides in next to me with concern written on her face.

Her curves are a familiar road map. My body is a live wire on high alert with the heat of her body so close, but I need to stay focused and listen to what she has to tell me. She may fill in the gaps and trigger more memories.

"The stars are extraordinary out here in the woods without the lights of the city. As a child, I would take a blanket outside late at night and watch for shooting stars. I know the constellations by heart." Her face glows from the fire, and her eyes sparkle with memories.

"It is not the stars to hold our destiny but ourselves," I whisper close to her ear.

"How very romantic of you to quote Shakespeare on a starry night." She smiles and sips her coffee.

"We are even in the battle of the quotes, as always." I chuckle.

I won't push her to tell me what I want to know. I need her to want to help me uncover my past. She needs to trust that I can handle what she has to reveal.

"Your foot is moving a mile a minute. You're eager for me to tell you what I know. How does it feel to want?" She laughs.

"You always were kind of a sadist."

She hums. "A couple of months before you disappeared, you and I had become close."

"What was the turning point? Because I remember us being adversaries." I turn my body to face her.

She takes another sip of her drink. "It's hard for me to talk about," she chokes on her words.

"After last night, there's no judgment here. Take your time."

She takes a deep breath. "Everyone at the office went out for happy hour on a Friday night. You were there too but stayed on the opposite end of the bar. One drink led to another, and we were feeling no pain. I was having such a good time; I must not have been paying attention to the people around me." She looks over at me with pain in her eyes that spears my chest.

"There was this guy who kept trying to talk to me during the night, but I wasn't in the mood for any company. Happy hour turned into more drinking and dinner as we stayed until the wee hours of the morning." She takes another sip.

"I left the bar to get a cab back to the office, hoping to sleep it off. I wasn't drunk, but I was buzzing from the alcohol. A man came up behind me and grabbed my arm. He said something about how dare I ignore him, and I was being a rude bitch. He pulled me into the alley and threw me down.

My head hit the ground hard, making me almost black out, but I managed to stay in the moment. He punched me in the face a couple of times, and I heard the zipper of his pants. I knew what was coming, and I was defenseless."

She sighs deeply, clutching her coffee mug. Tears shimmer in her eyes. "I turned and was trying to get up off the ground when suddenly I saw a dark figure beating the hell out of this guy. It's the last thing I remembered before I passed out."

She looks up at me as the flames from the firepit dance in her blue eyes. "I woke up the next morning alone in someone's bed. I felt the tightness of the stitches near my eye, and then you walked in." Her fingers float over the smallest of scars near her left eye I never noticed before.

"If you hadn't come in the alley, that man would've raped and killed me. You saving me was our turning point." Her fingers clutch my shirt.

She lets go and looks away. "We became friends. There was no more animosity, only respect."

Her story hits close to home as I remember waking up in a bed but wanting to scream from the pain of my burns. My head tries to dive into my memory bank to find where this happened, but I come up short. I can't get to this moment in time, but I should, given the significance of the event.

"There was always respect. But we were only friends, eh?" I get a feeling there's more to the story.

She nods. "You're right. In our work, there was respect, but we were just friends."

I lean down close to her ear. "Then why is your body so familiar to me, Petal? It's like I know every curve." She shivers as my breath caresses her ear .

"I don't know. Maybe you are having fantasies about something you can't have." She smiles, but she's a bad liar.

I take the mug out of her grasp and place it on the deck. "Who says I can't have you? There is something so familiar about you that screams more than friends. I don't think I'm getting the complete story, but I will eventually. I always get what I want."

Before she has a chance to answer, my lips crash down on hers, letting her feel my familiarity. I wait for her resistance but find none. My tongue demands entry as she fights back for control.

She grabs my hair with both hands, which spurs me on. She gives as good as she gets and won't be outdone. This is the way it's always been. A mutual respect with a winner-takes-all ending.

I peel away her jacket as my hand finds her soft breast. Her hard nipples push through her thin shirt. With her shirt and bra pushed out of the way, I roll her nipple as she lets out a moan. My kisses trail down her neck, across her chest, to their destination when I latch on to her nipple and play with it. She writhes underneath me, eyes shut tight. Her nipple pops out of my mouth, and I freeze.

"We need to stop." The words leave my mouth, but my cock wants this train to continue down the track.

"What? Why?" She pants.

"Poppy."

"What about her?" Her frustration shows.

"What if she gets up and wanders out here? That child is everywhere. We can't let her see us like this." I'm convinced I'm doing the right thing.

Liv rolls over and straddles me, so her sex is in line with my rigid cock. She takes off her shirt and bra, displaying her awesome tits and making me second-guess my restraint.

"Do you know there are people in the world who have

two children?" She puts her hands on her hips and she grinds down on my cock.

"Yes." I have no idea where she's going with this, but I like it.

"They have two children because they have sex whenever and wherever they can, praying their first child stays asleep. If she wanders out here, I guess we'll call it wrestling. So, are we going to continue, or are you going to wimp out?"

I roll her over onto her back, pinning her arms above her head. "Sounds like you're giving me another challenge. Remember, if she pops out here and wants to know what we're doing, you're gonna have to explain why you're wrestling Prince Declan."

We stare at each other as the fire paints us in a warm glow. Flames always seem to lick at my heels. She's not resisting being intimate, which gives me even more information. The push and pull we have together is a friggin' turn-on.

Licking her lips, I pick up where I left off. I suck on her other nipple as her body softens under me. Her hands travel over my back, skimming over my skin. I freeze, surrounded by layers of shame and fear, wanting someone to accept me for the way I look. At this moment, I forgot I haven't been with a woman in years, afraid to scare them away. Liv doesn't scare easily. She never did.

She understands my hesitation. "I want to see you and feel you. I already know the man you are and how you got here. There's nothing left to hide," she whispers. "Let go of your fear. Stop being the outsider and let me in."

I let out the breath I'm holding as she says the words, releasing me from my fears for the moment. I nod in acceptance. She pulls my shirt up over my head, revealing the scarred skin, bare in some spots and tattooed in others. Her eyes roam from one tattoo to the next as her fingers follow. She looks mesmerized.

"Your artwork is beautiful, and so are your scars. I like the feel of you. Smooth skin is overrated. It lacks texture and character."

With those words, I strip her out of her clothes as she tears me out of the rest of mine. We lie naked under the starlit sky, and I grab a blanket to cover us. The combination of heat from our bodies and the fire warms us, and we begin our slow dance.

My fingers roam across her soft, rosy skin and find her sex soaking wet. I want to be gentle with her as I insert a finger and rub her clit with my thumb. She rocks underneath me in rhythm with my strokes.

Grabbing my cock, she strokes me up and down and it takes everything I have not to come. I am on sensory overload. My heart pounds in my chest from excitement and fear. Action in the sex department has been nonexistent, and I question if I'll be able to satisfy her. I pull back.

"I need you inside me, please," she begs.

"I don't have any condoms."

Her eyes pop open. "How is that possible?"

"As hard as it is to believe, I haven't had sex in a long time." My smart mouth is tamed by the truth.

"Then, we need to fix that. It's been a while for me, too. I am protected and clean. What about you?"

"It's been so long; I think I've hit virgin status."

She smiles and guides my cock to her entrance. I slide in without resistance as we move slowly together. My eyes never leave hers as I kiss her and taste her lips. The calm I get when I swim comes over me. The rhythm between us is natural without awkward guessing. She's everything I didn't know I needed until this moment.

"I'm sorry," I say on the edge of an orgasm.

"For what?"

"I'm not going to last long."

"Good, neither am I."

I release five years of pent-up sexual energy to the woman who sees me for who I am and accepts the flaws of my character and skin. She arches her back and comes with me as lights explode behind my eyes. My body shutters with aftershocks. I fall on my elbows next to her head, not wanting to crush her as our hearts beat together and our breathing slows.

I have complicated things between us since I don't know how this mission is going to go. After what I've survived, I'm taking every moment I have to live to the fullest, and I want to be with her. When we go back to work, there will be many threats around us. Now, I'm even more invested in keeping her safe.

# Chapter Twenty-Two

Olivia

SOMEWHERE DURING OUR EUPHORIC STATE, we decide to go back to his master suite. I lost count of how many orgasms he gave me during the night, but I treasured every one of them.

He's gifted me with his precious secret as he rebuilds himself into a stronger man. Only an insightful person can be as vulnerable as he has been with me, shedding light on his darkest moments. I'm in awe of who he has fought to become.

He makes me feel more alive than any man I've ever been with and challenges me to be better. With each step we take, our trust for each other grows deeper roots. It doesn't take away from how new this is for both of us.

We behave like two sex-starved teenagers, groping each other and trying to get our next high. In the wee hours of the morning, we go from soft to hard and back to tender. We want to feel everything, afraid it might disappear tomorrow. I fall asleep sometime during the night while he wraps himself around me, so I have nowhere to go.

The door crashes open, and my head snaps up.

"Prince Declan, I can't find Mommy." Poppy is in a panic.

Poppy jumps on the bed and sits with her legs tucked under her in her nightgown, staring at both of us. Ozzie plops himself next to her. She looks back and forth between the two of us with unspoken questions.

"You're up," Declan whispers. "Good luck. I'll take notes for next time."

I pull the sheet up to my neck. "Declan and I were wrestling."

She laughs and face-plants on the bed as if it's the most hysterical thing she's ever heard. I'm so screwed. She's too young to figure this out.

"You weren't wrestling. You wanted to snuggle with a prince. Everyone wants to snuggle with a prince."

"That's not all princes want to do," he murmurs out of earshot. I elbow him in the ribs as he lets out a grunt and then laughs.

She turns her attention to Declan, who has the sheet down around his waist, and his fingers are clasped behind his head. He's so smug.

Her eyes get big as she asks the all-important question, while I hold my breath. "Can you make me Mickey Mouse pancakes again?"

He looks over at me while he gives her his answer. "Of course. Anything for Princess Poppy. We'll meet you downstairs."

"Okay." She hops off the bed and scurries out the door as Ozzie follows behind.

Declan laughs so hard he has tears in his eyes. I slap his hard shoulder and hurt my hand.

"What's so funny?"

"I think your child is smarter than you are. She so did not buy the wrestling explanation."

He pulls me into a hug and kisses the top of my head. "I haven't felt this much joy in years. Maybe I've never felt this much joy ever. Thank you." His mouth is buried in my hair.

I look up at an open, happy, and content face. We might as well enjoy it now because we have no idea what waits for us down the road.

I throw back the covers and step out of the warmth of the bed. Turning around, I try to cover the stretch marks on my lower belly, which is ridiculous considering he's seen me naked already.

Declan grabs my hands before I can cover them. "Don't you dare cover those or say a negative word about them. They are the most beautiful marks I've ever seen, considering the little redhead is the one who made them."

He knows something about skin marks, and his words allow me to lose my self-consciousness. He grabs my ass from behind and begins kissing each stretch mark, one by one. I'm at a loss for words as I run my fingers through his hair. My heart wishes he will decide to stay, but I know it's a long shot given his history.

"What happens when your mission is over?" I whisper.

He stares up at me. "We'll cross that bridge when we come to it. We need to take one step at a time."

Those are the words I was afraid of, but he's right. There's no sense in jumping ahead since we both know the future is a fair-weather friend.

The hot spray of the shower washes away his scent, which is the last thing I want to do. The steam envelops me, and I hear the shower door open as he slips in. Music plays from his phone as Drake White sings about the "Power of a

Woman" and "Luckiest Man." No words are spoken. The songs speak for him.

He pours shampoo in his hand and begins washing my hair with great care. His soapy hands trail down my body, leaving a wake of heat in their path. He pushes the right buttons with tweaks and caresses, verifying we have the right chemistry.

He knows how to make me wet as he pushes into me from behind with ease. We rock into one another without effort. Our bodies recognize each other from years before. He's right. We were never only friends. We were lovers at least one time, but I don't need to reveal that yet. I need to see where this goes because I have other people to think about.

We come together and collapse against the tile wall. He rinses the soap from every part of my body and leaves behind tender kisses.

I'm tired in a good way, not drained but sated. I'm going to ride this pony for all it's worth because I don't know how long this is going to last. When his mission is over, will he leave me again? I swallow down the thought, not wanting to think about it.

After breakfast, he shows me to the small barn where his SUV is parked. He calls her Gal. It is a Mercedes-Benz G wagon with the number 63 at the end.

"You officially own one of the ugliest cars ever made." I make a face. "Why do you call her Gal?

"I didn't know you had opinions on cars. For your information, you might think she's ugly, but she's useful in many ways. She has gadgets on her, including bulletproof glass and body armor. The rest of her weapons are a secret. She's as beautiful as Wonder Woman." He winks at me.

"If she can get me to work on time, I don't care what she

can do." To be honest, I'm a little miffed she's named after one of the most beautiful women in the world.

She has matte graphite-gray paint with black trim, making her somewhat attractive. Gal screams out of the driveway and onto the highway. He never lets up on the gas as we travel at what feels like Mach 10.

"Are Poppy and my mom going to be safe at your cabin? Are Frederick and Henri going to check in on them?" The farther away we get from his cabin, the more anxious I become.

"Yes, and yes." He grabs my hand and rubs his thumb over my knuckles. "I have everything covered."

"Funny, I don't remember you being covered last night."

"You might say I've accepted my skin again." He smiles a real smile.

Our banter is a comfortable place for us and calms my nerves. I enjoy the view of the countryside as we drive back into Cologne. We pass the enormous poppy field with large buds waiting to open.

"What are you smiling about?" he asks.

"I pass this poppy field every day on my way to work."

"I love poppies. They are my favorite flowers."

"Mmmhmm."

Declan doesn't park in the company garage. Instead, he parks in a smaller garage down the street, and we walk to the office. We make our way to the sixth floor, and things are unusually quiet. My colleagues look up from their work and quickly look away as if someone is watching them.

Lara wears a serious face as she approaches us. I throw my bag on the floor and hang up my coat. She comes in and closes the door behind her.

"If I didn't know better, I'd say you got laid this

weekend." Her eyes scan Declan up and down as if he couldn't have possibly helped in the effort.

He gives her his stone face, revealing nothing.

I wave my hand in the air, brushing off her comment. "What's going on out there? It looks like everyone's on pins and needles."

"Well, if you would answer your phone on the weekends, which is so unlike you, you would know we have a visitor from the ivory tower."

"What are you talking about?"

"Dr. Zahara Ugana is in the house, so to speak. She's making the rounds with the scientists on every floor, asking them questions. People are nervous. Word is, she's going to make some cuts."

"Why? She's visited before and usually ends up on the eighth floor. Our research is important and legitimate."

"She's asking questions she doesn't normally ask. Oh, by the way, she's looking for you."

# Chapter Twenty-Three

Declan

"This is an interesting development. Why is Zahara looking for you?"

Liv is deep in thought.

I obtained a scrambler from Fredrick and set it up in her office, preventing our conversations from being recorded.

"I don't know. I guess it's time I find out." Liv trades her overcoat for a lab coat. "What's that?"

"A scrambler so we can talk freely."

Lara looks at me. "Who are you, some secret agent?"

Liv and I look up at her at the same time and say, "No," in unison.

I grab Liv by the shoulders and turn her toward me so Lara can't hear what I'm saying. "Be careful. We don't know what Zahara's up to, and she has plenty to answer for. I'm going to keep a low profile. While you're looking for her, I'm going to call the office to see if I can get some things going."

I nod to Lara as they leave the office. She does not know

what's going on, but she gets the message loud and clear: protect Liv.

I call Pippa, our top-notch dark web expert, and she answers on the first ring. "How's it going?"

"Hey, Red, I have something you can get your claws into."

"Is that any way to refer to the woman's nails who held your hand in the cabin in Afghanistan?"

I chuckle. "It's meant as a compliment. No one messes with you. Besides, you spooked me. You remind me of Kendall. You're like a sister to me. But I could use your claws to dig into Zahara's emails."

Pippa would love nothing more than to find some dirt on her arch enemy. Zahara was responsible for poisoning her boyfriend, Beck, and killing his parents in Zambia.

"Oh, do tell. This sounds interesting." I hear her rub her hands together on the other end.

"After a series of life-threatening encounters, details to come, she has shown up at the company unexpectedly, asking for Liv. I need you to hack into her emails. Maybe even copy something with the letterhead."

"Do you mean Dr. Olivia Marcel? Calling her Liv seems awfully cozy. Is there something you want to share?" She never misses a beat.

"I'll save it for when I see you, but I need to get to Zahara sooner rather than later."

"I like how you think. You have a plan up your sleeve already, don't you?"

"You know I do. Once you get into her emails, I need you to send individual emails from her to me and Liv, giving us permission to get key cards to the eighth floor. Got it?"

Silence greets me on the other end as I wait for her to respond.

"What's on the eighth floor?"

"Not sure. They have it locked down tighter than Fort Knox, and I need to get up there to see what's going on. There is no sign of her working down here on the memory drug."

"Roger that. I'll let you know when I get into her account and when I've sent the email."

"Thank you."

"Declan, be careful."

"Always. I may have something to live for after all." I hang up before she has a chance to ask; keeping her in suspense is my specialty.

I shrug on my lab coat and begin studying the files Liv wanted me to go through. The research she's doing is fascinating and groundbreaking. If she can get this to work, it will be a major breakthrough.

The door burst open, and Liv's face is red. She slams the door behind her and stands in the middle of the office with her hands on her hips.

"What flew up your ass?"

"A big bird named Zahara."

"What does she want?"

She steps closer to me. "She wants a full report about every drug in development for my department."

"Her request isn't unusual. I don't see what the problem is."

"She has never asked for reports from my department, mostly because she could care less about any pediatric drug development. To top it off, she wants it in by the end of today. I have to get everyone together to call a meeting and tell them what we're in for. It's going to be a long day."

She plops herself down in the chair next to me. "I'm

going to have to work for twenty-four hours straight to get this done."

I smile.

"What are you smiling at? This isn't funny."

"It's the old divide-and-conquer method."

"She knows I'll help you with this report, and it will keep us here in the office, away from the cabin. My guess is she doesn't know about the cabin but is pulling out all her resources to find out where your mother and daughter are so she can use them as leverage. I'm still not sure what she wants other than me gone. She must know I'm here looking for the memory drug."

I hold her hand in mine. "We're going to get through this together. Meanwhile, I'm going to get us some key cards for the eighth floor," I whisper, hiding my mouth in her honey-scented hair.

"How?"

"Pippa, the other redhead in my life, is working on hacking into Zahara's email and getting us permission via company letterhead."

"You must have some talented friends because I don't think it's going to be easy."

I smile. "I have very gifted friends."

I move back from Liv as the office door opens and a tall woman enters with two men at her side. She's dressed in a cream suit, accenting her ebony skin.

"I didn't have the pleasure of meeting you last time you were here. I'm Dr. Zahara Ugana." She holds out her hand.

I'm hit by her voice. There's something familiar about it, like I've heard her speak before, and yet I've never met her. She has a British accent with something else mixed in. She is charming but smiles with the look of the Joker as if she knows my innermost secrets.

"You disappeared on us last time you were here. Where did you go?"

Silence stretches between us to see if I can make her uncomfortable. I shrug. "Here and there."

She nods, knowing she's not going to get the full story from me. "Nice meeting you. I would love to hear about your travels. Maybe you and Olivia can come to my place for dinner."

"Sure thing," I reply with a smile.

Zahara leaves with her bodyguards in a whirlwind, and the office grows quiet.

Liv stands there with her mouth gaping open. "She's never called me Olivia. Did you just get an invitation to have dinner with her? No one ever gets invited to dinner, and I don't know of anyone who's ever been to her penthouse."

"I wouldn't consider it a good sign. She's onto me. This dinner can either go in our favor, or it could mean she is one up on us, depending on how it plays out. Does she always have bodyguards? Seems kind of odd."

"I've never seen her with bodyguards. What do you mean she's onto you?"

"She may have resources to deep dive into my background and blow my cover. We need to push up the timeline. I'm going to need you to go to the eighth floor with me when we get the key cards."

"What? No. I didn't sign on to get wrapped up in this super spy crap. This is all you."

I hold her by the shoulders, turning her to face me. "You know this place better than anyone. You know what computers to go to and what programs to look for. I haven't been in this building, so I don't know the layout as well as you do. We need to get her memory drug formula and try to wipe out her computer at the same time."

She pulls my hands away from her shoulders and backs away from me. "Right now, I have reports to put together with my team. If you want to be part of our work, great. If not, you do your thing, and I'll do mine. My life's work is at stake, and it's going to take laser focus."

Someone needs a decaf coffee. She walks past me and out the door, leaving me in silence. Silence used to be the thing I treasured most. What a difference a few days can make. I've never had an op with this much on the line.

I need to protect Liv and her family while trying to get the memory drug formula and destroying the programs they built it on. Accepting an invitation to Zahara's house may be one step into the lioness's den. Getting out may be a different story.

# Chapter Twenty-Four

### Declan

I DON'T WANT her to be part of this, but I have no choice. This op was a solo operation, but the tide has turned. The two of us must work together to get hold of the memory drug formula to shut down Zahara and cripple Deep 8. I won't share my intel on Deep 8 with Liv. She will run for the hills.

The timing is perfect to make good on Zahara's dinner invitation. I leave Liv's office, and the floor is a ghost town. Everyone is in the meeting except one tech.

I approach him from behind. The ginger hair makes me think of my brother. "Excuse me. Do you know where Dr. Zahara Ugana's office is?"

He turns around, and I'm surprised, recognizing his face. "Campbell?"

He gives me a wide grin and talks through his teeth. "Remember, they have cameras everywhere and can probably read lips."

"Right. Meet me in the bathroom."

"No can do." He bends his head down as if he's reading a

document. "They have this place covered except for one bathroom. Besides, Zahara's office is on the eighth floor, inaccessible by you or me. Her secretary has a large office on the seventh floor by the elevator."

"The fact they have cameras in the bathroom is gross. I may never pee here again. I'll be in touch," I talk to my shoes.

"The blonde is gorgeous and feisty. Dr. Olivia Marcel? I like them like that."

I look up and move into his space. Giving him a big smile, I say, "She's off-limits. Don't even think about it."

"Someone's touchy."

He never knows when to keep his mouth shut. "As in no touching, and if you make a move, it's on."

He laughs because he loves to push my buttons. I'll catch up with him later. At least I have backup if this goes sideways, which is looking like a good possibility.

Someone heads for the door to the stairwell and uses their key card to gain access. I sneak in behind them and take the stairs to the seventh floor, looking for Zahara's secretary. She sits in a large corner office. A view of the Rhine is the backdrop with windows across the front. The setup seems a little over-the-top for a secretary.

I knock on the glass door, and she waves me in without looking up.

"Can I help you?" Her eyes are glued to her screen.

"Dr. Ugana extended an invitation to have dinner at her penthouse. I would like to take her up on it if she's available this evening."

This gets her attention. "Who are you exactly? Because I've never seen you here."

"I'm Dr. Declan Craig, and I work with Dr. Olivia Marcel

in the pediatric department. They hired me a couple of days ago."

She nods her head and looks back at her screen to check Zahara's calendar. "She has a note here about you and an opening this evening around nine." Her fingers fly across the keys, and the printer behind her spews something out. "You need to understand this is a formal dinner. Dress appropriately. Here is the address to her penthouse. Her location is highly confidential, so please don't share it with anyone."

She focuses on the screen and hands me the paper over the top of her monitor.

"Thank you."

*Confidential location? What are you up to, Zahara?*

My eyes linger on the elevator door next to her office. The elevator is private and requires a key card. Whoever works on the eighth floor must use this elevator regularly.

I make my way back to Liv's office and continue to work on the Rett Syndrome files. From the look of it, it will be years in development and trial before there is a cure.

The afternoon drags on, and I decide to book a hotel room since we can't go back to my townhouse, too many eyes. The late night won't allow us to go back to the cabin and take a chance of being followed.

Liv comes back to her office with a look of defeat. Her box full of papers lands with a thud on her desk. She walks over to the window as the sun disappears behind the city skyline dotted with clouds.

I join her at the window. We speak in hushed tones. "What's going on?"

"She can shut down my entire department. I won't be able to take the research with me because it belongs to them. My contract states that I won't be able to work for another pharmaceutical company for at least a year. I'm screwed along with everyone else in my department." Her fingers curl into her arms, and angry tears make an appearance.

"Lucky for you, we have an appointment with her tonight. Maybe you can convince her to keep your department intact."

She sighs, rubbing her upper arms.

"I'm sorry. Part of this is my fault." Guilt tears at me. I want to wrap my arms around her, but there are eyes and ears everywhere.

"I'm not sure it is. We haven't had a drug approved in a long time. You know how difficult it is to run trials large enough and get approval depending on the side effects."

My hands, stuffed in my front pockets, curl into fists. "I got us a room at the hotel. It's going to be a late night."

She turns to me as her eyes widen. "What about Poppy and my mom? We can't leave them alone."

"I've already called Frederick and Henri. They are going to spend the night with them. Your mum and Poppy will be safe. Trust me."

She nods, accepting her fate in Act Two of this play. I'm trying to race toward Act Three and the final curtain call, hoping to leave Cologne behind, but this city has a grip on me.

The ride to the hotel is quiet. She leans her head on her hands and stares aimlessly out the window. I pull up to the front of the hotel, and she turns to me with a surprised look on her face.

"You booked us in the Excelsior?"

"I did. I wanted to treat you and get you to unwind and relax. It's been a rough day."

I get out of the car and throw my keys to the valet as I round the back end to help her out of her seat. The back of the

SUV is packed with boxes, which I instruct must be taken to our room.

Check-in is easy as I grab the key card and head for the elevator to the penthouse suite. My Petal is fading. She'll be mine before she has time to think about it.

The elevator opens to a large living room, bedroom, and bathroom. The suite has colors of dark blue, cream, and gray, giving it an old-world feel.

I take her by the hand and lead her to the bathroom, accented with veined marble tile. The bath is drawn and steaming with rose petals floating across the surface.

"You should soak for a bit before we have to get ready."

She spins around with a look of horror on her face. "I have nothing to wear for tonight."

"Yes, you do. I picked something out, and clothes will be delivered for both of us. I'll order something for us to nibble on."

She stares at me for a moment, as if she can't believe what I'm telling her. "You took care of everything."

I hold her face in my hand and stroke her cheek with my thumb. "I take care of the things that are precious to me."

Tears form in her eyes as she places her hand on my heart. Without a word, she turns and clicks the door shut to the bathroom. I'm dragging her into the hornet's nest, but I need her to have her head in the game.

Going to Zahara's for dinner is not without careful planning. I need to find out what she knows about me and what she plans to do with Liv's department. I doubt she'll give up anything on the memory drug.

# Chapter Twenty-Five

Olivia

MY CLOTHES LIE in a pile on the bathroom floor. The reflection in the mirror reveals a woman with saggy breasts and stretch marks along the lower abdomen, and yet he is undeterred. He made love to me as if I was his lifeline, but I think he's the one saving me.

There is a life beyond my job without sacrificing everything I've worked for. The bags under my eyes show the stress of the last couple of days. I've been caught in a yo-yo between home and work for too many years to count.

I slip into the warm water with scattered petals and sink in up to my neck. There's an inflated pillow behind my head, and my eyes flutter closed as I fall asleep. I have vivid dreams about the night Declan and I spent together five years ago. The events of one night changed the course of my life. The depth of emotion I felt with him wasn't like anything I've ever experienced then or now.

A hand grabs my shoulder and shakes me awake. I hear myself moan as I'm in the middle of a love scene between

Declan and me. He is the most passionate man I've ever experienced because he gives everything he has while being the most infuriating.

"Hey, Sleeping Beauty, it's time to get up. We need to get ready for tonight. You must have had a kinky dream. You've been moaning for a while." He smiles. "No doubt I was the leading man."

I open my eyes. "I wouldn't be so sure you were the star. Some hot-looking guys work on my floor."

He leans in close, a whisper away from my lips. "Maybe, but they don't know how to push your buttons to make you come. I have that secret locked up tight."

Heat rises to my cheeks, and I'm not one to get ruffled, but his words do things to me.

His lips feather across mine, and he bites my lower lip enough to get my attention. "Let's go. I can't wait to see you in the dress I picked out."

Move over Versace, Declan's a design consultant. He holds my hands as I get out of the bathtub, sprays me with bath oil, and pats down my skin.

My heart pierces, knowing this will end and he may leave again without us. I can't see any other ending to this as hard as I try.

I grab the terrycloth robe from behind the bathroom door and tie it around my waist. A splash of red color covers the bed from my beautiful evening gown. There is a strap on one shoulder as my eye follows the dress down to the slit on the other side. Layers of fabric start at the waist and go to the floor.

"It's beautiful," I gasp. Then I give him a questioning look.

"Zahara wants this to be a formal dinner. I'm not sure why." Declan stands behind me. "The fabric resembles the petals of a flower."

I whisper, "Oh, I see it now."

I turn around and put my arms around his neck. "Thank you for the dress. It's perfect. What do you say we make the most of the evening?" I wiggle my brows.

He exhales through his nose and pushes loose strands of hair off my face. "This evening is going to have to be navigated carefully. I need you to focus on what I'm saying and what I'm not saying. She may have questions for you."

I nod. "Got it. Now, what about getting you in a suit?"

He kisses the top of my forehead and turns to leave.

He included everything from earrings and shoes to a clutch. The dress fits like a glove, and the pearl earrings are a subtle elegance. I loop my hair around in a French twist to complete the attire. I walk out into the living room and stare.

Declan is dressed in a tuxedo and is better-looking than any James Bond. His smile lights up from across the room, and I soak it in. I want to treasure every moment with him until our goodbye.

"Let's go, James."

"Bond, James Bond. You look beautiful tonight," he says in his best Sean Connery.

A town car picks us up in front of the hotel and takes us across town, over the river. We're whisked up to the penthouse, which takes up the entire top floor. A butler answers the door and invites us in.

The view of the city and the river is incredible at this time of night. I don't know any researcher or scientist who makes enough money to afford these digs, but I guess when you're sitting on the board of directors, the job has perks.

We're shown to the dining room where Zahara sits at the head of the table flanked by two bodyguards.

She gets up to greet us. "I'm glad you accepted my invitation. Please, sit down."

"What's with the heavies?" Declan gets straight to the point.

"You can never be too careful these days. The world is a dangerous place." She goes back to the head of the table, and we sit next to each other, facing the windows.

Tension in the room crackles with energy. They each have an agenda I doubt will match. The test will be who can outmaneuver the other one.

Zahara fires the first shot across the bow. "Declan, to what do we owe the pleasure? Why have you come back, besides the obvious?" She nods in my direction.

Declan takes a long pause to collect his thoughts. "Liv asked me to come back to work on her Rett Syndrome research, which was convenient considering I'm in between jobs."

"Really? Where have you been for the last five years? You seemed to have disappeared." She snaps her fingers and takes a sip of her white wine.

"I took some time off to travel. A little life reflection goes a long way as I tried to remember the year I lost." Declan doesn't even look at the wine.

She leans forward, interested in his lost memories. "You lost memories of a year? How did that happen?"

"After my accident, I spent a long time in and out of consciousness. I'm not able to remember the time before and after the accident."

She glosses over his comment about having an accident. Odd. "Did you have any other symptoms with your loss of memory?" She's hooked.

"Not that I can recall. Why? What symptoms should I have had?" He frowns.

She leans back and blows out a breath. "You can have headaches, dizziness, vomiting, among other symptoms."

Declan leans his elbows on the table. "I was a burn victim. I didn't hit my head. Why on earth would I have those symptoms?"

Her eyes grow cold. "In the research I've done, some of those symptoms can occur after a traumatic event, causing memory loss. It's a type of retrograde amnesia."

Declan plays to her ego. "Have you done a lot of research on amnesia? I would love to pick your brain on the topic. You may have some therapy we could use so I can get my memories back."

She clears her throat. "Perhaps."

I'm not sure who won that match, but they seem to be feeling each other out.

We've already gone through the first course of salad, and we're on to the main course. She asks about his accident, and he recites the details. This time, he talks about the accident as a matter of fact, as if he's outside of himself.

After the main course, she focuses on me by asking questions about my daughter. As I answer them, I realize she is gazing at the stem of her wineglass, stroking it up and down as if bored by the topic.

"By the way, I got most of the reports from your department. I've made a decision."

She's captured my attention. My career rests in her hands, not a place I want to be.

"How can you decide when you don't have the entire department's reports?" I shoot back.

She ignores my question. "I'm going to recommend shutting down the pediatric department for this company."

I can't help myself. "What? Why?"

"Your department is not profitable. Things take way too

long to get to market. Research, development, and trials take years, sometimes decades. Keeping it running is not in the company's best financial interest."

I stand up, almost tipping the chair behind me. "I thought the company's mission was to help people find cures to incurable and life-threatening diseases. Some of those diseases can cut short the lives of children. In the end, it comes down to the almighty dollar. I hope you realize what you're doing. You're firing scientists who have a passion for helping others. It's not about the money for them. It never is."

"We will compensate you handsomely with a golden parachute package. I am certain other pharmaceutical companies would gain from your intelligence and passion for your work. Bio2Chem is going in a different direction." Her voice lacks emotion.

I fight not to say anything about the memory drug she has used on people for evil. This battle is not over. I'll be contacting certain individuals on the board of directors.

Declan gets up and buttons his jacket. "Thank you for a lovely evening. I'm sorry you're going to have to close the pediatric department. The scientists who have worked hard for so many years will be devastated."

I can't get out of there fast enough, as I'm one stride off running for the elevator. She walks next to Declan as she sees us out.

"Tell me, Declan, have you ever been to Zambia?"

"No. Is it worth a visit?"

"Indeed, I just got back from there. Have a good evening. We might get a chance to talk about your memories."

She sneers at us right before the elevator doors close.

# Chapter Twenty-Six

## Declan

THE RIDE back to the hotel is cloaked in silence with a red mist of anger filling the air inside the car. Liv crosses her arms, embedding her fingernails into her upper arm. Her mouth draws a tight line as she avoids making eye contact with me.

"I'm so sorry. Maybe I should call Neil and end the op. You might have a shot at keeping your department intact." I'm desperate to keep the peace and make her happy.

Her head whips around like something out of *The Exorcist*. "Are you fucking kidding me right now?"

Her F-bombing me is not a good sign. I'm in deep shit with no escape. I would open the door and roll out, but the car is moving way too fast.

"You're not going anywhere. We're not aborting anything. I am one hundred percent in on this one. I want that bitch to go down, preferably screaming at the top of her lungs." Her fingers open and close in fists. "Who does she think she is? I've worked for this company for ten years, and suddenly I'm thrown to the curb like garbage. How many guns do you have? I might need some knives, too."

"Enough for a small army, but you're not getting any of them. Besides, you're scaring me. You need to calm down."

"I. Will. Not. Calm. Down." Her face is crimson.

*Okay, so that was the wrong thing to say. Note to self for the future: don't tell her to calm down, ever.*

"What is the plan, and how do we get to the eighth floor? Do we need explosives?" Her body turns in my direction as crimson moves to her neck and chest. She makes Attila the Hun look like a beginner.

"You need to slow down. Things like this need a precise plan."

She burst into tears, holding her face in her hands and leaning into my shoulder. For the love of God, I'm going to need a motorboat to navigate these waters. Holding her to me, I let her cry it out. Offering any words of comfort would not be in my best interest. I could lose my balls. I'm in uncharted waters without a life jacket.

We pull up to the hotel, and she peers up at me with a mascara-streaked face. I wipe the black smears away with my thumb. Her nose is red, and her eyes are bloodshot and swollen.

"Tell me we're going to bring her down," she begs.

"There is a plan, but not the one you mapped out thirty seconds ago." I go for some levity.

She leans on me in the elevator as we ride up to the suite. I get her settled on the bed, stripping her out of her dress and pulling off her shoes. I tuck her in under the sheets and go to the bathroom to grab a washcloth.

I wipe the makeup off her face as she sits against the headboard in a semi-catatonic state.

"I need face moisturizer."

"What?" I'm stunned this is at the top of her to do list.

"My skin will dry out, and I'll get wrinkles."

Typical Liv. Always thinking about the way she's going to look.

I grab the hotel moisturizer from the bathroom and hand it to her.

"God, this is utter crap."

"It's what they have. Do you want me to run down to the lobby?" I'd swim across the Rhine not to incur her wrath.

"No." She dumps some out in her palms, rubs them together, and pats her face down with the cream. "This can't be happening. I've put in over ten years in research, development, and trials. We are so close to making some breakthroughs for children in a couple of areas. The last time my world was upended was when I found out I was pregnant with Poppy." She stares down at her lap, and I try to keep up.

"What happened?" I ask gently.

"I don't want to talk about it." Without looking at me, she lies down and turns her back to me.

One minute she needs me, the next minute she shuts me out. My motorboat is running out of gas. No matter what I do, I'm on the losing end.

We were supposed to work through the night to get the reports into Zahara, but that seems pointless now. I can't imagine how devastated Liv must feel.

I peel out of my clothes and curl in behind her, wrapping my arm around her waist. Despite everything, I want her to know I'm still here for her. She lets out a stuttered sigh as her fingers interlace with mine. We fall asleep, wiped out from the day's events and disappointments.

. . .

THE SUN STREAKS in through the window, and I consider it a good sign. I'll take anything at this point. The first person I need to call is Campbell to find out what he's doing here. I sneak out of the bedroom and make my call in the living room.

"Are we on a secure line?"

"Always, big bro." I can picture him smiling on the other end with his ginger hair in every direction, looking like something akin to Ed Sheeran on steroids.

"How you outranked me in the military is beyond me. What are you doing here?" My voice is laced with irritation.

"Neil sent me because they were looking for a nuclear engineer. As it turns out, it's a small, newly created department. I'm in the office a couple of days, and I work remotely."

"Since when do you know anything about nuclear physics? I thought you were a cryptologist."

"I was, but I've always been interested in science. I studied nuclear physics and engineering. Excelling in science seems to run in the family."

"Mac must have missed that gene because he's about a scientific as a rock." Mac butts head with me every chance he gets.

"Maybe, but he's got a wife and a kid, which is more than you have."

"Thanks for pointing out the obvious. In case they haven't filled you in, I need to get onto the eighth floor. I think it's where Zahara has the formula for the memory drug, and we need to get a hold of it." I pause. "Things could go south fast, and I need you to take care of Liv, Poppy, and her mum."

"Who's Poppy?"

"Liv's daughter. You two share the same mentality. You'll

get along great with an almost five-year-old." One point for me.

"Says the Dark Lord." He snickers on the other end. Okay, we're even.

"Haven't you heard? I've upgraded to prince; long story for later. I need you to promise me to take care of them."

There is silence on the other end. "Always. They must mean something to you. You don't need to ask. What's the plan?"

"Pippa is working on getting us up there, but I haven't heard from her."

"Wait, *us*?"

"Liv and I are going up. She knows her way around the company and the technology platform better than I do. She's agreed to help me. I can't do it without her. She's a woman on a mission since she found out Zahara is closing her department."

"That sucks. Bro, I have a bad feeling about this. You shouldn't be taking a civilian on an op."

"I don't have a choice. She's my best shot at getting to the memory drug."

"Keep me in the loop. I've got your back. Good luck."

"Thanks."

"Who was on the phone?" Liv says from behind me.

She's wearing my dress shirt from last night and nothing else. My sweats won't be able to hide how hard I am for her. The last thing I want to be thinking about is my brother.

"My brother, Campbell. He's going to be our backup if things go wrong. Liv, are you sure about this?"

She struts over and puts her arms around my waist. "I told you I'm in. Things didn't change overnight. I know she is shutting down my department to get you to leave, or maybe out of spite, but I want you to take her down more than ever.

Maybe your friend, Pippa, can find my contract on the hard drive and make it disappear."

"Are you sure you're not a trained agent? Because you think like one."

"It's not the strongest of the species that survives, nor the most intelligent that survives. It is the one that is the most adaptable to change." She grins.

"Nicely done, Charles Darwin."

"Thinking like an agent is probably genetic from my uncle."

"Do you know what happened to your father?"

She hesitates, tracing the ink on my chest with her finger. "He spent many years in the military, but when he got out, things didn't go well for him. Shortly after I was born, he left my mother and became homeless on the streets of London. Years later, Uncle Neil told us they found him dead in an alleyway. Someone had beaten him to death." There is no anger or resentment in her words.

"I'm sorry for your loss."

"There was nothing to lose. He was never part of my life. Uncle Neil was there for me in every way."

The Lego pieces in my brain click together.

"Does anyone in the company know who your uncle is and what he does for a living?"

"Not that I know of. I was always told to never speak about him with anyone."

"I bet Zahara knows, which is why she's running scared."

# Chapter Twenty-Seven

Declan

"WHAT DO YOU MEAN?" She frowns, looking confused.

"I think Zahara went on an expedition and found out who your uncle is and who he works for, especially after what went down in Zambia."

"She mentioned coming back from there last night. What happened there?"

"One of our teammates was poisoned with the memory drug. We think she developed the drug. He survived and got his memories back, but she disappeared. She was baiting me. There is no way she knew I was in Zambia."

Liv walks over to open the slider to the balcony. The tail of my shirt falls below her fine ass, teasing me. I follow her out to the balcony and lie on the lounger next to her.

"If your theory is right, she is after you because she thinks you were in Zambia or knows what happened in Zambia, but she wants to get rid of me if she knows my uncle is the head of MI6."

She curls up on the lounger, tucking her hands inside the

long sleeves, and gazes out over the city skyline, cool as a cucumber. I don't have to worry about her when we get onto the eighth floor, but I have everything to lose if this goes ass up.

The look on her face is fierce, and she's not backing down. She's out for blood, but so is Zahara. My money is on Liv in this showdown.

"Do you think we can take the day off and go to the cabin to see Poppy and my mom?"

I give her a look of surprise.

"What? Can't I take a day off?" she responds.

"Of course, but I think we need to make an appearance at the office at some point. I don't want Zahara to think she got to us."

She nods. "Good point."

I order more clothes from the shop in the lobby, purchasing her a pantsuit and me the usual black jeans and a T-shirt. With the warm weather fast approaching, they don't have any long-sleeved T-shirts. This will be my official coming out with my scars on display in a short-sleeved T-shirt.

Liv steps out of the bedroom and stops as she looks at me. "Are you going to be okay wearing a short-sleeved T-shirt?" Her words are gentle. "I noticed you only wear long sleeves."

"I have to come to terms with this, eventually. I've got bigger things to worry about. Besides, wearing long sleeves in hot weather sucks." I shrug.

We take an Uber to the parking garage to pick up the G wagon. I check for trackers and find none. As we follow the road out of town, Liv holds out her hand to me. I lace my fingers with hers and hold on tight. I'm never letting her go.

I check my rearview mirror for a tail and see none. We're in the clear for now. I call ahead to let everyone know we're coming home. *Home*. Interesting how much power that word holds for me.

Up ahead, at the end of the driveway, Poppy jumps up and down on the front porch. Ozzie jumps with her. Frederick and Henri left to go tend to things on their farm, knowing we were on our way.

"Mommy, Mommy, Mommy!" she screams from across the driveway and charges toward Liv.

She jumps up into her arms as Liv twirls her around, feet flying behind her. Poppy's giggle seeps into my veins. For the first time, I yearn for a family, someone I can come home to and a child who will jump into my arms. On instinct, my hand touches a tattoo of a poppy inked on my chest. The symbol has taken on a new meaning. All poppies are my favorites. These are the memories I won't forget, no matter what happens.

Once inside, everyone goes their separate ways. Poppy and Ozzie go back to playing on the floor with Prince and a puzzle. Margot gives Liv a look, and they disappear upstairs. I stay with Poppy, making sure to keep an eye on her, but I also want to get my guitar from upstairs.

I climb the stairs to the second floor and hear muffled voices from Margot's room. Inching closer, I'm able to make out some words.

"You can't go on like this. You need to tell him," Margot's voice is hushed.

"It's not for you to tell me what I should and shouldn't do. I need more time," Liv replies.

The talking stops, my cue to get up to the third floor to get my guitar. Margot must be talking about more memories from my past. Liv is not comfortable sharing. All in due time.

As I come down the stairs with my guitar, Liv comes out

of the room, red-faced and flustered. Margot is behind her with a long face as she casts her eyes away from me.

I followed them downstairs and find Poppy where I had left her. I sit on the couch with my guitar, and her head whips up from the puzzle she's focused on.

"Would you like to help me write a song?" I ask.

Her eyes get wide as she stares at the guitar. "What's the song going to be about?"

"You," I strum a couple of chords on the guitar.

"Oh, we should call it Poppy and the Prince."

I play a couple of chords, and she starts laying down the words. We're laughing and playing, having a good time, when my phone rings. I hand the guitar to Poppy.

"Be careful with it and see if you can play a couple of notes."

I go out to the back deck and take the call. "Pippa, what's up?"

"I'm in, of course. But you're not gonna like this. We had to crack the code to get into her email. It uses the same encryption as Deep 8."

"I figured as much. What are our next steps?"

"I need you on-site before I can get the email to you. This requires me to request an email password change from her, but after she resets her password, things are going to happen quickly."

"Roger that. Give us an hour to get on-site. I'll call you then."

Breathing deeply, I look out over the mountainside, knowing we have one shot at this. The situation is make or break. One I don't want Liv involved in. The slider behind me opens, and I know who it is without turning around.

"What's going on?"

"We got word from Pippa, so we're heading back to work sooner than we wanted to be." I peek over my shoulder at her.

Her lips form a tight line, and she nods. "I'm ready. Are you?"

"I have my plan, and I'm ready to go. There are some things I need to tell you about before we go to the eighth floor."

## Chapter Twenty-Eight

### Declan

WE SAY our goodbyes and get back in the G wagon. The air is heavy with anticipation, and she gives off nervous energy. If anything happens to her, I will never forgive myself, and then Neil will kill me on sight. I can't imagine a world where Poppy would be without her mother. Her father not being part of the picture is bad enough.

"Once we get back to the office, things are going to run at a quick pace. I need to put some things in place in case we get separated."

She turns in my direction with wide eyes. "What do you mean if we get separated?"

"I'm going to need you to get into the main server on the eighth floor so you can download everything we need about the memory drug formula. I will scout out the rest of the floor to see what I can find. Before we go up there, the fire alarm is going to go off. While they're going down, we'll be going up."

She nods as her eyes scan the horizon. I can see her mind taking notes as she swallows. "Okay."

"If we get separated, I'm giving you my phone, the keys to Gal, and the code to the cabin."

"I will need none of those because we are not getting separated. You can keep your phone, and I don't need the keys to... Gal. I don't need the code for the cabin." Defiance comes before submission.

I pull the car over to the side of the road before we enter the city limits. I shut off the engine so I have her undivided attention.

"You need to listen to me. There's always a backup plan in case something goes sideways. You've got to follow the backup plan, no matter what. If we're on the eighth floor and you have everything you need off the server, then count for ten seconds, and if you don't see me, you need to make a run for it back downstairs to the sixth floor. Go to the bathroom near the supply room. There are no cameras or bugs. Stay there until everyone comes back into the building."

For as tough as Liv is, she's being pushed to her limit. Tears crest her eyes, and her lower lip quivers. I hold her hand in mine and try to give her some reassuring words.

"You can do this. You're made of tough stuff, and you're brilliant. Don't worry about me. Get word out to Neil if you don't see me after everyone reenters the building from the fire alarm. Do you understand?"

"Yes, but I'm not ready to lose you or have you taken prisoner by some crazy woman who probably wants you dead." For the first time, there is real fear etched on her face.

"I have complete faith in you. You have the most important job of this op, to get the formula off the hard drive. I can take care of everything else. I don't know what lies ahead, but we've got this."

I hold her beautiful face in my hands and kiss her tenderly on the lips. Nothing aggressive or possessive, only tenderness and love. *Love?* I've been entrenched in her family, getting to know each of them, including a dog, a cat, and her mother. They hold a special place in my heart, a heart I never thought would ever beat again for any other reason than to keep me alive.

Life has proven me wrong so many times. I don't know how this will end, but I know I want Liv, Poppy, Margot, Ozzie, and Prince to be part of it. I've never felt surer of anything in my life.

Words escape me because I don't want to scare her away or put more pressure on her about potential outcomes I have no control over. If I make it out alive, I'll give her a quote she'll never forget.

Our kiss solidifies a connection I believe we made a long time ago, even if she won't confirm it. Our connection can't be broken. Nothing has broken it in five years. Neither one of us will forget what happened between us or how deep we feel for one another on so many levels.

"Are you ready to take this on?"

She holds her chin up defiantly. "I want Zahara gone and to put her in a position where she has no choice but to leave the company. I am ready. I want my department back, my research, and my scientists. Let's do this."

I hand her my phone and the extra key fob for the G wagon. "Here is the code to the cabin, along with a spare key in case you need it and can't get a hold of Frederick and Henri. Be gentle with Gal. She's sensitive." I smile.

She rolls her eyes and holds out her hand as I slip her the key and a piece of paper with the code on it. Her hand closes over both, and then she dumps them in her purse. She looks up at me like she wants to say more but remains quiet. The only sound in the car is our breathing in sync as we stare at each other. I break our moment to get my head back in the game.

The engine starts with a rumble, and I pull out onto the road. My words didn't help lessen the tension in the air. She needs to do exactly what I tell her to do. Campbell's words echo in my head, "I have a bad feeling about this."

He's not the only one. What I don't tell her is many things can go wrong, many variables unaccounted for, and I'll need to improvise along the way. MI6 agents are trained to think on their feet.

If I get caught, I doubt Zahara will show me any mercy. She has the upper hand and knows my background, but I don't think she has all the pieces in place. She'll want to know what we know about Deep 8, and that is nonnegotiable.

I park my SUV in the same parking garage as before, in the same parking space. Liv will be able to get to the G wagon easily if she needs to get away without me.

We walk a couple of blocks from the parking garage to the Bio2Chem building. I rub her lower back for reassurance. I may need more reassurance than she does. Her shoulders drop, and some of the tension leaves her back and neck. The warrior in her locks it down and appears before we get into the building.

The elevator takes us to the sixth floor as we make our way down the hall to her office. She doesn't take time to talk to anyone on our way. People's eyes look up at us from what they are doing and then dash away as if they're unsure of what's going on. Tight energy vibrates on the floor, possibly from fear of losing their jobs and the tension Zahara has brought with her.

As soon as the door closes to Liv's office, I make the call, changing our destiny, putting everything in motion. Liv will make it to see another day, but I may not. Part of my job has always been about sacrifice, lingering in the background, waiting for its turn.

I link my earbuds with a voice scrambler. "We are on-site and ready. Give us the go and tell us how to proceed."

I say the words as I watch Liv's face across from me. There is fear in her eyes and something else I can't quite pin down, but her determination takes over. As much as her life's work is at stake, she understands the significance of shutting down something as detrimental as the memory drug set to destroy soldiers.

The implications for the use of this drug are massive. If Zahara gets the drug to work, soldiers could be turned into machines, erasing their memories of wartime events, especially for special ops, and returning them to the field repeatedly until there is nothing left. After seeing how it affected Beck, I would do anything to make sure they don't use this drug on another human being.

# Chapter Twenty-Nine

### Declan

I HAND LIV AN EARBUD, stuff the phone in my pocket, and open a file in front of both of us to make it look like we're working. Without Liv knowing it, I set up the scrambler with a remote to mask our voices.

"Once I get into the mainframe, I'm going to send a directive to Zahara asking her to change her password because of a security breach. When she resets her password, it will allow me to write a clearance letter to get your key cards upgraded to the eighth floor," Pippa instructs.

"How much time do we have?" I ask.

"When she receives the directive to change her password, she has a limited window of time, so she will do it right away. As soon as I get her password. I will email you the letter."

"That will give us time to go down to security and get our key card clearance upgraded for access to the eighth floor. Is there anything else I need to know, like where Campbell is in this? Did you do any snooping into their security system?"

"Campbell is going to stay as our inside contact. You

two will go without him. Snooping is what I do best. There are a couple of things you need to know. You might say I've done some cyber recon. There are no security cameras or bugs on the eighth floor. The crew up there must be tight, and they don't want anything recorded about what's going on, so you don't have to worry about getting caught on video. I'm sending you the schematics for the eighth floor."

Pippa's experience as a hacker on the dark web gives her the edge when it comes to a security breach. She used to work in the gray area but now wears the white hat and works for the good guys.

"Fascinating. I guess they're not expecting visitors. I hope they like surprises." I turn to Liv. "Do you have questions for Pippa?"

She shakes her head and has been quiet on the call, taking everything in and maybe realizing how serious this is about to get.

"We'll wait to hear from you." I end the call and take out my earbud. "Are you okay?"

She takes my hand, pulling me to the bathroom, and closes the door.

"There's something I have to tell you."

"I know, and it's okay. We can talk about it later. Now is not the time to have this discussion."

"You know?" She looks baffled.

"It's fine. I figured you would reveal everything when you were ready."

She seems surprised by my reaction to her important announcement. I'm in the zone and need to stay here to make sure everything goes according to plan. I can't get sidetracked in a heavy discussion about my past.

She looks at me with something resembling adoration.

I'm torn between wanting to ravage her and knowing I have to lock it down.

I opted for something in between. The air between us is electric and something I've never experienced with anyone. Our lips crash on each other, and we kiss with passion and fire, dueling tongues and biting lips.

I don't want this to be our last kiss, but my mind goes there anyway. I'm not ready for the L word yet, but my actions have a louder voice. She needs to feel how much she means to me. My hands roam her body, grabbing her tender areas as if mapping out the places they've already been, not wanting to forget.

I hold her to me, so we're touching from head to toe. The curves of her body meld into mine. I don't want to let her go, but I have no choice. I trust she can make the right decisions and get herself to safety if she needs to.

Maybe we weren't meant to be together in this lifetime. Standing here with her makes me feel alive. My life has purpose, but not without the bumps and valleys where it flatlined before. She pulls away from me and looks up with questions in her eyes.

"You'll be fine. Everything will work out." I can think of a hundred things that could go wrong.

"I hope you're right because we're just getting started. I don't want to lose you before I have a chance to get to know you again." She sniffs her tears back.

I smile and kiss the tip of her nose as my phone goes off in my pocket with a text message. It's game time.

"What do you have for me?" We leave her private bathroom.

"I got into Zahara's email and wrote your security clearance letter. I have a bad feeling about this. Her emails are clean, as in too clean. There's nothing in there connecting her to Deep 8. She uses this email for Bio2Chem business only. I'm working to locate the email she's using to communicate with the organization. I'm giving you thirty minutes to get your key cards before I set off the fire alarm. Can you make that window?"

She's the second person to tell me they have a bad feeling about my op, but I can't back out now. There's too much on the line, with no turning back. I will never let down a fellow soldier.

"Got it. We're on our way to the security office now. Talk soon."

"Be careful." For a moment, I hear Kendall talking to me, and my heart listens. She always watched out for me. Maybe she'll be with us.

I turn to Liv. "It's time to go." I lead her into the hallway, where there seems to be a gathering of people, so our voices won't be recorded clearly.

"There can't be any missteps from now until the fire alarm goes off. We have thirty minutes, which should be more than enough time. Once we get our key cards, we'll come back here and dump our phones."

"Dump our phones?" Liv says, alarmed. "Don't we need them to stay in contact with each other?"

"No, if either of us gets caught, the phones will be a direct line to the other people in our lives. We can't give them any advantages or leads."

We get in the elevator, and she takes several deep breaths, closing her eyes.

I lean down and whisper in her ear, "It would be best if we were in an argument when we go to the security office. If there are questions later, it won't look as though we are a cooperative team."

She smiles with her eyes still closed. "That shouldn't be too hard. We used to be fantastic at arguing."

"I knew you'd see it my way. You always came around to my way of thinking in the end."

"Sorry to disappoint. Women are masters at making men think they make decisions."

I laugh. She's right, and I can't argue, given my track record with women.

We step out of the elevator, making our way to the security office. We're a few steps away from the door, and she starts the argument.

"I don't even know why they hired you back. You weren't any good when you were here. Why would they give you any kind of security clearance?"

"Oh, so now I'm not any good. I was good enough five years ago, and I'm better now." I open the door to the security office.

"I covered for you and cleaned up your reports. You're a mooch at best. Maybe you should pack your bags and leave like you did before. Running seems to be something you're superb at."

A woman from behind the desk approaches us with caution. "Can I help you?"

I ignore her, keeping my focus on Liv. "You think I should pack my bags and leave? Well, newsflash, I'm not going anywhere. You're stuck with me. Maybe your life will become unstuck."

Liv's throat moves, and she swallows as if I said something that hits too close to home.

"Excuse me." The woman tries to get our attention.

Liv responds to me, "I'm not stuck. I've carefully made all the choices in my life and planned out every step along the way, except for one."

I get the feeling we're no longer having an argument about me working for the company. We've veered off into another area, and I'm not quite following. I turn my attention to the security officer.

"We both received a letter from Dr. Ugana giving us security clearance for the eighth floor. We'll need our key cards upgraded."

"I'm going to need to see the letters she sent you." She puts her hands on her hips.

Both of us reach for our cell phones, opening the email with official company letterhead from Zahara. She reads each letter, hands back our phones, and nods.

"I'll need your key cards. This might take a couple of minutes. Clearance to the eighth floor is complicated."

We hand her our key cards and stand back away from each other, but I'm not sure if she's playacting anymore or we're having a real argument.

The air around us is stagnant with anticipation. Either way, we're a team on a mission to take down Zahara, despite how we feel at this moment.

# Chapter Thirty

## Declan

WE'VE MADE it this far and need to push through to the end. I try to catch Liv's eye, but she won't look at me, simmering underneath the surface. I have no idea where I took a wrong turn, but it's not the time to figure it out. The security guard looks up as her eyes bounce between us, but she doesn't say anything.

She steps out from behind her computer. "Here you go. I have reconfigured the key cards so you have access to the eighth floor. Good luck."

"Good luck?" Liv questions.

"Some people get security clearance for the eighth floor and never come back, but you didn't hear it from me. You two seem like a nice couple."

Liv surprises me with her quick response. "First, we're not a couple. Second, we are always running trials in different departments in the building. Maybe someone signed up for a trial and requires a longer stay than outpatient."

She doesn't look convinced and shrugs. "All couples

argue. It goes with the territory. You two have fire." She smiles.

"Do you have a list of the personnel who have access to the eighth floor? I want to make sure we're connecting with the right people," I inquire.

"Unfortunately, I don't have that list, and I'm not sure who keeps track of it." She turns to go back to her position behind the computer.

"Thank you." Liv waves to her as we leave.

We take our time walking across the lobby so we don't draw attention to ourselves. Liv's body is stiff, given our new piece of information.

"Someone's quick on their feet," I mumble. "You would have made an excellent spy."

"I didn't want her to suspect anything, so I gave a logical explanation. This needs to happen soon and be over. I hope we find what we're looking for because people disappearing does not sound good. We have very few people in patient trials that I know of."

"I thought the same thing. When we get back to your office, we'll dump our cell phones and wait for the fire alarm." I hesitate to continue with my next thought. "You're either a really good actress, or we were arguing about something I have no clue about."

She rolls her eyes. "Men."

I've learned my lesson and refuse to take her bait. I refocus on our next move.

Adrenaline pumps through my system as we get one more clue to what's going on above us. Someone's leaving breadcrumbs without knowing it, but why are people disappearing?

We stand together, silence suffocates us for the entire ride back to the sixth floor. Liv stands in the corner with her arms crossed in front of her. She aims her angry waves at me. I don't blame her. Trouble seems to find me no matter where I try to hide. I cannot change the course we are on.

She bolts out of the elevator, and I tag behind. Once we're in the office, I create smoke with two chemicals that won't set off the alarm, and it fills the room, moving up. The smoke will block any cameras without it looking obvious.

Liv unlocks the bottom drawer of her desk and throws her cell phone in the bottom.

"Do you have any packing tape?"

"Yes, why?"

I shut down my phone and stick the packing tape to the back. I reach up underneath and secure it to the bottom of the drawer above it. I do the same thing with her cell phone.

"Lock them up."

She locks the door and puts the key in her pocket. Moving to her computer station, she grabs a mini two terabyte hard drive and hooks it up to the computer. I shake my head.

"Not now. Later," Those are the only words I can use, telling her she can download her research after we hit the eighth floor.

The fire alarm goes off as the lights dim, and a blaring sound penetrates the air. Sprinklers wet down the chem lab as people take cover and run for the stairs. They use their lab coats to cover their heads as protection, and we do the same.

The key cards will get us into the elevator and the stairwell leading up to the eighth floor. Since elevators don't work when a fire alarm goes off, we head for the stairs with the crowd. I push Liv through the door ahead of me and follow her up the stairs as others head down.

I memorized the schematics Pippa sent me, and I know there are two stairwells. One leading from the eighth floor down to the seventh and sixth floors. There's another one going from the eighth floor down to the lobby. My guess is that's the one they will use in case of a fire.

We pop open the door to the eighth floor. The lights are off, along with the sprinklers in the labs. This floor seems to be on a separate system, but no one is here. When I memorized the schematics, they made little sense. There is a chem lab and offices on the far side. The other half of the floor seems to be a wide-open space not being used. Why take over an entire floor and not use the space?

"I need you to find Zahara's office. My guess is the bulk of the research on the memory drug is being stored there. See if you can get in and download it. Remember, if you don't see me, make a run for it." I take my leap of faith and throw her a quote. "Love is composed of a single soul inhabiting two bodies."

She shakes her head and presses her lips between her teeth. "I'm not giving you the name of the person you quoted until I see you again."

She turns to find the biggest corner office or anything indicating it's Zahara's space. I keep an eye on her through the glass partitions. She settles in behind a huge desktop screen and taps away on the keyboard.

My attention goes back to scouring the desktops for anything having to do with the memory drug or the disappearing patients. I lift papers and files having to do with trial results, but the files are labeled with numbers. Moving from desk to desk, careful not to disturb anything, I open a drawer and find a large file folder labeled "Patient Profile".

I lay it on the desk and flip through it. Every one of the patients listed is ex-military from various branches and countries. Most of them are at the top in their field.

My heart stops when I come to a name I recognize: Paul Ritcher. We worked together for MI6. He was a top operative, well respected, and earned many accolades and medals along the way until he went MIA about a year ago. He disappeared without a trace while on vacation. Going on vacation is a rarity in this business and would be a brilliant cover if you were going to disappear.

The agency tapped every resource they had to find him but came up empty. They presumed someone got to him and killed him. We had a service for him with full honors. Everyone thought he would be the last agent who would be captured by the enemy. He was a magician when it came to getting in and out without a trace.

His disappearance was a turning point for me. As agents, we're not infallible, even though we're made to believe we are. We're broken down, built up, and our egos are stroked to build confidence. The best of the best can get killed at the drop of a hat or vanish. Paul may not be dead, but he vanished.

I put the folder back together and have a sudden realization about the empty space on this floor. Moving across the space, I get to a metal wall with double doors. There's a scanner pad, and I pray with everything I have my key card will work. I press my key card to the pad and watch as the red light turns green and the door clicks open.

Cool air hits my body, and the lights are dim. My eyes adjust to the sight before me. Rows of beds with men hooked up to IVs fill the room. The door closes behind me with a click as I walk down the aisle, observing the men who seem to be asleep. They are dressed in white gowns, under the sheets, covered in blankets. Most of them are pale and thin, lacking muscle tone. Some look as though they have recently arrived in hell. My throat goes dry. This is something out of a bad horror movie.

For whatever hell I thought I endured, this is the real

purgatory where life is suspended at the hands of a madwoman bent on controlling humans like machines.

Up ahead, I see the face I'm looking for. Paul is alive, but I'm not sure how well he's doing. His mop of brown hair has thinned out. His face is gaunt and pale with his eyes closed, but there's a grimace on his face as if he's trying to fight whatever is going on.

The hair on the back of my neck stands on end. I can feel someone behind me. Before I can turn around, someone hits me on the back of the head, and my world fades to black, a place I'm well acquainted with.

# Chapter Thirty-One

## Olivia

I HEAD for the largest office on the floor and assume it belongs to Zahara. Her office feels high-end from the furniture to the accent pieces, but I don't take time to catalog it. I need to get to the hard drive and download the formula for the memory drug if it's even on here.

Her computer isn't in sleep mode, so she was here when the fire alarm went off. I scan the document section, looking for a huge file. She labeled them starting with the word Zambia, followed by the numbers one through three hundred and twenty-three. Nowhere on her computer is the word memory drug.

I click on Zambia 22 to see what's on it. The document contains a chemical formula using some sort of plant. I read the formula and recognize the chemicals, wondering why anyone would put them together. This combination of drugs in a human nervous system could be catastrophic, with amnesia as a side effect.

Opening other files titled Zambia, I notice variations in

the chemical formula. There are a few notes on the results of the trials. It doesn't look as though she started her trials on animals. She went straight for humans.

My stomach turns at the thought of what anyone might have gone through during the early stages of this drug and the aftereffects. I don't condone using animals in trials and never do, but in this case, the human nervous system would take an irreversible hit.

I'm so absorbed with the formulas on the screen that I forget to watch for Declan. I push the two-terabyte zip drive into the USB port and begin the download process. Each file labeled Zambia is separate. She didn't put them into one file, so I click through each one to download them. I start with the most recent Zambia file and work backward toward Zambia one.

As I near the end, I hear the click of a door. I can't call out to Declan in case someone is up here. I stop the download before I've completed copying the files to my zip drive. My nerves get the better of me, and I can't see him through the glass partitions. I unplug her computer from the outlet, hoping she thinks she tripped over it on the way out. When she plugs it in, it will go to reset.

My pace quickens as I make it to the other side of the floor. There are metal walls with double doors. The only way in is with the keypad, but I notice the fire alarm has stopped blaring. I don't want to leave Declan behind, but I have no choice. My countdown from ten is about to hit zero. I have to get out of here before everyone comes back up to the eighth floor.

I run down the stairwell until I reach the sixth floor. As I open the door, the sprinklers are still on, and I pull my lab coat up over my head. Declan's words come back to me. *Always look calm*. I make it to the private bathroom. He told me to go where there are no sprinklers and lock the door. My back hits the wall as I slide to the floor.

My heart beats in my ears, and my lungs are desperate for air. I'm not sure if I'm having a heart attack or a panic attack. Either way, once people stream back onto the floor, I need to make it to my office and get out. Closing my eyes, I try to bring down my heart rate by breathing deeply. I can do this. I have to do this, even without Declan. *Where did he go? Did they capture him?*

Muffled voices come from the other side of the bathroom door. People amble back to the floor and clean up the soggy mess left behind by the sprinklers. My lab coat is damp, but the prized possession is secured in my front pocket.

I open the door and peek out, looking for my entry into the stream of people. My pace is even with theirs as people trudge toward their desks, sifting through wet papers and puddles on their keyboards. The disappointment and frustration on their faces pains me, but this was for the greater good.

My office door closes behind me, and with shaky hands, I take the key out for the drawer where our cell phones are hidden. I catch myself before I unlock the drawer, remembering Declan's smoke screen. I've got to pull myself together.

Once the smoke rises, I grab the phones and stuff them in my laptop case. My computer calls to me to get the research I've been working on for years and download it to a zip drive, but I don't have time. Time is the one thing I keep running out of. I need to find out what happened to Declan. I hang my lab coat on the door and head out to the hallway.

I take my time getting to the elevator, appearing calm and stopping to talk to several of my colleagues to see how they're doing with everything. Most complain about cleaning up the mess but are thankful their research is backed up to the server. Little do they know that they don't truly own their research. Bio2Chem owns the server, which means Zahara owns their research.

The elevator doors open to the lobby, where a maintenance crew cleans up the water. Zahara, flanked by two of her bodyguards, approaches me, blocking my exit out of the building.

"Dr. Marcel, is everything okay?"

"Yes. Where was the fire?"

Her lips draw a taut line. "There was a malfunction in the system, triggering the alarm." She looks at me through suspicious eyes.

She scans the people in the lobby. "Where is Dr. Craig? Isn't he with you?"

I hear Declan in my head again. *Give them the unexpected.* "No. It wasn't my turn to watch him. If you'll excuse me, I have an appointment to get to." I walk around her and her bodyguards and decide to turn around to give my final blow.

"If you find him, could you tell him he's fired? I have little need for someone as incompetent as him." I smile and wiggle my fingers to wave. Her reaction is one of surprise. I need to throw her off our trail.

Outside, the sun shines, and a warm breeze blows down the street, ruffling my hair, a stark contrast to the assault on my nervous system. I pass by several cafés on my way to the parking garage where Declan parked the G wagon. I haven't worked up to calling the SUV Gal.

Out of the corner of my eye, I glimpse the reflection of someone following me in one of the windows. They are not even trying to be inconspicuous.

I duck into a café and order a sandwich for takeaway.

Once my sandwich is ready, I head for the back as if I'm going to the bathroom, looking for a back door exit. The kitchen is a way out as I get questioning looks from the cooks.

I point to the front of the café. "I have a stalker out front."

They nod their heads and go back to work.

Once I hit the street, I run for the parking garage while looking for the key fob in my purse. I take the stairs to the third level and hit two buttons. One to unlock the car and one to start the engine. Ripping open the door, I throw my bags in the front seat and lock the doors. I need to make it out of here as quickly as possible.

I take several turns to get to the road, taking me out of town and back to the cabin. This SUV is amazing and handles nicely in traffic as I dodge in and out of cars, vans, and trucks. In my rearview mirror, I noticed a black BMW keeping up with me. I squeeze the steering wheel.

"Hold on, Gal. It's about to get wild." I know I've lost it because I'm talking to a car and called her by name.

She responds. "Did you want to go to Fit Club?"

"What the hell?"

"I'm sorry. I didn't understand. Please repeat the command."

"Cancel."

"Would you like to cancel the destination?"

"Yes," I yell, taking out my frustrations on a voice in the car.

The system must have brought up Declan's destination list. I'm arguing with a car while trying to lose two idiots behind me, but this might work in my favor.

"Call the cabin."

"Calling cabin."

"Hello?" Poppy answers the phone. I bite my lower lip to keep myself from crying.

"Hi, honey, it's Mommy."

"Hi, Mommy. Are you coming home?"

"Yes, but I need you to do something for me. Remember when Prince Declan showed you the button you need to push in case of an emergency?" I choke on my words.

"Yeah."

"I need you to push the button now, sweetheart."

"Why?"

"I'll explain everything when I see you. Go get Grand-mère and push the button for me, okay?"

"Okay." She hangs up on a mission to find my mother. I hope my mom doesn't panic.

"Call Neil McFadden."

"Calling Neil McFadden." Gal is irritating and perfect.

"What's up?"

"Uncle Neil, it's Olivia. I need help because I'm scared shitless and running for my life."

# Chapter Thirty-Two

Olivia

"TALK TO ME." Uncle Neil's voice is the calm in the storm.

He's the person I need to be talking to right now to keep me focused because this is insane. Somewhere, my life has taken a drastic turn. I don't recognize myself.

I bring him up to speed on everything that's happened since we left the cabin, including Declan's disappearance and my run-in with Zahara.

"I've got a familiar black BMW on my tail, and I'm heading to the cabin. I called ahead and had them push the panic button to lock the cabin down. Tell me what to do."

"How close are they?"

"They're getting closer."

"You can outrun them. You've got more horsepower in the engine."

"I have no experience driving a car at over a hundred miles per hour."

He replies, "Do the best you can."

I push the gas pedal to the floor. I'm cruising at over one

hundred and twenty miles per hour and well out of my comfort zone, but the need to get away overrides my fear of driving at a high speed. Poppy's face keeps flashing before my eyes as I fight the tears blurring my vision.

Bullets fly, hitting the back window with a thud. I scream, fighting to hold it together.

"They're shooting at me!" I yell.

"Weave back and forth. Use the entire road. It's harder to hit a moving target. Frederick and Henri are on their way. Drive past the cabin for as long as you can until they get to you. I'll stay on the line."

Gal flies down the road and past the cabin. This car has a mind of its own. I don't let my foot off the gas.

In the distance, I can hear the high-pitched sound of motorcycle engines. They exchange gunfire with the men in the BMW. The scene unfolds in my rearview mirror. Frederick and Henri shoot the tires of the BMW, blowing them out. The BMW goes end over end across the road and into a field, where it lands and blows up. I guess that a bullet hit the gas tank.

I take my foot off the gas and pull over to the side of the road. My fingers are so tightly wrapped around the steering wheel that it hurts to uncurl them. The muscles in my shoulders and neck are stiff from holding them up by my ears. I hear my uncle's voice asking me if everything is okay, but I'm too dazed to respond.

With the engine off, I fall out of the car and collapse in the grass. My body shakes uncontrollably as my heart races and the tears flow. I hear the motorcycles stop behind me, but I'm not paying attention. Henri speaks to me in French.

"Have you been hit? Are you okay?"

I nod my head and wave them away, continuing to sob and taking big gulps of air to calm down. My tears have little to do with being shot at and more to do with the fact I have no idea what happened to Declan. I'm terrified of what Zahara could do to him. He's already been through so much. Could he endure hell again? My chest aches as I try to rub away the pain.

Frederick kneels next to me and rubs my back. "Are you able to drive?"

"Yes," is my only reply, and my body shutters. "Maybe not."

Frederick holds my arms. On shaky legs, I walk back to the G wagon. There are several holes in the glass surrounded by spiderwebs, but the glass held together. Gal did her job of keeping me safe. Declan would be proud. I climb into the passenger's seat as Frederick starts the car.

"Henri will be behind us, and I'll drive us back to the cabin." He squeezes my upper arm for reassurance. "You'll be fine."

He turns the G wagon around and heads back to the cabin. Uncle Neil has left the call. My body comes down from the adrenaline rush of the car chase, and I'm hit with sheer exhaustion. The up and down of adrenaline from the day's events has worn me out.

The gravel driveway to the cabin kicks up dust around the SUV, blocking my view. When we park and let the dust settle, I can see the safety measures Declan put in place. The cabin looks nothing like it did before. Black metal shields cover the windows and front door with slits in them. No one was going to get to Poppy and my mother.

"Mommy?" I hear Poppy, but I can't see her behind the steel curtains.

I turn to Frederick. "How do we get to them?"

Frederick pulls out his phone and taps on it a couple of times. The shields go up, revealing the windows. Poppy opens the front door with my mom behind her. She runs down the stairs and into my arms. I've never been so glad to hold anyone in my life. The next person I want to feel like this with is Declan. Ozzie comes running out behind her, almost knocking my mom off her feet.

My mom seems unfazed by the entire experience. Her reaction must come from being married to a former agent, but I also see the worry as her eyes scan the G wagon. She hasn't lived this life in a very long time, and her granddaughter is her world.

Henri comes up behind us. "Let's get everyone inside. We need to talk. Frederick is going to park the vehicles out of sight."

Poppy takes my hand in both of hers as we walk toward the cabin.

"Mommy, where's Declan? Why did I have to push the button? It was fun."

"Absolutely nothing happened. Thank goodness Prince Declan made you a fortress to keep you safe. He'll be back soon." I choke on my last words. Thank God she's young. Otherwise, she would hear the lack of confidence in my voice.

"I told you he will always keep me safe." A big smile comes across her face.

We get inside, and I find the nearest place to sit down. My mom offers to make me some chamomile tea, and I gratefully accept, wishing Declan could make his special coffee. Poppy runs off with Ozzie, and Prince pads over to sit in my lap.

Henri sits across from me with a look of concern on his face. "Frederick is checking your vehicle for trackers. When did you notice they were tailing you?"

"Not long after I left the parking garage. They had been

following me from the company building. They must have been waiting for me on the street."

He nods as if he's put two and two together. I tuck my legs under me and cross my arms to get warm. The chill is a reaction to coming down from a high-stress event. I pet Prince for comfort.

"We need to get back in there and get Declan out," I demand.

The front door opens, and Frederick comes in, shaking his head, indicating there were no trackers found. Henri acknowledges this with a nod of his head and turns back to me.

"Neil needs to be consulted on the next move, which will be crucial. This is his op. The mission has been compromised, and we need to get Declan out safely. We also want Zahara, preferably alive. We have yet to get anyone from her team alive."

This gets my attention. "You are both ex-operatives. Surely the two of you can get to the eighth floor and rescue him. We can't leave him there. He's been through too much already." The pitch of my voice gets higher.

Henri reaches out and covers my hand with his. "He's trained for this. He knows what to do to stay alive. We have to trust him, and now Neil is calling the shots.

I shake my head. "No, you don't understand."

"I do understand. I know more than you think I know." He smiles.

# Chapter Thirty-Three

Neil

DECLAN IS A SURVIVOR, but I don't know how long he can stay alive under Zahara's thumb. She's wicked, smart, and, based on her activity in Zambia, she has no remorse, a dangerous combination. There's one call I need to make.

"Sean, we need to get the team together. The mission's gone south."

"Details," Sean replies.

"We think Zahara and her team captured Declan. He went on a recon and didn't come back with his contact." I don't tell him I didn't want Olivia anywhere near this situation, but Declan convinced me it was the only way.

"Hold on." Time ticks by in what I'm sure are minutes but feels like an hour. The men on this team have become family to me, which is dangerous for a man in my position. I could make decisions based on emotions rather than intel.

Sean comes back on. "We're here. I've got Mac, Dean, Beck, and Antonio. Pippa is up to her eyeballs in another

194

project, which is why I brought on Antonio. Campbell is your point man and is also on the line."

"Got it." This is the point at which I go easy because I know how Mac is going to react.

"Declan's contact at Bio2Chem is my niece, Olivia. They breached the eighth floor of the building, which has the highest level of security. Their mission was to seek out and get the formula for the memory drug. At some point, Declan got captured, but Olivia got away and downloaded some information on the memory drug."

There's dead silence, and then the eruption. "What the fuck are you talking about? Why isn't Campbell going in? Why haven't you called for backup?" Mac raises his voice to a superior. Correction, a former superior. I don't blame him. I'm on the verge of losing my shit too. Over the years, I've taken care of Declan. He feels like a son to me.

"You need to calm down because getting pissed off will not get us anywhere."

"Declan was a top agent. How did he get himself into this?" Mac's voice is desperate.

"You're right. Declan was a top agent and one of the best in the business. Mac, there are things about Declan you don't know."

Mac snaps back. "What are you saying?"

"It's not my story to tell. What's happened to him in the past needs to come from him. This is why I'm calling you. Get packed up because it's wheels up in an hour. I'm flying out of London tonight. I'll meet you in Cologne tomorrow. We'll talk about logistics then."

Dean, the wild Aussie of the team, speaks up. "You're meeting us there? Kind of unusual for you. You always leave the dirty work to us." Leave it to Dean to bring everything out into the open.

"Olivia and her mother, Margot, are the only family I have. We think Zahara knows about Olivia's connection to me, and this could get personal. I won't let anyone get near my family, just like Mac and Campbell aren't going to let Declan take the fall for this mission."

"Roger that," replies Beck, also ex-MI6. He returned from a trip to Zambia, where he found his biological family and cracked into more information about Deep 8.

"I'll see you there. This could be rough, so be on point."

I end the call without saying goodbye. It's become my signature closing. I hate saying goodbye. I've been saying goodbye my entire life. For once, I'd like to say hello and stay longer than five minutes before I jet off to my next assignment. Being M, head of MI6, is an all-consuming job. It may be time to hang it up and get a life beyond the next mission.

I call Olivia. "Hey, how are you doing? Are you back at the cabin?"

"Yes, we're at the cabin. The guys in the SUV blew up. Shouldn't Frederick and Henri be going to get Declan?" Her words run together in a panic.

"I'm flying in from London tonight. I've also called in Declan's entire team so we can put together a rescue plan."

"So, the only way we get you to visit us is to have someone get kidnapped? I need to remember that." She's being cheeky to alleviate the tension.

"Don't get any ideas. I need you, Poppy, and Margot to stay at the cabin in lockdown until the team arrives. Is there enough room for us?"

"How many are coming?"

"Seven, including me."

"We'll make it work. This place has five bedrooms. I'm

going to need to go to work tomorrow," she says with defiance.

"Not going to happen. I can't risk you going to work and having them take you, too. Your escape is not making Zahara happy if she knows you are part of the plan."

"I saw her in the lobby on my way out. We exchanged words. I said some things to make her think Declan and I are distanced."

"Good. How much did you download of the formula? Have you looked at it yet?"

"I don't know. I haven't looked at the files."

"Let's leave it for Antonio. He can sift through it when he gets there."

"Sounds good because I'm way too tired to deal with anything right now." I hear her sniffle. "Are you going to rescue Declan? I know how serious this is. Just a minute." I hear her move to another room and close the door. "You need to bring him back, preferably alive."

"I know. We will. I don't want to get your hopes up about what condition he will be in. They may torture him for information about you and me."

"No, you don't understand. He has to come back." She sobs, "He's Poppy's father."

"I know, and I want nothing more than to bring him home."

Her sobbing takes over, and she doesn't question how I know.

"Stay locked down at the cabin. I'll see you soon."

There are bad days and terrible days. This is worse than both of those.

# Chapter Thirty-Four

### Declan

THE BACK of my head pounds from where I was hit. My eyes open through slits and I see dim lights above me. The first thing I do is try to move my arms and legs, and that's when I realize I am chained to the bed. My arms and legs move about six inches from where they are attached.

Panic sets in. Being immobilized is one of my weaknesses. During my training as an agent, I had to find strategies to quell my anxiety. I use my breathing technique while closing my eyes and going to my happy place. *Liv and Poppy.* My head needs to stay in the game so I can get back to them.

I lift my head to look around the room. Paul Ritcher lies next to me.

"Paul, it's me, Declan."

His head turns in my direction, but his stare is vacant. A piece of me breaks in two. He looks nothing like the agent I remember. God knows what they've done to him in this place. He frowns.

"Declan? What are you doing here?"

I'm amazed he remembers me. "It looks like I'm doing the same thing you are. Being held prisoner."

"I'm not being held prisoner. I'm part of the trial to test a drug to help with PTSD."

"Paul, when was the last time you saw the light of day? You went MIA about a year ago. No one knew what happened to you." I try to appeal to his logical side.

"They know exactly where I am. They recruited me for this trial." He remains committed to country and queen, looking at me as if I'm the one who's nuts.

I lie back and stare at the ceiling. On top of being Zahara's victim, she's brainwashed Paul, probably along with the others. I take deep breaths to keep myself calm. I'm sure I will get a visit from Zahara. I'm her new favorite patient.

Paul continues to talk. "It doesn't surprise me you got recruited. You are one of MI6's finest. Where did you disappear to? You fell off the radar about five years ago."

I don't want to strain my neck to look at him. "It's a long story. We'll get into the details later. Right now, we need to focus on getting out of here."

"It's all good, mate. The data they're collecting from the research will be invaluable for the soldiers in the future. We're committed to the cause."

"You are so mis—" I stop in mid-sentence as I hear the door open at the far end of the room.

Heads turn in Zahara's direction. Everything is quiet except for the clicking of her shoes on the concrete floor. She does a runway walk down the aisle flanked by two bodyguards. She buries her hands in the pockets of her designer pantsuit as she stands next to my bed. Always the fashion diva.

"Hello, Dr. Craig. It's so nice to see you again." Her words are encased in ice.

"Aw, Z, I wish I could say it's nice to see you again, but it really isn't. By the way, you can call me Prince Declan." My eyes never leave hers.

She leans down, getting close to my face. "You're hardly a prince. You will tell me what I need to know or the consequences maybe your royal demise."

I lift my head closer to hers, and I whisper, "First off, you need to get a sense of humor. Second, if you kill me, you'll never get the answers you're looking for."

Her face squeezes together as if she's bitten into something sour. "Who were you with when you got onto this floor?"

I laugh hysterically, forcing tears to my eyes. She rears back, surprised by my reaction.

"Why on God's green earth what I ever bring anyone to this place? I would never jeopardize anyone's life but my own. Coming up here was an enormous risk." I yank on my arm, making the chains clank. "You seem to be an expert at taking prisoners. How many do you have here, over fifty?"

She wraps her fingers around my throat, putting pressure on my trachea. "The number of soldiers I have here is none of your concern. This time, there is no escape for you." She squeezes my throat and smiles.

There is something seriously wrong with her. She could be the poster child for psychopaths everywhere. She lets go right before I pass out as I take gulps of air and cough.

Her stare is frightening, and she continues to smile.

"You lost me when you said this time." I force my words out through the coughing.

She leans down so her mouth is near my ear. "Who do

you think put the holes in your hazmat suit? I was hoping you would burn to death, a fitting way for you to go, considering you thought you were so hot. But here you are, once again a thorn in my side. This time I need to find out what you know before I give you a slow, torturous death."

I react instinctively by trying to reach for her. The chains and cuffs on my wrists halt my motion and clank. She stands back and laughs.

"Your humor is a little off, but I don't think you're laughing at the fact your cancer-causing drug didn't pan out." I might as well dig the knife in deeper. She knows why I was at the company five years ago, which makes me think MI6 has a mole.

Unable to get away from her, she drags her fingertips along my arm, running over the bumps of my scars. She is twisted beyond nine kinds of hell. Whatever hatred Liv has for Zahara, mine has tripled. I want to kill her more than I've wanted to kill anyone in my life, and I've run across some bad dudes over the years, but none quite as psycho as her.

"I thought Dr. Marcel might be involved in this, but when I ran into her in the lobby, she didn't seem too impressed by you. She told me to fire you. Her mind doesn't work that way. She's too focused on her kiddie research. One way or another, I'll find out who's working with you."

She turns away from my bed and continues to walk down the aisle to the other side of the room.

That's my girl. Always thinking on her feet. Liv put some distance between us, throwing Zahara off track. She hasn't connected Neil and Liv, a point in our favor.

Everyone lifts their heads during our exchange to see what's going on. They look at me with curious eyes, some even frown. I've already been identified as the rebel. Let's see if I can get them to stand with me and work against Zahara.

"What the hell was that about?" Paul says to me.

"Long story short, five years ago, I was in a chem lab in a hazmat suit with holes in it. My arms and legs burned and left me in limbo for months. I had several skin grafts, and the recovery was extensive and painful. I just found out who was responsible for my agony, and she's going to pay."

"No, it can't be Zahara. She's been nothing but wonderful to us."

"And I have some property I'd like to sell you in the Sahara. What planet are you living on? I told you she tried to burn me alive. Oh, and by the way, you're being held captive whether you want to believe it or not. You did not sign up for this. There is no British government program testing a memory drug for PTSD. How sick have you been during this research?"

Paul gives me a look as though he's swallowed something that tastes bad. The look on his face tells me he's not sure what to believe. It may take a while for me to undo the brainwashing Zahara has put in place. She must feel confident she has them snowed, otherwise, I would be by myself in a holding cell.

"It's been dreadful. Sweating, headaches, vomiting, and a host of other symptoms. We have been told it's in the name of research for our government." Paul starts to lose color in his face. He has no idea where he is.

"What country do you think we're in?"

Paul stares at me and blinks several times. "England," he says in a tentative voice.

"I don't know how to break it to you, mate. We're not in England. We're nowhere near there. We are in Cologne, Germany."

His eyes widen and then squint. "Are you sure?"

I've got a long road ahead of me on both fronts. I need to convince Paul and the others of what is really going on. Then I need to find a way to get out of here. I'm guessing that at this point, Neil has called for backup. I pray they have a plan because from where I'm lying, I don't have many options.

## Chapter Thirty-Five

Olivia

AFTER THE DUST SETTLES, I tuck Poppy in, with Ozzie at her feet. I shuffle back to my room and collapse into bed. I lie staring at the ceiling, wondering where we went wrong. One minute, Declan was there with me, and the next minute, he vanished. If someone was there and took Declan, did they know I was there too?

Questions swirl in my head. I worry about what's happening to him and how much he can endure. Even trained agents have their limits. My father was a prime example of a broken soldier.

The door to my bedroom opens, and I hear small feet pad across the carpet. Something big and furry lands on my bed with a thud.

"Mommy, we're going to sleep with you tonight." Poppy gets herself under the covers as Ozzie lies at the end of the bed. She offers no explanation.

I wrap her in my arms, holding her close to me. My most precious gift was given to me by an incredible man. He needs to live long enough to get to know his daughter. They've had very limited time to be with each other, and I'm hoping it won't be the only time they have together.

Poppy is asleep within minutes, and Ozzie snores at the end of the bed. The silhouette of my mother appears in the doorway. She moves across the room toward the bed and lifts the covers.

"Move over. I'm coming in."

She lies next to me as we huddle together. "He'll be back, you know. You and Poppy have his heart."

"I hope you're right. Uncle Neil told me his team has some of the top agents in the world. They should be able to bring him home."

She squeezes me. There's nothing like a mother's love, which I hope I pass along to Poppy. Sleep takes me as I feel secure, knowing that almost everyone I care about is in bed with me.

Morning comes way too early as Poppy scampers out of bed, whipping back the covers and jumping onto the floor. My mom is the second to leave the comfort and warmth of our nest.

"I'll take care of her. Why don't you try to get more sleep?"

I drift back to sleep, dreaming about Declan, Poppy, my mom, and the animals together in a field of wildflowers. The sun shines through, warming our faces. Dark clouds form as torrential rain pours from the sky, and someone grabs my arm from behind. The people I love disappear as I stare into Zahara's cold, evil eyes.

She screams, "What have you done with my formula?"

I jerk awake and sit up in bed, panting, clutching the

sheets to my chest. This isn't the kind of panting I want to be doing.

Voices from downstairs get my attention as Poppy screams, "Uncle Neil!"

I force myself out of bed and get dressed in a pair of sweats. As I round the corner, I see my mom with my uncle standing in the kitchen.

"It's so good to see you." She pulls him into a hug.

They stand back from one another with loving eyes as if they want to kiss but are aware of Poppy. My daughter sits at the island, eating her breakfast, not watching the scene unfold before her.

I clear my throat to let them know I'm here. Uncle Neil jumps back away from my mother.

"Oh, I didn't see you there," he comments.

I smile. "I bet you didn't."

My mom covers her blushed cheeks with her hands, then grabs her coffee cup, looking at her brother-in-law as if they've gotten caught in the act. I'll be addressing that with her later.

I grab a mug from the cupboard and pour myself a cup of coffee. Any coffee other than Declan's doesn't taste good.

"Did you just get in?"

"Yes, there were some delays. The rest of the team will be here either later tonight or tomorrow. In the meantime, you and I can debrief about the details of what happened yesterday." He's been here five minutes, and he's already in work mode.

I nod. "Let me wake up first."

Quiet comes over the kitchen as we sit at the island and have breakfast together. I need to address the awkwardness between my mother and uncle without Poppy's busy ears.

"Poppy, why don't you and Ozzie go to the living room and find five things beginning with the T sound?"

"I love this game." She hops off the stool and runs into the living room with Ozzie close behind.

I turn to the two teenagers sitting quietly, staring at their plates. "So, would you like to tell me what's going on because the elephant in the room is about to explode?"

They look at each other, guilt written on their faces.

My mom speaks first with her chin held high. "I don't know what you're talking about."

"Denial is always the first line of defense. Try again." I sip my tasteless coffee.

"Oh, for Pete's sake. Your mother and I have been seeing each other for about a year. We didn't mean to keep it a secret, but we didn't want to upset you."

"Why would you think I would be upset? I'm an adult woman, not a child. There are many reasons I can think of why the two of you would be together. I'm surprised it took you this long." I smile. This explains how he knew Declan is Poppy's father.

My mom reaches out to hold my hand. "Do we have your blessing?"

"You don't need my blessing, but yes, you do. I'm happy for you. You're both too young to be alone." A knot forms in my chest. I'm also too young to be alone.

"Good. Let's get down to the debriefing." Uncle Neil leans over and kisses my mom on her temple, and she smiles. I haven't seen her smile with such warmth in years, and it warms my heart. It explains her intimate phone calls at odd hours of the day and night.

My uncle and I move to the dining room. Declan's cabin is beginning to feel like home, but without him here, it feels vacant. The playful energy he has with Poppy and his overall presence is what's missing, like the cabin has been unplugged.

We get settled in, and I relay as many of the details as I can remember from the time the fire alarm went off to being shot at in the car.

I ask the question I'm not sure I want the answer to. "Do you think Zahara knows you and I are related?"

He sits back as his fingers stroke the handle of his coffee cup. "I don't know. She may have been putting the squeeze on you to get to Declan, thinking the two of you are in a relationship. Our family connection has been buried deep for years."

This information strikes me as odd. "We never showed each other any signs of affection. If five years ago is an indication of what our relationship is like, she would've known it didn't end well. We argued in front of the security guard while we were getting our key cards upgraded."

"If she talked to the security guard, she knows you had access to the eighth floor, as well as Declan. I don't mean to frighten you, but she and her team are looking for you. They will search high and low to find you, especially if they suspect someone had access to the memory drug formula."

A chill runs through me as I shudder to think what would happen if anyone on her team found us. She never struck me as a forgiving person.

"We need to get Poppy and my mom out of here to a safe location and out of the country."

"No. Any movement would raise a red flag. We can protect them if they're under our wing. You'll see what I mean when you meet the team. No one will get through them."

## Chapter Thirty-Six

Olivia

THERE'S NOT a cloud in the sky as the sun sits higher with each passing day. Poppy can't understand why she can't go outside. The shades are drawn on every window in the house, except for the sliders opening to the back deck.

My uncle thought it was best if we stayed inside, considering the car wreck happened a few miles up the road. Zahara and her team may search the area, and he thinks they will use drones.

I set my laptop up on the dining room table and check my email. Most of the emails are asking about their backed-up research and the fire alarm from yesterday. I answer a few of them, but I'm distracted. Focusing on work was never a problem for me until Declan entered my life again.

My attention gets pulled back to the zip drive I used to download the files from Zahara's computer. Curiosity gets the better of me as I plug the drive into my USB port and wait for the files to load. I save the files to my hard drive, starting with Zambia three hundred, until I reach the computer's storage limit.

What appears before me is nothing I can understand. The files have been encrypted, and since I'm not a hacker, I won't be able to get into them. I close my laptop and go in search of my daughter and her furry beast.

The sun beats through the slider in the kitchen. She and Ozzie sit on a beach blanket on the floor, both wearing sunglasses while she sips lemonade.

"Mommy, do you want some lemonade?"

"I would love some lemonade. Should I get sunglasses, too?"

"Of course." She bounces up, gets a glass, and pours some lemonade for me. I reach for the extra set of sunglasses on the counter.

"When's Prince Declan coming home?" She misses him.

My little girl has a way of throwing me for a loop with a few words. I'm stuck on the word home. Her home is where her heart is, and her heart is with Declan.

"I don't know. He has some things he needs to take care of before he comes back." I take a sip of lemonade to prevent myself from saying more.

She looks at me for a bit too long, as if she can sense my trepidation. I want to protect her as much as possible since I don't know the outcome of this adventure.

They say children are resilient, but events that happened to us early on have a habit of staying with us for the rest of our lives, let alone the trauma we may endure as adults.

I need her to remember him in the best light if he doesn't come back. Although, the thought of him not coming back could send me into a crying jag.

We hear stomping feet outside the front door, and I clutch Poppy to me. Ozzie runs to the front door, barking and growling. Uncle Neil runs downstairs from the second floor and opens the door.

"That's the last friggin' time you're driving. You're a goddamn maniac," one of them says with a Scottish accent.

I put my hands over Poppy's ears. The team has arrived.

"Well, ever since you had a kid, you drive like a little old lady. With your precious cargo and all," the Aussie snarks.

Poppy wiggles out of my arms to run toward the action. I follow behind her to see what the commotion is about. She stops in the middle of the living room, throws her arms in the air, and screams with joy at the top of her lungs.

The six giants standing by the door take a step back, stumbling on each other, unsure of the screaming small person. Ozzie stops barking long enough to give his warning and sits in front of her.

She counts each of them using her pointer finger. They stare at her wide-eyed and curious, afraid of what's coming next.

"Mommy, there are six princes here."

I wonder when she'll grow out of seeing men as princes. Maybe we don't grow out of it. We end up changing the parameters, always looking for the prince underneath who fits us.

She runs up to the large black man and cranes her neck to look up at him. Ozzie follows her and sniffs him. "Are you the Chocolate Prince?" Her eyes grow big with excitement.

I'm horrified. "Poppy Victoria, you're being rude."

She glares at me over her shoulder and frowns. The man throws his head back and laughs.

"I've been called worse," he says with an aristocratic British accent.

He gets down on one knee and holds his hand out to her.

He pets Ozzie with his other hand. "My name is Beck, but you can call me Prince Chocolate."

She puts her tiny hand in his and gives him a firm shake. "Do you know where Prince Declan is? He needs to come home."

Everyone stands still as the air feels like it's being sucked out of the room. Their eyes turn in my direction.

The one with the Scottish accent holds up his hand to me and gets down on one knee, too. "I'm Prince Mac, and we're here to find my brother, Prince Declan."

"Is he lost?" She doesn't care that Mac is Declan's brother.

The rest of the men get down on one knee. The Aussie speaks, "I'm Prince Dean. This is Prince Sean. Prince Campbell is Prince Declan's other brother, and over there is Prince Antonio. Yes, your prince is lost, and we're here to find him."

She grabs his face, mushing his cheeks together. "You have to find him. I miss him."

I cover my mouth with my hand to prevent a cry from escaping. The men nod in agreement with tight lips. She lets go of his face.

"Oh, we're going to find Prince Declan, and when we do, we're going to—" Dean starts.

"Okay, thank you, Dean," my uncle cuts in. "Why don't you guys go upstairs and find a bed? We'll meet back here in thirty and start strategizing a plan."

The men slowly rise from the floor. "My God, my knees can't take being in a kneeling position," Mac groans.

Campbell, their chauffeur for the day, coughs, "Old man."

They lumber up the stairs. "I think I want one of those. She's adorable and smart. Do they always scream?" Dean asks.

Sean smacks him on the back of his head. "Having a child would require you and your girlfriend to be on the same page. Remember, women carry the child. And there's a lot more than screaming involved."

"I've never been a prince before. I'm usually the joker of the group," Campbell laughs.

Poppy watches the men go upstairs and then turns to me. "Why is Prince Declan lost? Doesn't he remember how to get home?"

How do you explain to a four-year-old that someone we love is being held against their will? Someone may be torturing him or, worse yet, having the memory drug put into his veins.

Images flash through my mind, making me want to break down and cry. I need to hold it together for her and for him if we're going to get him out alive. I know I won't have much of a role in this, but a weepy woman is not what is called for in this situation.

"It's a long story. Why don't you come to the kitchen with me?"

The rogue team of oversized men looks fully equipped to rescue Declan. They also look angry and ready for battle. I'm going to have a lot of mouths to feed and a lot of food to cook.

I pray that whatever plan they come up with, they do it quickly. The more time Zahara has him, the more damage she can do. I need Declan to come back to us in one piece.

# Chapter Thirty-Seven

### Declan

FROM MY CALCULATIONS, I've been here for over forty-eight hours. The team must have landed and is planning my extraction from this sterile hellhole.

I trust my teammates more than anyone in the world. Despite two of my brothers being part of the team, every member feels like family, and we have a solid bond. Training as an operative forms bonds that never die, but I never thought I would like being part of any team again.

I fidget and get antsy, missing Liv and Poppy. Images of them are what I hold on to, keeping my sanity intact. I replay the moments we had together, so I don't forget them. Fear claws at me that, somehow, I will lose them and the memories we had together. There's always anxiety around trying to remember things from the recent past.

Poppy sparked something in me I'd never imagined for myself. I have a new outlook that includes a family. God willing, Liv and Poppy will be a part of my life when I get out of here. They give me something to live for and a reason to survive. Otherwise, I wouldn't care, risking everything for the mission.

Liv's soul is who I'm in sync with, no matter what we argue about or who is battling for control. Because of them, I've never wanted out of a situation so much.

This place runs like a prison, but everyone being held is convinced they are here for the greater good. They are friendly to the med techs, even laughing and joking with them. When they are not hooked up to IVs, they take walks around the floor, behind the metal walls, and out of sight of the other scientists working in the labs.

They don't find it unusual they haven't been outside in I don't know how long. I assume the lights above us are UV lights to help regulate our biorhythms, but that doesn't seem to matter either. Every couple of hours, they escort another patient to a back room. I assume they are testing their memory functions. They return smiling, happy they can't remember the horrors of war.

They keep me chained up and give me enough food and water to sustain myself. If this is the best they've got, they need to up their game. I've been in worse situations, namely my recovery from my last murder attempt. My threshold for pain is quite high, and I've been trained to conserve my energy. I don't think they have a lot of knowledge about the extensive training of a special forces warrior.

Zahara hasn't been back to grill me, which makes me suspicious. I know she's hunting for Liv, and the thought of anyone hurting Liv and Poppy makes me crazy. I distract myself by talking to Paul, but our conversations go in circles. He's so far under he can't see the surface through the bubbles being blown up his ass.

I haven't been able to convince him he's on the wrong side of this mission. Occasionally, one of the medical assistants comes around and injects something into the men's IVs. What's curious is there are no women, only men. The injections are different for each of them. Based on my observations, the injection contains a different strength or variation of the memory formula as the trials continue. The drug must contain a sedative because they are out cold after they administer the drug.

As I stare at the ceiling trying to think things through, the double doors open, and her royal highness enters with her bodyguards. There's pep in her step and a scowl on her face, which means she hasn't gotten what she wanted. Her cool demeanor is in jeopardy.

"It's so good to see you again, Z." I grin, showing my teeth.

She stands at the side of the bed with her hands gripped together in front of her. Her calm demeanor has left the building.

"Who was with you when you breached this floor? Don't say no one because someone has downloaded the Zambia files with the latest formula I need." Her lips form a thin line.

"Is that what you're calling a drug that makes soldiers ill and wipes out their memories? Your drug may be taking away their PTSD, but it's also taking everything else with it. You should rename it the Wipe Out Drug."

She waves her hand across the room. "Do you see anyone ill?"

"Of course not. It's why you use Compazine and painkillers. You forget who you're talking to, Z."

She purses her lips together and leans down. "How do you know my memory drug would make anyone ill?" She smiles as if she's finally got me in a corner.

The best defense is a killer offense. "Let's cut through the bullshit. You know who I am and why I'm here. My teammate, Beck, had serious side effects from your drug when he was in Zambia. It almost killed him, which is probably what you were hoping for so you could gain control. The question is, what the hell do you want with me?"

She snaps her fingers and curls them as a signal to her henchmen. One of them gets a chair for her as she makes herself comfortable next to me and crosses her legs. She leans back in the chair and folds her hands in her lap.

"Let me tell you a little story. You were patient zero for my first round of the memory drug, as you like to call it. When you didn't burn to death, I thought I would use you as a guinea pig for my latest drug." She props her elbows on her knees and leans her chin on her laced hands. "Tell me, what do you remember after your recovery?"

I strain at my chains, trying to get to her and wrap my hands around her neck. I have a distinct memory of her voice from right after my accident. As I floated in and out of consciousness, her voice was the one thing I could hold onto, but not anymore. "Why would I tell you anything?"

She smiles. "Because I can reverse the effects of the drug and get your memories back if you play nice." She lays on the charm, but her hood is showing, resembling a king cobra before it strikes.

"I don't play well with others. You can't reverse the effects. I lost years of my life, and time hasn't brought back the memories. If you haven't gotten the memory drug to work the way you want it to, why would I think you have a drug that can reverse its effects?" I won't play dumb for her.

She tries a different tact. "You know, Dr. Marcel has not shown up for work. Says she has a stomach bug. I think she's hiding out somewhere. I think she has my formula. If I find her, there's no telling what I will do to her. Are you willing to take that chance?"

I smile. "Do whatever you think you need to do. I'm not playing by your rules, and I don't give in to terrorists."

She stands over me. "What a brave little warrior you are." She turns to one of the techs. "Hook him up to a line. Maybe some sodium pentothal will help jog your memory of where she is and who else is here looking for you."

The med tech comes over and inserts a needle into my vein with a line. Fighting at this point will make the situation worse and might even rupture the vein. I have to think fast because sodium pentothal is deadly if it's administered at a high dose.

"What I know is, by now, Dr. Marcel has probably left the country. There would be no reason for her to stay."

"You're wrong. My men chased her out into the country until two of your men drove them off the road, and their vehicle blew up. I think she's still in the country. I doubt she would leave you behind."

I frown at her as if she knows something I don't.

"What an interesting reaction. You must not know. It doesn't surprise me. I'll save that tidbit of information for another day. In the meantime, I'll make you my latest patient for the memory drug, without anything to ease the discomfort, and see how you deal with the side effects."

"Tell me, who was the mole that blew my op?"

"I would never give up someone on the inside. They are way too valuable. Take care."

She walks away and says something to the med techs on the way out. They come over, tilt my bed upright, and begin injecting something into my line.

Depression falls over me like a heavy weight at the

thought of having any more of my memories ripped from me. I've made new memories I want to hold on to for a lifetime. I don't know how to fight this as I slip under and let the darkness take me.

# Chapter Thirty-Eight

Olivia

THEY'VE BEEN SITTING around the dining room table most of the day. There doesn't seem to be a set plan. Poppy keeps running in and out of the room. Campbell chases her out and then tickles her into fits of laughter. Their playfulness makes me giggle. He doesn't realize he's only encouraging her to keep coming back into the room. They are two peas in a pod.

Seeing her with her uncle makes the pieces fall into place, from her looks to her personality. She is one of them, but I see so much of myself in her as well.

Declan's cell phone burns in my pocket. I've been carrying it with me since I grabbed it from the drawer. I'm not one to snoop, but I'm curious about his playlist. I swipe to open it, but it's password protected. The lock screen makes me catch my breath.

There's a photo of Poppy and me laughing in the wildflower field, and underneath are the words from Adele's song, "Go Easy on Me." I crumble into the nearest stool at the island in the kitchen and play the song. The radio played it for weeks on end, but this time I really listen to the words. Tears roll down my cheeks.

I've made a horrible mistake not telling him about Poppy, and now it may be too late. Nothing was in his control five years ago, and decisions were made for him. I've been holding on to the idea that the decisions were made by him. We need to get him back. I wipe my wet cheeks.

As I walk past the dining room, I try to pick up on any part of the conversation to find out what their rescue plan is for Declan. Words like *not possible*, *out in the open*, and *inside person* litter the conversation but never hook onto anything.

Giving up, I enter the room, and their heads turn to look at me.

"Maybe you need a fresh set of eyes on this. What did you come up with so far?"

Their heads turn back in my uncle's direction for the final word on my participation in this mission. He nods his head in acceptance.

"Mac, tell her what we have so far."

"We've got jack shit. It doesn't matter what angle we hit the building from; we will be detected and more than likely outnumbered. Some approaches are better than others, but what we really need is a distraction. The bargaining chip we have is the memory formula. Our guess is Zahara doesn't want anyone else to have it for good reason. If it works, it could be a global game changer."

The table gets quiet, and their eyes plea with me for an answer I doubt I have.

"It's worse than that for her. I downloaded her most recent trials, and unless she backed them up, I'm the only one who has the formula. What if I was your inside person? I could contact Zahara and let her know I have the memory drug formula in exchange for Declan."

They blink several times without saying a word, but I know what they're thinking.

"What? I watch a lot of action flicks like *Jack Reacher*."

Beck speaks up, "We can't let you do that or put you in harm's way. You have your daughter and mother to think of. You're not a trained operative. Although, I hear you can drive the hell out of a car, not unlike Pippa, who scares the shit out of me when she drives." His white teeth are brilliant against his ebony skin as he grins.

I smile. "I appreciate your concern, but I need to be a part of this. Poppy's life is so much better when her father is in it. They bonded before Zahara captured him. She needs him, and I think he needs her."

I've exposed a bombshell. Uncle Neil looks away from me and grimaces.

Mac looks at me and frowns. "What did you say?"

Campbell smiles. "I'm an uncle again."

Poppy stops at the doorway to the room. "Prince Campbell, I'm coming in there. You better not tickle me."

I lean over the table and whisper, "She doesn't know about Declan or you and Mac. Please don't let on about it. It may be too much for her."

Campbell gets up to chase Poppy out of the room, exactly as she wanted. That's what uncles are for.

Mac turns to me. "Does Declan know?"

"I tried to tell him before we went up to the eighth floor. He acted like he already knew and was okay with it." I shrug and frown.

"I assure you; Declan does not know. There will be hell to pay when he finds out you kept it from him," my uncle booms from the end of the table.

I stand up. "Funny how no one asked about the path I've walked for the years he's been gone. Was I supposed to welcome him back with open arms and say, 'By the way, you have a daughter.'? How did I know he wouldn't leave again? As far as I was concerned, he had a habit of disappearing. I wasn't going to put my daughter or myself in that position." No one says a word, but Mac looks at me with understanding. "I need some air."

The fields of wildflowers call to me as I throw on a sweater and walk among the sunflowers, reaching for the sun. I stand in the middle of the field with my face to the sky, trying to wrap my head around what the next steps are for my family and me.

I hear heavy steps coming from behind me, but I don't acknowledge them.

"I'm sorry he left you," Mac says. "I have a daughter too, and I understand it couldn't have been easy for you to raise her on your own for these past years. Declan hasn't been in a good way over the last couple of years. This is going to sound crazy, but knowing he has a daughter might save his life. She will give him a reason to live."

I grab the sweater at my chest, knowing I hold one of Declan's secrets he hasn't told his family. They will rescue him, and when they do, he can share what has happened to him and made him who he is today. I nod, accepting Mac's information, not revealing the complete picture.

"We need to rescue him from the crazy bitch who's holding him, and then he can meet his daughter. I'm not sure how he's going to feel about me not telling him right away. He and I grew close, and as they say, it's complicated."

"Forgiveness is an interesting maiden who's voyage always starts from the inside. I hope he will be able to see your side of the story. This won't be an easy transition for the two of you," Mac replies.

"Is that a quote from someone?"

He looks at me with curiosity. "No. It's a quote from me." He smiles.

I shake my head, and tears form in my eyes. "I've fallen in love with him again. I'm not sure I ever stopped loving him from the one night we had together. That's the night we created the wild redhead who Campbell keeps busy. We were always at each other and one night changed everything."

"Trust me, it only takes one night. She reminds me so much of our late younger sister, Kendall." Mac stares off at the horizon.

I wiped the tears from my cheek and smile. "He might've mentioned her a time or two."

"Let's go back inside and see if we can come up with a plan to get Poppy's father home."

# Chapter Thirty-Nine

Olivia

AFTER SPENDING twenty-four hours inside the cabin, I beg my uncle to let us go outside. We're getting a little stir-crazy. Poppy needs fresh air and to run around in the sunshine. He agrees reluctantly and tells us to watch for anything unusual.

Poppy is excited to go outside, and Ozzie joins us. She asks if Prince Campbell can come with us, but he needs to stay with the team as they come up with the final details of their plan. He also needs to do some work remotely for the company to keep his cover.

She looks disappointed for a second, but runs out onto the deck, and into the fields where the wildflowers swallow her. Ozzie lopes behind her as I follow them out. The sun does nothing to thaw my cold heart. Declan is the only one who knows how to warm me from the inside.

"Mommy, I am going to pick flowers for all the princes, especially Prince Campbell. He's a good tickler."

I'm thrilled she has retained her innocence and optimism throughout this whole ordeal. We have turned her world upside down and it seems to have little effect on her. When Declan comes back, it may be a different story. She will finally know who her father is. I'm not sure if I'll end up being the good guy or the bad guy, but Declan will remain a prince.

We pick flowers along the way, and she hands them to me, climbing our way up the mountainside. As we step inside the tree line, I notice a drone hovering toward the back of the cabin.

Goosebumps cover my skin, and the hairs stand up on my arm. On instinct, I push Poppy farther into the cover of the forest. She wanders over to a log and sits down.

I grab my cell phone out of my pocket and hit one number.

"There's a drone at the back of the house." Before I have time to finish my sentence, the drone fires at the house.

"You need to come back to the house before we put the shields up." Uncle Neil is calm as I'm on the verge of hysteria.

"No, we can make it to the little cabin and hide there until you come for us. Take care of my mom." Two black military vehicles barrel down the road toward the cabin. They're outfitted with guns.

"They're coming up the road now." I end the call and get Poppy, pushing her ahead of me.

The shields come down covering the windows and doors of the cabin. I'm cut off from anyone who can help me.

My heart beats like a hammer in my chest and my adrenaline kicks in, but I have to stay calm for her and Ozzie. Ozzie will be the first to detect any fear from me.

I turn to Poppy. "Do you remember when we came up here with Declan?"

"Yeah, he showed us the baby cabin. Can we go there?"

"Yes, we have to hurry. We're going to play a game of hide-and-seek with Prince Campbell."

She's thrilled with this idea as she runs ahead. Ozzie stays by my side and looks up at me for a moment.

"No worries. We'll be fine."

He runs ahead, making sure Poppy doesn't get too far away. I run to catch up with them and have to lean on the cabin, out of breath. I really need to work out more, especially if I'm going to keep up with Declan in the bedroom.

We get inside and close the door, putting the iron bolt in place. I take her over to the far corner and we sit on the cot. The gunfire begins, but I can't tell where it's coming from. Gunfire is returned as the team defends the fort.

Poppy huddles close to me as Ozzie hops up next to her and lies down. "What's that sound, Mommy?"

"I don't know. We'll have to wait for Prince Campbell to come and find us." I kiss the top of her head and stroke her hair.

Never in my lifetime did I think I would be hiding out with my daughter and our dog in a cabin in the middle of the woods. I never thought Poppy would get to know her father, but the thought of her never knowing Declan as her father has my stomach in knots.

This was supposed to be a simple mission. I bite my lip to stop the tears. Things are never simple with him. He doesn't lead a boring life, but this time, life may call his bluff. Zahara will use everything she has to find out who has her formula. Her lack of ethics has no bounds.

She must have gotten information out of Declan on where we're hiding. Her methods probably included some sort of drug. He would never give us up. I am sure of that down to my bones.

We wait in the cabin for what seems like hours. The heat rises as drops of sweat travel down my spine and my hair sticks to my forehead. Poppy is getting tired and complains about the heat. She thinks we should surprise Campbell in the woods. Ozzie pants and we have no water.

Blocking out the sound of gunfire with an explosion here or there is impossible. My nerves are raw as I wait for it to end and for someone to come and get us. Just as I think I've reached the end of my rope, there's silence. My imagination gets the better of me, as I have visions of dead bodies and blood.

Outside the cabin is the crunching sound of footsteps, and the knock at the door startles me.

"It's Campbell. You can come out now," he says with a heavy Scottish accent.

Poppy jumps up and races to the door, trying to slide open the iron lock. I help her and the door flies open.

"Prince Campbell, you found us." She throws her hands up and jumps into his arms. Her energy is boundless, as mine wanes.

I look at Campbell. "Is everything okay?"

He gives me a look indicating something has gone wrong. I nod and follow him down the mountain. Poppy insists Campbell carry her piggyback to the house. He doesn't argue with the princess.

As we get closer, the house comes into view riddled with bullet holes. The shields are up, and it looks like the cabin has been to war and lost. There are two Hummers in the driveway, but I don't see any bodies.

We walk in the front door as some of the men are putting the furniture upright. There are a few holes in the walls, but nothing that can't be patched. The shields did their job.

Everyone looks up as I enter the cabin and then look at each other. Something is wrong.

"Where is Uncle Neil?"

Mac approaches me. "I don't want to upset you, but your uncle has been hit. He'll be fine. He's upstairs with your mother."

I turn to Campbell. "Can you watch her for me?"

He nods. I run upstairs to my mother's bedroom. My uncle lies on the bed with a bandage around his leg. My mother sits next to him, holding his hand.

"I'm getting too old for this shit, Margot. I need to think about retiring."

"Sounds like a great idea to me." My mother would love to have company at the farm.

I sit on the other side of the bed next to him. "Are you okay? It looks nasty."

"I'll be fine. It's a surface wound and may need stitches. I'll get one of the guys to do it. How are you and Poppy doing?"

"I feel like I'm running a marathon without a finish line. This seems to go on and on. Do we have a plan to get Declan home?"

"We need to up the timeline. They started with Frederick and Henri's house and then moved here. We were evenly matched, but we need to move out of here. Zahara will send others with more firepower."

"Doesn't sound like you have a choice about including me. I'm going to have to be part of this and offer her the formula for Declan's life. At least I can serve as a distraction while the team enters the building."

He takes my hand in his. "I've tried so hard to keep you away from this lifestyle, the way of life that took your father away from you. I also see the determination on your face, and

I think you may be right. We'll have to talk to the team and come up with a solid plan. In the meantime, Frederick and Henri are scouting for a new location. Be ready to go."

For the first time, my uncle's face looks tired. His eyes are weary. I know I have what it takes to help them get Declan. Getting him home is my one goal, and it's all for my daughter.

# Chapter Forty

Declan

As I slip under, I feel as though I'm floating. A tunnel pulls me backward in time. I look down, and I'm wearing dress pants and a button-up Oxford shirt, the clothes I wore years ago when I worked at Bio2Chem. The way I dressed was always of major importance. I had to look good for the ladies. Time changes everything.

Liv stands next to me in a floral dress. She's smiling and laughing with rosy cheeks. The evening is warm, and the banner up ahead says Oktoberfest. People are milling around, most of them with beer flights, enjoying the last of the summer-kissed autumn nights.

We walk up to the bar and order a round of Warsteiner Dunkel beer for her and a Guinness for me.

"Is this your way of apologizing?" she asks coyly.

"I never apologize when I'm right, and I'm right most of the time." I sigh.

She smirks. "You're rarely right."

This feels like a first date, but I've known Liv for almost

a year. She doesn't like the name Liv, but it suits her and irritates her at the same time. We are always arguing or disagreeing about something going on in the lab. She thinks I'm a party boy out to get laid as much as possible, and she's not wrong. What she doesn't know is I'm here undercover.

I'm on a mission to uncover information about a drug used to cause cancer. As evil as it sounds, it would be a gold mine for pharmaceutical companies the world over. Those holding patents for medications to cure cancer stand to benefit the most. Depending on how it's administered, it could also be used to reduce the world's population.

The thought makes me sick to my stomach. As a scientist, it goes against every fiber of my being, and it needs to be shut down, which is why I took the assignment.

So far, the few leads I've had are dead ends. I narrowed it down to a few scientists, but nothing concrete. As my frustration builds, I've been taking risks, trying to get into the mainframe, which might trigger someone I'm snooping around where I don't belong.

We meet up with some people from our department, and they are surprised to see Liv and me together. We tend to stand on the opposite side of almost every issue. Tonight, I'm comfortable with her, and something significant has shifted between us since her incident in the alley.

As the night goes on, things become fuzzy. This memory feels like an out-of-body experience. There are moments when I am not sure if it's a memory or a dream. Everything looks and feels real, as if I could reach out and touch it, but the people look like ghosts. I stay in the moment, wanting to see where this ends.

Liv slips her hand through my arm to steady herself. She'd had a couple of drinks, but not enough to be drunk. I'm slightly buzzed, which is usual for me on my way to getting hammered, but tonight, I need to stay closer to sober. Liv is the one woman who's not impressed by my good looks and intellect. She has evaded every attempt to be captured by my charm. I plan to change her perspective. She's different from any woman I've ever met, and in many ways, she terrifies and excites me.

She puts her head on my shoulder. "Do you think you're going to charm my panties off, Dr. Craig?"

*And now she can read minds, too. I'm screwed...maybe literally.*

"Panties, bra, shoes, and dress. I'm conducting an experiment to see if your beautiful blond hair covers your perky tits."

She throws her head back and laughs. I know I've got her where I want her, but I'm getting stage fright. What if I don't live up to her expectations or mine?

"I'll let you in on a secret. My hair definitely covers my tits." She says the word tits like she invented it, and there's a hardness behind my zipper.

"Further research is going to have to be done. I'm going to need hard evidence, maybe even photos, to prove my hypothesis." I continue to play her game.

She steps in front of me. "There will be no photos. This is a private showing, a one-and-done."

"Music to my ears."

One-and-done is the only game I play these days. No attachments work for me. She looks up at me with lust in her eyes, but her jaw is set. We will be a good match for each other. I bend down to taste the sweetness of her lips before I wreck her for anyone else. Fear tickles my stomach. *Will she wreck me?*

Her lips are velvety soft as I lick and nibble them. In

between my assaults of her mouth, she whispers, "You're a tease."

"Oh, baby, this is just a warm-up. If it's going to be one night, I've got to make it last."

"You wouldn't want to disappoint a first-timer."

"I thought you were a virgin. I promise to be gentle." I smile.

"Wishful thinking. Maybe I don't want gentle."

There's a part of me that begs to step away. She checks too many of the boxes. I won't be able to get out from under her if I allow myself to be fully present. Curiosity gets the better of me. What would it be like to be with a woman who hits most of the things you're looking for? It's not like I'll be sticking around for very much longer. I could dive in and never come up, at least for a couple of hours, to have a taste of what it's like to connect.

"Let's take this back to my place."

"I thought you didn't bring women back to your place," she scoffs.

I whisper in her ear, "The most beautiful thing we can experience is the mysterious. It's the source of all true art and science."

She shivers in my arms. "Albert Einstein."

"Yes, and you are a mystery."

"Hardly."

The war of words continues between us. The battle may justify the outcome. I enjoy having the upper hand when it comes to her. She's always so confident, without doubt or trepidation. People flock to her for advice and to be around her. They're around me for other reasons. I'm the fun one. She's the leader.

We take a car back to my penthouse that overlooks the city. I demanded comfort for this assignment. The reason I don't bring people here is so they don't see how much I have. My taste for the finer things would raise a red flag. Top researchers are the ones who get paid to live like I do, not your average lab scientist.

I light her wick in the car, caressing the places where her skin is showing, arms, legs, and my favorite, neck. Kisses, touches, and tongues work together to stimulate her nervous system and get the endorphins flowing, creating sparks along the way. She'll be begging for release by the time we get there.

She moans and hums, returning my advances with her own.

"I don't think you are who you say you are."

I stop mid-kiss. *Does she know I'm MI6?* "What do you mean?"

"You come across as a player, but underneath, I think you're a softy. You don't want people to get too close and find out who you really are. It's easier to keep them at arm's length. No harm, no foul. You play it safe. Declan Craig would never put his heart on the line."

This is going to be one hell of a crash and burn. "Maybe I haven't found the right person to put my heart on the line for. My needs are very specific."

"Most people have specific needs, but you have to take a chance and find out if they fit the parameters, so to speak."

"Says the woman who lives for her research and nothing else."

"You make me want to take a chance." Her voice is breathy.

"I'm going to give you so much more than that." I kiss her as if she's the last woman on earth. This one is going to hurt.

# Chapter Forty-One

Declan

I UNDRESS HER SLOWLY, peeling her out of her clothes, unwrapping her like the best gift I've ever gotten. I skirt the edge of the danger zone with every stroke, caress, and kiss. Her skin is the color of lilies, and she smells like honey. Her eyes are bright blue and wide.

She moves with grace, and every touch seems to bring her pure joy. She's not performing like some of the women I've been with, but she's in the moment, focused on what's happening between us.

She stands before me without a hint of modesty and flips her hair forward to cover her breasts. I'm fully dressed and leaning back on the couch.

"See? I told you they would cover my perfect tits."

"I said perky." I fight a smile.

She holds them in her hands and looks down. "Nope. They're perfect."

My cock takes notice and strains against my pants, wanting to join the fun, but I have plans for Ms. Perfect Tits.

She tempts me at every turn by being herself, a true challenge.

"Come here." My voice sets itself an octave lower than normal. She obeys, curious to know what I'm going to do next.

"Straddle me." She does as I say, and I can smell her arousal.

I make her wait, watching her, trying to figure out how we came to this place. Her eyes are clear, and her lips curve up on one side as if she has a secret about me. I don't think I'm fooling her. She gets squirmy but doesn't say a word.

My hand brushes up her thigh and my fingers skirt the outside of her pussy, teasing her without mercy. I bend her toward me and push her perfect nipple into my mouth, sucking to the point of pain. Her fingers weave into my hair as she holds on.

My fingers find their target as she rides them like she hasn't had sex in years, which may be true.

She pants, "More."

My cord of control snaps, and I flip her over, holding her hands above her head. I continue to alternate sucking on her nipples until they stand at attention and undo my zipper with my other hand.

"Oh, no you don't."

"What? Are you saying no, now?" I release her hands instantly and fall back on my heels.

"I want the full platinum package."

"Which is?" I can't wait to see where this goes. My full platinum package is filled with kink.

"You. Naked. Now."

"Not. A. Problem." I rip my clothes off and throw them in a heap on the floor.

I lean over her, ready to pick up where I left off, minus the kink.

"Not so fast. Stand up and turn around. I want to see that tight ass I've been looking at for the last twelve months."

Of course, I make a show of it and start posing.

"Interesting. You don't have a speck of artwork."

"No point in covering up perfection."

She smiles, but I know something's coming. "Look at that. The perfect penis to go with my perfect tits." Her compliment is unexpected.

"Don't stop. I don't want to interrupt the compliment train."

"You need to get over here and finish what you started."

So much for being in charge. I hover over her but grab a condom from my wallet and slip it on before entry. My cock hovers at her entrance as we stare at each other. I brush a few strands of hair from her face and push into her with patience. My restraint is remarkable, considering I want to plunge into her and make her come for the rest of the night.

I cover her mouth with mine and invite her tongue to come out and play. A moan escapes her mouth, and it's what I need to send us both over the edge.

I grab one of the decorative pillows and push it under her ass, giving me a better chance of hitting her G-spot. Being selfish during sex never benefits anyone.

Her eyes glaze over, and she hums with satisfaction. I reach between us where we are joined and circle her clit with my thumb, finding my rhythm. She screams when she comes and grabs hold of my hair, which spurs me on. I thrust a few more times.

Somewhere outside myself, I hear her say, "I'm going to come again."

We come together, which is a feat most couples don't

accomplish, and my climax keeps going until there's nothing left. Sweat sticks us together, but when I pull away from her, there's a goddess with swollen raspberry lips, tousled hair, rosy skin, and satisfaction written on her face. Heaven has never felt sweeter.

Life is made of moments. At this moment, there is a rip in my universe. What she said earlier about not being who I pretend to be is true. I don't let people in because when I do, there's never a good outcome. She looks beyond my facade. Her attention to detail makes her a superior scientist.

I won't be able to hide from her, no matter how hard I try. There's a relief knowing I don't have to put anything on for her, but it also leaves me wide open. I rub the left side of my chest.

From the first time we met, there was never a moment I didn't trust her. I watched her interact with her team, listen to people's family problems, and go head-to-head with her boss. She's the real deal, but will I be enough for her? Can I let my guard down?

I pick her up and carry her to the bedroom, where we continue to make love on and off for the rest of the night. She pays attention to what I like and what I don't like. I make sure I satisfy her with every turn and touch. The flow is natural and easy. I haven't felt like this with anyone in years.

Somewhere during the night, we fall asleep. I never stay with a woman through the night, but I'm comfortable in this place with her as I wrap her in my arms and legs. I may have to rethink this, being a one-and-done guy.

I wake up the next morning, and she is sound asleep beside me, probably worn out. As much as I want to go for round thirty-two, I let her sleep. She doesn't seem to get much of it. Besides, we can't be seen walking into work together.

I slip out of bed, take a shower, and get ready for work. Heading out the door, I'm happier than I've ever been. This will put a strain on our work relationship, but I'm hoping to be off the case soon, and I'll figure it out then.

Few people are at work this early in the morning, and I take advantage of it. I want to pick up where I left off with my trials from yesterday. They contain volatile substances, and I need to work in the chem lab. I get my hazmat suit from the locker and put it on. The ventilator is working, and I'm ready to go.

I begin to work with the chemicals, mixing them to get my intended compound. For this to work as a base, it needs to be stable, and it's not. As I am getting ready to put the chemicals away, my legs and arms become hot. I stand back and realize my suit is in flames. My last thought is of Liv sleeping in my bed.

I wake up screaming.

# Chapter Forty-Two

Olivia

UNCLE NEIL GIVES the order to pack up everything we can fit into our bags. Three SUVs wait for us in the driveway. We pile in one car with my uncle, my mom, Poppy, me, and the animals. Frederick and Henri head for the second SUV, filling it with guns and other weapons. The rest of the team fills the last vehicle with a lot of controversy about who's driving and dibs on shotgun. I see why my uncle holds these men so close.

There is an uneasiness among us, and I'm not sure if it's from the attack or if everyone is contemplating our next moves. We're on edge for different reasons.

We head out to a new location north of Declan's cabin. We drive for thirty minutes and turn onto a dirt road. Potholes, rocks, and debris cover the road. The three Range Rovers manage the obstacle course without a problem as the climb becomes steeper and steeper. Someone would have a hell of a time getting up here without the right vehicle.

At the top of the mountain, where the road ends, is an

enormous cabin. Declan's cabin is small in comparison. We exit the vehicles and head for our new temporary home. My uncle informs everyone that the cabin has eight bedrooms, each with a bathroom.

The space on the lower level has an open floor plan where the living room, dining room, den, and kitchen flow together. The deck wraps around the cabin, and on the backside is a hot tub. Everyone heads to claim their room.

I meet up with my uncle in the kitchen. "I would say you went overboard."

"If you knew these guys like I do, you would know they shouldn't share a room. They get cranky." He pauses and looks at me. "Do you mind if your mother and I share a room?"

"Not at all, as long as I get the master suite. I'll be with Poppy, an oversized dog, and a cat."

We laugh together, which gives levity to the day.

"When are we going to talk about the plan to get Declan out?" My nervous system is in overdrive, along with my brain. I'm eager to see him again.

"Why don't you leave that to the team and me? I would prefer it if you weren't part of this. I don't want to lose you, too." Sadness covers his eyes at the memory of my father, his brother.

I reach up and hug him, knowing I want to be part of the plan anyway. I'll do whatever it takes to get Declan back home. The word home fills my heart.

The house is quiet except for Poppy and the animals. She's playing a game with them, but I can't figure out the rules, and neither can they, while they stand in the middle of the room watching her with rapt attention.

I catch Mac in the den, video chatting with his wife and baby. Eavesdropping has never been my thing, but I can't help myself when I hear the conversation. I tuck into the other side of the doorway.

"Da, da, da, da," Dalia says over and over again as she puts her hands on the camera.

"Hi, sweet girl. Daddy will be home soon," Mac replies. "I'll bring Uncle Declan with me."

"How are things going?" his wife asks.

"I won't give you the gory details, but getting him out is going to be a challenge. I get the feeling I don't have the entire story when it comes to Declan."

"Your relationship with him has never been easy. I hope you two can keep trying once he comes home." Her voice is meant to soothe him.

"Leannan, I miss you something fierce, and it's only been a couple of days."

"Highlander, are you getting soft on me?"

"You need to cover our daughter's ears because I'm about to tell you how not soft I am right now," he growls.

This is my cue to leave and find out what the commotion is in the living room. His conversation makes me want a relationship with Declan if he can ever forgive me for not telling him about Poppy. The other half of me worries about what condition he's going to be in when he comes home. If she gives him the memory formula I uncovered in the files, he won't be well.

I wander to the back porch with its cathedral ceilings as Campbell throws Poppy in the air and catches her as she screams with delight. My first reaction is to stop him in case he drops her, but I back off. I need to have faith he won't drop his niece. I realize there is an adjustment with having this many men around.

"Princess, my arms are tired. I'm going to need to rest."

He sets her on the floor. They have come to call her princess. Not my choice.

My daredevil daughter moves to the next action park ride and asks Sean to throw her up in the air. Of course, he agrees. He throws her in the air, not too high, until she sees me.

"Mommy!" she yells.

He puts her down, and she runs over. "Did you see me flying?" She looks up at me with my own blue eyes.

"Yes, you were very good. I'm sure the men's arms are tired."

"Princes, Mommy."

I roll my eyes. "Of course, princes."

My cell phone dings with a text, and I look at it. The words are poisonous, and I bite my lip to avoid saying anything. Uncle Neil walks in behind me, and I show him the text.

He announces, "It's game time. We need to meet right now."

I bend down in front of Poppy. "Sweetheart, I need you to find Grand-mère. I think she would love to play a card game with you."

"I wanted one of the princes to throw me in the air again." She puts on her pouty face.

Beck steps up. "I'll throw you in the air later. We have some things to discuss."

She smiles. "Since you're the biggest, you can throw me even higher." She kisses me and runs away.

"Bigger is not always better," Dean quips.

"That's what some men tell themselves to feel better," Beck replies. The men laugh along with Dean.

Everyone sits down around the dining room table as Mac shuts the French doors.

"What's going on?" Mac asks with a worried look on his face.

"Zahara texted Olivia. She wants an exchange. Declan for the formula. She also says she knows Olivia has it. Declan gave her up. If she doesn't get what she wants, she will make Declan's death slow and painful."

My uncle turns to me. "The only way he gave you up is if she gave him a truth serum. Declan is a rock-solid agent."

"I have no doubts."

"We need proof of life before we make a move," Sean demands.

Uncle Neil's fingers fly over the keys on my phone. "I told her you need proof of life, and you will do the exchange." He hands me the phone.

He turns to the team, who look angry. "Calm down. This will give us time to figure out how to get him out while Olivia makes the drop."

"You're including me?" I'm stunned.

"We have to. She's going to expect to see you and make sure she gets what she wants."

"Okay. Has Antonio gotten in and through the encryption?" I ask.

"Yes, the encryption isn't a problem. I need you to work with him to rewrite some of the formula. Either you have the only copy of her latest formula, and she doesn't have it backed up, or she doesn't want anyone else to have it."

"While she's making the drop, we'll have her covered, and the rest of us can target the roof and get Declan," Dean explains.

"Are we sure she hasn't moved Declan somewhere else?" Beck says.

"Maybe we can pick up on some clues from her proof of life photo about where he is," Sean counters.

"I doubt it. She didn't get to be where she is by being stupid," I reply.

My uncle turns to me. "Even the brightest people make minor mistakes that can change everything." I'm not sure if he's aiming his comment at me or Zahara.

"If she wants to meet up off-site, Declan won't be at Bio2Chem. He'll be with her," Mac comments.

The room gets quiet for a beat.

"I think she wants Declan dead. The last time we were together, she and Declan had an odd exchange." My voice is soft, and I let my words settle in. "Maybe we should demand to meet her at the office. What if I can get you in the front door before the exchange happens?"

"How are you going to pull that off?" Dean asks.

I smile. "You forget. I still have a key card to the eighth floor. I can get you in as visiting scientists, and you can take it from there."

"Mac dressed in a lab coat and a pair of goggles. There's a stretch." Dean laughs.

Mac slaps Dean on the shoulder, and he turns away.

Uncle Neil has been sitting back, listening. "I think it could work. We can even give you credentials in case they run a background check."

"I'll put a call in to Pippa to work on it as a top priority," Sean offers.

My uncle turns to me. "I need you to work with Antonio on the formula now until it's done, and let me know when she texts you again with proof of life."

I couldn't be more thrilled and scared shitless at the same time. Timing will be everything, and even then, it may not be enough.

## Chapter Forty-Three

### Declan

SWEAT DRENCHES MY GOWN. Cuffs are still on my wrists and ankles, anchoring me to my reality. There's not a spot in my skull without a need of relief as my head pounds. The pain makes me nauseous as I try to breathe through my mouth.

Lack of nutrition and fighting through the pain have made my body weak. My nervous system is shot. I pray my team can get to me sooner rather than later as I hang on by a thread.

"Well, look who's back from Fantasy Island. Did you have a good time?" Z smiles with the look of a feral cat.

I laugh on the inside because what she doesn't know is that her memory drug works in reverse. I didn't talk to Beck about the effects of the memory drug on him, but based on my experience, I'm remembering things from my past that have been lost to me for years.

"The best time ever. I find it curious that you always wear white or cream. Do you think you're the good guy in this? Because you're not. You're evil incarnate."

Her face twists with anger, and her jaw muscles tick. She bends down over me.

"Sodium pentothal works wonders. You gave us all kinds of information, some of it we didn't need." She scrunches her nose. "We didn't need to hear about your sex life, although some of my techs enjoyed the stories." I hope my rendition was rated triple X and they learned some moves. "Thanks to you, we found who we were looking for. However, there needs to be an exchange. You for the formula. Of course, Dr. Marcel and your team want proof of life."

She stands up, puts her hands in her front pockets, and sighs. "It's all so annoying. But if this is what I have to do to get the formula, then we need to send proof of life so I can get rid of you."

Nausea rolls in my stomach as it makes its way up and out. I projectile vomit on Z's cream suit as it slides down her pants. She steps away and looks down at her suit in disgust.

"Oops. I wish I could say I was sorry, but I'm not. I'll take Compazine now unless you'd like me to puke on you again."

She makes fists by her sides and walks away with her two Frankensteins. One of the med techs pushes something into my line, abating my nausea. Paul turns to me for the first time since I've been awake.

"I've been watching what you've been going through, and it's not right. You screamed in pain like I've never heard before." His face turns pale.

"The reason you don't have my symptoms is because they're giving you painkillers and something to hold down the nausea. You're a guinea pig in a scheme to bring down soldiers and use them again and again. This is not a government-sanctioned medical trial."

"I get it now. It's why I got the keys to your cuffs." He opens his hand to reveal the keys.

"Put the key in my hand. My team is on their way, and I have to time this just right. I promise you, they will not leave you behind or anyone else."

He nods, and his eyes glisten. He realizes the severity of the situation and how twisted she is. When no one is looking, he gives me the key as I fold it into my palm.

Z walks back in the room, dressed in a deep red suit. At the sight of her, I shove the key under the sheet for safe keeping.

"Oh, thank God. You look so much better in red. It really accents your eyes for the devil in you." My smart mouth may push her limits, but I don't give a shit.

"How did Dr. Marcel ever put up with you?"

"I amazed her with what I could do with my mouth. I'm extremely talented."

"Enough!" Her voice echoes off the walls in the barren room. I need to throw her off long enough to have her make a mistake.

She signals to one of the guards to unlock my wrist and ankle cuffs. One of them shoves a newspaper in my hands with today's date.

"Here. Hold this in front of you under your face and smile for the camera as if you're on holiday."

"You need to work on your accommodations and hospitality. I believe they call this modern sterile, and it's not really to my liking. I was expecting a back and foot massage, a facial, and warm towels. I need to speak to the manager about a refund."

She grimaces with every comment, but I can't help myself. I know how to push her buttons, and it brings me joy.

I've been here before, but I know she needs me. Let's see how much she can endure.

On the front of the paper, there is an article about Bio2Chem she must have missed. My distraction is working. I position my fingers so they point to the headline of the article. Maybe someone will pick up on the clue that I'm being held here and not off-site.

One of her goons takes a picture with his cell phone, and I stick my tongue out. I'm sure my pale complexion is even paler, and my eyes are bloodshot. Anyone looking at the picture will see my condition.

"Once they get proof of life, the exchange will be made, and Dr. Marcel can have you back. Thank God. I can't wait to get rid of you."

"You're sure she wants me back. She never really had nice things to say about me. It hurt my feelings. You know what those are, right?"

She smiles like the cat that ate the canary. "You don't know, do you?"

"What am I supposed to know, exactly? You keep hinting at some big secret you have about me. Why don't you tell me? I can't take the suspense," I say dramatically.

She sits on the edge of the bed, with one skinny butt cheek. "That little redheaded child of hers has a father." Her eyes sparkle.

"I'm sure she does. That's how babies are made. You might have missed that tidbit in biology class. You probably haven't been touched in years."

She's still smiling, which is freaking me out. "Her child is yours. It's why Dr. Marcel wants you back, so her child can finally get to know Daddy Dearest."

"That's not poss—" Her words sink in, and bells go off in my head. "How do you know for sure?"

"Because I keep careful tabs on every employee." Z laughs maniacally, gets up, and walks away.

The dream I had before I woke up wasn't a dream. The one night Liv and I shared could have produced a child. I have a vague recollection of a condom breaking during one of our sexual exploits, but I didn't pay any attention to it, given the odds of her getting pregnant were extremely low. Apparently, not low enough when you have sex all night.

I stare at the ceiling, wondering why Liv never told me I was Poppy's father. Everything clicks into place about the time I spent with her. We had formed a bond. The knowledge she's been lying to me shatters the memory of Liv and me together five years ago at Oktoberfest. I taste my sadness as I slip under once again.

# Chapter Forty-Four

Olivia

THE MEN GET ready by applying prosthetics so they won't be recognized by a camera or any identification software. They each alter their chin, nose, and jawline. By the time they're done, they're unrecognizable even to me.

Poppy gives them a strange look, trying to figure out why they are wearing masks. I worry about how confusing this is for her.

A text comes in from Zahara requesting we meet at an off-site location. She sends the address of a warehouse in a run-down part of Cologne. With my uncle looking over my shoulder, I respond to her and suggest we meet at the company headquarters since I'll be there anyway. I go so far as to say it may be a safer location for both of us.

The communication stays silent for a while until she agrees to meet at Bio2Chem. She is specific about meeting on the seventh floor of the building, calling it a neutral zone. I'm not sure what is on the seventh floor or if it's neutral.

The team meets in the dining room after everyone is suited up and ready to go.

Uncle Neil maps out the timeline. "Pippa created a set of scientific credentials for Mac and Dean, which will get them in the front door. Campbell is working for the company undercover, so he's going in ahead of everyone else. We're going to get Declan out by taking him up. Beck and Sean will fly in a heli to land on the roof."

He hands me a small bud. "This goes behind your ear, out of sight. I will hear everything going on, and you can talk to me. You won't be alone. Someone will be nearby at all times. Trust me."

I nod, looking down at my lifeline, the size of a kidney bean. Great things come in small packages, as Poppy screams in the living room, playing a game. The Kevlar vest under my dress adds a layer of false security.

Mac and Dean remain quiet as they sit across from me, dressed in suits, covering up their Kevlar vests. A low hum vibrates in the cabin as we get ready to do the exchange. While my energy is nervous and anxious, they are calm, inward, and focused.

"Frederick and Henri will be in a maintenance van outside the building in case we need them," Uncle Neil explains. "I will stay behind here at the cabin and be on the ready, should anyone need me."

After we've gone over the final details of the plan, we pile into Gal, Declan's baby, who has had a makeover since the shooting. The ride to the city limits is quiet. Mac is in front with me, and Dean sits in the back.

"You know it's going to be okay. We'll get him out safely. Our second goal is to bring Zahara in alive so we can question her. We need a break in this case and be able to question somebody about what's going on in Deep 8," Mac says quietly.

"I've never done anything like this in my life. I'm scared and excited. Mostly, I just want to see Declan again. His daughter needs him." I bite my lip to keep from crying.

I need to put on my big girl panties and do the job that needs to be done to get Declan back. I've always had a spine of steel. Now is not the time to bend and weaken. My uncle must see something in me I don't, otherwise, I wouldn't be here.

We park in the garage where Declan left his car the last time. This will be my rendezvous location with Fredrick and Henri. The walk to the office building is short, and no one will see us get out of the vehicle.

We enter the lobby, and a guard stops us. "I don't have authorization to allow these two men in the building." He looks at them with suspicion.

I step forward and lower my voice. "If you would like to call Dr. Ugana, be my guest. You can even use my phone. She can vouch for these scientists, who need to be in an important meeting in fifteen minutes. You can verify their credentials."

He swallows and nods. Mac and Dean hand him their identification papers so he can run a background check. He focuses on the computer screen while I make a point of looking at my watch several times to indicate he's running out of time.

He hands their papers back to them. "They check out. You need to go to the security office to get badges for them as guests. They'll have a level one security pass."

Mac and Dean don't say a word and nod as we walk by the guard station and into the security office. The security guard, who's been notified by the front desk, makes quick work of putting together guest badges.

I turn to the guard. "I need clearance to get to the seventh floor. It should be on file."

She looks up the file on her computer and reaches out her hand. "Let me get you access."

I hand her my badge. I'm sure it'll show up. I also have access to the eighth floor. My hands sweat, and my heart beats faster. I would never make it as an MI6 agent. I'm better in a lab doing research, away from the action. I've had enough action to last me a lifetime.

Our first stop is the sixth floor to go to my office. Mac and Dean follow behind me, with suitcases in their hands. Their suitcases are filled with files, but hidden compartments contain everything they need to get to Declan. As we arrive at the floor, I nod and smile at my coworkers, who ask where I've been. I need to remember to be myself and not get caught up in my head over what is about to happen. I stop to answer their questions.

I set Mac and Dean up at a desk in my office and give them some files to look over. We need to make it look official. A text comes through from Zahara, indicating she is ready to meet on the seventh floor. I get my nerves under control, remembering the ultimate goal is to get Declan out of here.

Campbell joins us, and we walk to the stairwell door. I use my key card to buzz us through and walk them up to the eighth floor to get them access. The security guard didn't comment about my clearance for the eighth floor.

Mac and Dean bound up ahead of me as Campbell and I take our time to reach the top floor of the building. I scan my key card and get a red light as a response. I scan it several times, but the results are the same.

Dean curses several times. "Now what do we do, mate? What's the next step in the plan?"

Campbell steps up. "I have an idea. Wait here."

He runs down the stairs and out the door. When he returns, he has a lovely lab tech in tow. I don't recognize her, so she must work in a different department. She's laughing and giggling at something he's saying to her. He pushes her up the stairs ahead of him with his hand on her lower back.

"This group needs your help. The security guard downstairs must've made a mistake. They're wanted in a meeting in about five minutes. The meeting revolves around a top-level research project." Campbell lays on the charm.

I hang my head down so my hair serves as a cover to my face. I don't want her to see I'm here, trying to get on the eighth floor, in case she recognizes me. She may become suspicious.

He opens the folder in his hand and shows her the paperwork inside. Her eyes get big.

"I see you're part of the research on the eighth floor. The drug is our top priority, and we're on the verge of a breakthrough. We are trying to minimize the side effects and get greater efficacy from the drug," she rambles.

"You're an absolute doll for helping us out like this. I won't breathe a word of this to anyone. I would love to take you out sometime." He grins.

She blushes, scans her key card, and the door opens. "I would love to. Here's my number." She passes him a card with her name and number on it. We wait until she goes down the stairs, and we hear the door shut.

Dean rolls his eyes. "What is it with you Creighton men? Do you charm the pants off every woman you meet?" He sounds sour.

*Creighton?* I thought their last name was Craig. I'll deal with that later.

Mac and Campbell turn to him and grin from ear to ear, giving each other a high five.

"What can I say? It's a gift. Probably genetic," Mac responds. "Nice work, Campbell. I guess you know the players in this game better than anyone."

"I've been watching who goes in and out of this door for a while. It doesn't hurt to have options. I had Antonio print the latest file of the Zambia research."

Mac turns to me. "This is where we part ways. We'll see you on the other side with Declan. You need to get her talking long enough so we can get to him. Good luck. I know you can do it."

He's holding the door with his foot. The three of them slip between the door and the frame, and they're gone. Why do I feel like I'm truly on my own?

# Chapter Forty-Five

### Declan

I'M STILL STRAPPED to the bed and feel like a truck has run me over as another twenty-four hours tick by. My head pounds more than before, making me disoriented, and sweat continues to pour from me as my temperature rises.

I shake intermittently, which could be from the drug or my lack of food and water. Staring at the ceiling, I try to focus on something to center myself and wait for my team to enter. They won't come quietly.

My thoughts go back to what Z told me about Poppy being my daughter. I don't think she's lying to me. Why didn't Liv tell me? We spent days together. There must have been a moment when she could've told me Poppy was mine. What held her back?

The connection I have with Poppy makes sense. She also has an innate ability to learn languages quickly, another thing we share. I want to make it back so I can get answers from Liv, answers I deserve. I want Poppy to know I'm her father.

I try to move my body, but my muscles are weak, as I

struggle to move even a bit. My mouth feels like cotton. If I thought recovering from being burned was bad, this runs a close second. Life seems to be a series of tests to survive. I have had enough challenges to last me a lifetime. The goal is to make it out of this alive. Maybe I'll retire and open a coffee shop.

"Paul, you've got to unlock the cuffs on my wrists and ankles. I don't have the strength to do it. The key is under the sheet. We can try to make a break for it if my team doesn't show up soon."

He nods and looks around for the med techs. Slipping the key out from under the sheet, he unlocks the other three cuffs but leaves them in place and puts the key back in my hand.

"I've been spreading the word to the others about what is going on. Needless to say, they are angry and ready at your command. Do you think your team is going to be able to extract all of us?"

Fear rests in his eyes I've never seen before. He was an outstanding agent who wasn't afraid of anything or anyone. Once you've been brainwashed, you question everything, including your abilities and perceptions. When this goes down, I hope his military training kicks in. The team is going to need his skill set.

"They will get you out, one way or another." I lock eyes with him so he understands my commitment.

The sweet sound of gunfire comes from behind the steel wall, my team's calling card. They always make their presence known with a lot of heavy artillery.

The warriors being held prisoner react instinctively and look around for the nearest weapon, tipping over beds as cover. Paul drags me off my bed and onto the floor. My feverish body hits the cool tile, and I don't want to move. The chill is a welcome relief.

The scene unfolds as the guinea pigs being held captive use their superior military training to take out the untrained med techs. They use scalpels, tubing, and trays without mercy, cutting the throats of anyone who comes toward them. The look on their faces tells me they're in the survival zone. It's a kill or be killed scenario.

The unarmed fall one by one. Anger is a powerful tool, as if the gunfire has triggered a memory for them and woke them up. The scene may change once Z's trained men enter.

The gunfire ceases on the other side of the wall. Bullets hit the steel doors until they open. Three men enter with faces I don't recognize at first, but four of the eyes are the same as mine. They're splattered with the blood of other men as they split up and survey the room.

After they assess the situation, they frown and look at each other with questions. The suits are a nice touch but out of character. They look like they're going to a wedding.

I let out the sound of a wounded animal at the sight of them. There's a reason we wear combat gear and not suits. Fish out of water.

After the last med tech falls, Paul approaches them with his hands in the air and talks to them. They follow him as he points to me on the floor. Worry covers their eyes, but it's the most welcome sight I've seen in days. I know how bad I look because I feel ten times worse, but I gather enough energy to smile.

Mac bends down next to me. "See something funny, Dark Lord?"

"Didn't you hear? I'm a prince now. You guys look funny in suits." I start to hallucinate and laugh out loud as delirium sets in. Their faces morph into funny shapes.

Campbell kneels next to Mac. "Declan, we're here to get you out. Nice touch on your fingers pointing to the words

Bio2Chem in the newspaper. We have the remedy to get this out of your system. I gotta ask. What the hell is going on here?"

"Welcome to the land of Z's guinea pigs. We need to get them out for medical evaluation." I continue to laugh.

"What the fuck?" Dean mumbles under his breath.

My brothers hoist me up under my arms and realize I'm dead weight. I can barely walk. My feet drag behind me.

"There's a helicopter waiting for us on the roof. We have a limited amount of time to make the rendezvous. We'll come back for them," Mac says.

"No. At least take Paul with us and then come back. Where is the rest of the team?" My voice sounds far away, as if I'm not in my body.

"Everything is under control. We've got Beck and Sean topside and Frederick and Henri on standby out front," Campbell says. His eyes focus on the door they fired through moments ago as it hangs on its hinges.

We're fifteen feet away from freedom and an escape to the roof when two gunmen rush in. My brothers drop me like a sack of potatoes and fire on both men. Paul pulls me behind the nearest bed as cover.

I welcome the low temperature of the tile floor again, but my body heats it too quickly. The firing goes on for a few minutes until Mac and Campbell come back to get me. They hoist me up again as we make our second attempt for the door.

The bodies of four of Z's men lie on the floor, bleeding out, their semi-automatics clutched in their hands. They weren't as well-trained as I thought they would be. I tuck that note away for a discussion with Neil.

Wisps of smoke hang in the air, leftover from the gunfire. Lights flicker from being shot at, and the silence is a warning.

The hairs on the back of my neck stand on end. It's too quiet. Something's not right. I can feel it. Danger is always deathly quiet before it enters. When you've been on enough missions, you know this feeling, and you set yourself on high alert.

Paul and Dean are ahead of us as Dean gives us an upright fist, a sign to stop. He may have a smart mouth, but he knows what he's doing. A door on one hinge falls to the floor, revealing what's on the other side.

We stop cold in our tracks at the sight before us. I swallow down my scream.

# Chapter Forty-Six

Olivia

I SLIP the bean-size ear comm behind my ear. The zip drive feels warm in my hand as I drop it into my front pocket. As much as I don't like Zahara, meeting her on these terms puts us on a different level.

She thinks she's superior to me, but she agreed to my terms, giving me a slight edge. I have always known her to be a brilliant scientist, but I didn't realize how dangerous she could be.

I rid my mind of the ways she could torture Declan. I can't let myself get angry or seek revenge. Anger will distort my judgment. My vision and ability to make decisions need to be crystal clear going into this meeting with her. I take a few deep breaths.

My key card scans the pad, and the light turns green to open the stairwell door. I trudge up the stairs on shaky legs to the seventh floor, my final destination to get Declan back. This won't be easy. There will be some negotiating on both our parts.

I scan the card again to get through the door and onto the floor. The entire space is dark and empty. In the far corner, I see a woman standing by the window. Her silhouette is unmistakable.

My feet move me forward with my heart in my throat. There are many situations where my nerves are rock solid. This isn't one of them. I'm out of my comfort zone. This is a game where I have limited knowledge. I'll rely on my instincts and the advice my uncle gave me.

She's wearing a purple pantsuit as she leans against the window with her arms and legs crossed in front of her, an interesting expression of body language, considering she sees herself as powerful. Her hair is pulled in a tight bun, accenting her sharp cheekbones and full lips. I stop in the middle of the room, a suitable distance from her.

"I see you took my advice and came alone," she sneers, as if she's already won the battle.

"I didn't have a choice. There's a man's life hanging in the balance. I won't have his blood on my hands."

She pushes away from the window and walks toward me. "You may end up having his blood on your hands, anyway. Did you ever think of that?"

She circles behind me, and I become aware of the comm behind my ear, remembering it's hidden by my hair.

"Such a pretty woman. It's no wonder he fell for you." Her finger strokes my hair, sending prickles of fear down my arm. I want to run but stay put.

"I'm not sure he ever did fall for me. He's a one-night stand kind of guy. Why don't we cut to the chase? I believe the deal was the zip drive for him."

She's face-to-face with me, looking at me through ebony eyes as if she's trying to figure something out. "I doubt he's interested in a one-night stand when it comes to you. Sodium pentothal revealed some interesting secrets." Her mouth quirks to the side.

I can't let her know about my feelings for Declan. Showing vulnerability will jeopardize everything. I need to trick my mind into going back to when I couldn't stand him. My heart pounds, and a drop of sweat makes its way down my chest. I don't respond to her comment in hopes she'll reveal more. Saying nothing can be a powerful tool.

She steps into my personal space and whispers in my ear, "Do you know the bad things Declan has done? Has he told you what he's been up to for most of his adult life as an MI6 agent? He's no white knight in shining armor." She's right; he's not a knight; he's a prince.

"As he serves the Queen, it's none of my concern. I'm sure he did what he had to do to make the world a better place and survive." I hold her stare.

She throws her head back and laughs. "The Queen? You think the Queen has power? The Queen doesn't know what power is. We're going to make the world a better place, not the heads of state."

"Who is we, exactly?" I look her in the eye, demanding answers.

"Deep 8."

"Never heard of them."

She smiles. "No, you wouldn't have. We don't advertise. We work covertly toward our objective."

"What is your objective?" Curiosity gets the better of me.

"We will be making decisions for people where everyone is equal. Individual freedom is overrated. The world order needs a change, and we need to live under one umbrella for peace and harmony. We need to adhere to the same rules." She says it as if she's reading off a prompter.

"Freedom is what we fight for, what we sacrifice for, and

what we live for. I believe the world you're talking about is called communism. Most people in the world wouldn't agree with a one umbrella approach. Besides, so far, that hasn't worked out for anyone living in a communist country."

"Freedom is an illusion. Nothing is free, so why not make it so everything is free for everyone under one rule? We have the means to control the energy of the world, sickness, health, and money. We are working toward making things better for people, but they need to give themselves to us in return."

"History repeats itself, first as a tragedy, second as farce."

Her face falls as I use a quote from Karl Marx, the father of communism. No matter how hard I try, I will not get through to her. She lives by a philosophy not shared by me or most people in the world. I hope my uncle is listening to this through my earpiece.

"We are not a farce, and you will see soon enough. Things that make the world run will be under our control, food, money, energy, and firepower. This is one link in the chain to taking over." Anger rips through her words. "You had so much potential. I almost considered bringing you into the fold, but you were set on saving the kiddies of the world, showing your weakness."

"Where are we without investing in our future?"

"Our future is now. Children are only good to us if they are useful. Otherwise, they are obsolete."

I take a step closer to her. My rage is boiling. "Who is stronger than a child who has survived a life-threatening disease or the physically or mentally challenged child who brings light into our lives? They teach us lessons we wouldn't learn any other way. You don't get to decide the soul's journey."

The tick in her eye gives her away as she winces from my

words. She has a story that would take years of therapy to unearth, but I'm not interested in any of it.

"Where is the zip drive you used to download the formula?" She changes the subject as I hit a bit too close to home.

I tilt my chin up. "I have it. Where's Declan?"

She waves her finger in front of my face. "It doesn't work that way. You're not in a position to bargain with me. I need to make sure what's on the drive is the original formula or Declan dies a slow, painful death, the one I planned for him originally."

Everything clicks for me as I realize she's the one who tried to burn Declan alive. I fight with the rage taking over my body. My fingers itch to punch her in the face, but this isn't going to help get Declan back. What I don't know is why.

I'm sure it had to do with his mission. She must have found out who he was and what he was doing at the company.

"I couldn't get to the formula or open the files because they were encrypted, but you already knew that. The drive is in my office."

Her lips form a tight line as we both stand still. Shots ring out from the floor above us. She grabs a gun from behind her back and points it at me.

"Looks like you brought friends. Too bad they are going to die along with your love, Declan. Move." She waves the gun toward the stairwell.

She shoves the gun in my back as we walk to what may be my death. "Try anything, and I won't hesitate to put a bullet in your back. There's no honor in war." Her words are crisp.

We make it up the stairs as the gunfire stops. She puts me

in a headlock and holds the gun to my temple. Fear courses through my veins, and I can't breathe. She drags me to a set of open doors that have been blown apart.

Mac and Campbell hold Declan up while a second man, I don't recognize, is with Dean. The world stops as we look at each other, waiting for the other one to make a move.

# Chapter Forty-Seven

### Declan

THE ENERGY I have left starts at my toes and rockets through the rest of my body at the sight of a gun to Liv's head. The terror in her eyes makes my heart race.

Can life be so cruel as to take away my happiness again? Twenty-four hours ago, I was angry at her for not telling me about our daughter, but my anger dissipates at the sight of her life on the line. If Z hurts a hair on her head, I will kill her with my bare hands.

Her fear doesn't only center around the gun being pointed at her head, but the condition I'm in. She's not used to what war can look like on a man who's been held prisoner and poisoned.

Soldiers never get used to it. We get numb and stow it away where we think it won't hurt us. What we don't realize is the minute we tuck it away, it is sewn into our souls and can never be ripped out. We carry those snippets with us to our graves.

My body springs forward as I'm held back by my brothers. "Get your fucking hands off her!" My voice is raspy.

Z's mouth ticks up on one side, but it's not a full-blown smile. Weariness covers her eyes. She's not sure she's going to get out of this one alive. Too bad. My tiny violins play for her. If I had it my way, one of my brother's bullets would make its mark between her eyes. We need her alive. Torture may be more fitting for her, giving her a taste of her special cocktail.

"What do you want, Zahara?" Mac asks, a bit too calmly for my liking.

She shifts her weight and grabs a tighter hold around Liv's neck. "What I want is to rewind time, kill Declan when I had the chance, and get out of here with my formula, leaving you nitwits behind. We know I'm not going to get that. Here's my compromise. I'm sure Declan would gladly trade his life for Dr. Marcel's. Then he and I can go to her office and get the zip drive with the formula. I'll need a helicopter on the roof in ten minutes where I will release Declan."

"If you hadn't drugged and half-starved him, that would be an option. I doubt you're able to carry a two-hundred-pound man. Your plan will not happen unless I go with him," Campbell counters.

Mac hits his comm. "We need a heli on the roof in ten, but not one minute before."

His request means he's waving off the heli until the time is right. Out the windows, in the distance behind Zahara, I can see the heli, but something is not adding up. How did they get a heli here this fast?

Z's control slips as she swears under her breath. "Okay,

you can come over here with Declan, and I'll give you Dr. Marcel. Unload every one of your weapons and put them on the floor. Move slowly, or I'll blow her brains out."

Campbell lays down his gun with his other weapons and puts his hands in the air. She nods in acceptance.

He lifts me up under his shoulder as I lean on him. I take a few steps but falter and stop, stalling for time. We're halfway to them when we stop and look up at the sound of the heli landing on the roof.

"Hurry up. Move it." Zahara panics.

Mac taps his comm again and says loud enough for her to hear him. "We have a present for you to pick up, plus an extra passenger. The passenger will give you specific directions on where to go."

The word present means there's something wrong. We always use the word package.

Zahara points to Dean. "You." She waves her weapon. "Go down to Dr. Marcel's office and retrieve the zip drive now. We'll meet you on the roof. Move."

Liv calls out. "Look in the top right drawer." Her hands hang onto Zahara's arm.

I make it to Z and take Liv's place. Relief comes over me when she is out of danger. Liv's face is red, and there's a mark around her neck. Zahara will pay for that and a lot more. Liv turns back to Z and says, "Never interrupt your enemy when she is making a mistake."

That's my woman. Wait, what? I think I'm still delirious. I know it's a quote, but I can't recall who's, and I'll never let her know. I don't want to lose the challenge. I must be somewhat coherent to even be thinking about our duel of quotes.

We shuffle to the stairwell as Campbell holds me up and

Zahara has the butt of her weapon to my head on the other side. We make it to the top of the stairs and push the door to get out onto the roof.

The rotation of the blades slows down on the heli, and someone is sitting in the pilot's seat. We take two steps toward the heli, and Campbell falls away from me. There's a blur to my other side as Beck puts a gun to Z's head.

"Let him go, or there's a bullet with your brain matter on it," Beck booms over the noise of the heli.

She lets me go as I fall into Campbell and puts her hands in the air, still holding her gun. Her ego won't let her die on a rooftop in the middle of Germany. She'll go down fighting, resisting interrogation.

Beck takes her weapon. "I should kill you for what you put the two of us through, but living the rest of your life in a black site cell might be more torture than being dead. You have answers to a lot of questions."

He has a lot more to kill her for than poisoning him. She killed his birth parents by sabotaging their plane in Zambia. Her evil has no bounds.

"What makes you think I'll tell you or anyone else anything?"

He grabs the back of her neck and jerks her toward him. Her eyes grow wide. "We have ways of making you talk you haven't even imagined," he says through gritted teeth.

Mac and Dean burst through the door with their weapons drawn.

Beck turns to me and Campbell. "Let's get you back to home base."

"Where's Liv?" I yell to Beck.

"She'll meet us there. No worries. Frederick and Henri have her."

My adrenaline crashes as they carry me to the heli, load

me up, and strap me in. We lift off and take a sharp turn, due north toward the mountains. I assume we're heading for my cabin. My eyelids are heavy, and I'm fading fast.

Napoleon. That's who she quoted. It's the last thing I remember before I fade to black.

# Chapter Forty-Eight

Olivia

I CAN'T STOP SHAKING and massaging my neck where Zahara had a hold of me. She held my life in her hands.

Fear crept through my veins like a vine, waiting to suffocate me. My body will never forget the terror. I don't want to go back there ever.

What scared me more than anything was how Declan looked. His gaunt face held black circles under his eyes, and his body couldn't hold itself. I don't know what she gave him, but I hope there's a remedy. I've never wished death on anyone, but she would make the top of the list.

Frederick and Henri come and escort me out of the building as quickly as possible before German SWAT, known as GSG 9, show up. They keep asking me if I'm all right, and I keep nodding.

This is an amusement park ride without an end. The adrenaline rush ebbs and flows. I'm never sure where the next peak is or the next valley, but I've hit my bottom. This was my one and only in the spy game.

We leave the van behind and get Declan's G wagon, Gal. I want him to know I took good care of her while he was gone. I bought into the fact that this car is a woman and even had a conversation with her. My mind is scattered, focusing on things that don't matter.

Frederick drives us out to the cabin, where he says we'll meet up with Declan. The cityscape becomes a blur as my mind gets lost in a fog until we drive by the poppy fields, which grab my attention.

Poppy. I have to talk with Declan as soon as he's better. We need to figure out how to tell Poppy her father is Declan. I don't know what her reaction will be after not knowing about him. It's hard to put myself in the shoes of a four-year-old. The trick is going to be how to explain where he's been this entire time.

The climb gets steeper the closer we get to the cabin, but Gal handles the terrain without a problem. The helicopter flies overhead after dropping off Declan and the rest of the team. I can't wait to get out of the car to see him.

Uncle Neil waits for me on the front porch with Poppy. She jumps into my arms and gives me a huge hug, which is exactly what I need. I can hear Ozzie barking on the other side of the door.

"Mommy, you're home."

"I am home and thrilled to see you."

She continues, "Prince Declan is back, too, but Uncle Neil won't let me see him." Tears well in her eyes.

I kiss her on the forehead and wipe away her tears. "That's probably a good idea. He hasn't been feeling well and needs some rest. Maybe one of the princes will play hide-and-seek with you. We'll let you see him as soon as he's feeling better. I'm sure he misses you terribly and will be very happy to see you."

"Okay." She is not convinced but slides down my body and out of my arms, scurrying inside to find someone to play with her.

As soon as Poppy is inside, my uncle turns to me. "I need you to go easy." There are those words again. "Declan is in terrible shape. We don't know how much of the memory drug she gave him. SWAT rescued the others being held, and they are receiving medical attention at a military hospital. We need to keep this out of the news. The German government will spin it to suit everyone's needs. Beck has Katoo here to help Declan recover."

I frown at him. "Who's Katoo?"

"He's an elder from Zambia who helped Beck recover from the memory drug Zahara gave him. He brought herbs and other things from his garden to counteract the drug. Part of the drug has a plant called panther's claw. This is more your area than mine." He stops to look at me. "I heard things got rough in there. Are you okay?"

"You'll be happy to know I don't want to become an MI6 agent, ever. The science lab is the only place for me for the rest of my life. Thank you for everything today. Your team was amazing." I hug him, then push past him, not wanting to talk about my near-death experience anymore. "I'll be interested to see what Katoo has to help Declan."

A man draped in black and red fabric stands in the middle of the kitchen. He has a presence about him that demands respect. He's chopping something on a wooden board, and the smell of rice and chicken permeates the air.

I reach out my hand to him. "I'm Dr. Olivia Marcel. It's nice to meet you. I hear you have some natural remedies to help Declan get better. I would love to be a part of his recovery."

He nods and goes on to explain the herbs Zahara used

with other drugs to create the memory drug. Herbs from his garden will counteract the effects of parts of the memory drug as well as clean the liver. I'm fascinated by the use of natural ingredients to flush out Declan's system, hopefully restoring his memory.

"Why don't you take this up to him? There's a very regimented schedule for the first couple of days between the meals and herbs. He will need to drink a lot of water in the first twenty-four hours." Katoo hands me a tray filled with food, a huge pitcher of water, and other things.

My legs move me step by step up the stairs to his room. The entire experience has left me with frayed nerves after worrying about him. I don't know what to expect or the effect the drug has had on him. Did he lose more of his memories? I know he recognizes me, but from what time period?

I inch open the door with my foot. The room is cast in darkness. The light from the hallway shines on him, and I realize he's hooked up to a saline IV. His eyes are closed, and his breathing is even, letting me know he's asleep. I set the tray down next to him, and his eyes open. His skin is flushed, and his clothes are damp from sweat.

"Hi," I greet him.

"Hey." His eyes are weary and unfocused.

"I brought you the food you need to eat with herbs put together by someone named Katoo." I test his memory, knowing he was in Zambia and probably met Katoo.

He hums. "Katoo is a fine man. He helped Beck get better. I trust him." He pushes himself up so he can eat. "I know you're worried I don't remember things, Liv, but you're impossible to forget." He gives me a weak smile.

I let out the breath I've been holding. "You can't blame me for wondering after everything you've been through."

"It's been an interesting couple of days. She had at least

fifty soldiers she was using as guinea pigs. I have no idea what condition they're in."

"They've been taken to a military hospital for a full evaluation."

"What about Paul Ritcher?"

"I assume he went there as well, but my uncle didn't mention him by name."

His shoulders fall. "I was patient zero, which explains what seemed like retrograde amnesia. She used the memory drug on me when I was recovering from the burns. She confirmed there's a mole in MI6, but she wouldn't reveal her source."

Words escape me at this moment. Her actions are incomprehensible to me. How did she even know... then I remembered what she said to me.

"She was the one who rigged the hazmat suit and set you on fire." My words tumble out.

Tears crest, threatening to fall from my lashes. The events surrounding not only his burns but his exposure to the memory drug come crashing down around me. I wipe the tears from my cheeks. He doesn't need my tears. He needs my help.

He continues, "After everything, it looks as though she has a formula that isn't going to be worth anything. I got some of my memories back from the time right before my accident with bits and pieces from the last five years. Her memory drug had the opposite effect. This could be a breakthrough for people suffering with amnesia."

He looks at me through hard, unforgiving eyes. I know what's coming, but I don't want to face it now. He has put two and two together.

"How about you focus on getting these herbs into your body and healing? We can talk about this later. No one's going anywhere. We're staying here until you get better. I promise."

"Trust me, I'm not letting you off the hook, but I need my energy back to have this conversation."

I help him eat and change his clothes, wiping the sweat from his body so he feels fresher. It's the least I can do, considering the bombshell I'm about to unleash.

# Chapter Forty-Nine

Declan

I WAKE up gasping for air. A collection of memories floods my mind, jumbled together. Some of them I would like to forget forever, and others bring me happiness. I sit up, and dizziness hits me, followed by a wave of nausea.

Liv has set up an air mattress on the floor beside me. She's been up every four hours to give me water and herbs. Her eyes flutter open. They're dark, puffy, and tired.

"What's wrong? Are you okay?" She leans on her elbow.

She is by my side before I answer her. My emotions are mixed with thankfulness, disappointment, and anger.

"I'm fine, just disoriented. The last couple of days have been rough. Memories keep coming to me in streams."

"I can imagine. Do you need Compazine?"

"Yes."

She hands me the pill, and I wash it down. A voice comes from behind the door. Our heads turn in sync.

"Mommy, can I see Prince Declan now?" she says in French, her comfort language.

Liv looks at me for an answer. I shake my head. I'm not ready, and I don't want her to see me like this.

She goes to the door and opens it enough to slip through into the hallway, leaving the door ajar.

"Not yet. Declan is still tired and not feeling well. His belly is upset. Maybe tomorrow, sweetheart." Liv's motherly intuition kicks in as she responds to her in French.

"Maybe I can help him feel better."

"You are so thoughtful and kind. He needs medicine and rest. He'll be feeling better in no time. You go ahead to the kitchen for breakfast, and I'll be down in a minute."

"Do you think Prince Declan will make my favorite pancakes?"

I close my eyes and visualize Poppy giving her mum a pouty face as her red hair falls on her cheeks.

"Of course, he'll make your favorite pancakes when he feels better. He loves to make those for you."

I listen to their exchange, and my heart weeps. Poppy brings so much joy to my life, and it kills me not to see her. I want to hold her and tell her she's mine. I've got four years to make up for it.

Liv enters our dark cavern and shuts the door. Silence swallows the emotions swirling around us. To her credit, she doesn't run from me but moves toward me.

"I guess you heard us," she says, barely above a whisper. When I don't answer, she offers a way to ease the heaviness. "Do you want me to open the drapes?"

"No. Darkness is my companion. I've grown used to it. My team calls me the Dark Lord for a reason." I slide back into my mode of self-pity and withdraw. A life without light is a safe place for me.

She can fill in the words I want to say. *Poppy is mine, and you never thought to tell me.*

I peel the tape off covering the IV insert and carefully pull out the line.

"What are you doing?" Liv asks, alarmed.

"I need to get back to normal. I have pancakes to make. Can you help me into the shower?" My words scream ambivalence.

"Sure." She doesn't look at me.

I swing my legs over the side of the bed, and a dizzy spell hits me. Breathing out through my mouth quells the nausea and centers me. The pill hasn't kicked in yet. I wave her over and use her shoulders to stand up. My legs are weak, but I'm able to stand on my own. She walks next to me as we make our way to the bathroom.

"I got it from here." I close the door without a glance.

"I'll be right here if you need anything." Her voice is muffled through the door.

The woman is hell-bent on breaking me. She hasn't faltered in her dedication to my health and well-being, but I won't go easy on her.

I strip out of my clothes. Being naked is a relief. A shower is welcome to wash away the smell of being held against my will. Damn it. My cock is like a heat-seeking missile straight to Liv. I want to be angry, but my body reminds me of how much I want and need her and how good it felt to be inside her.

Not today, buddy. She and I have some things to work out. I can't wait to hear the reasons she didn't tell me about Poppy. There are no excuses, and she had more than enough chances to tell me. I need to be open to what Liv says, but a host of other emotions get in the way.

The dirtiness of being medically induced and the antiseptic smell swirl down the drain. Hot water streams down my back as I let it warm my rigid body, loosening my muscles.

There's something about water that heals whatever ails me. The calm seeps into me and, in a weird way, grounds me. I miss swimming and as soon as I feel better, I'm going to take my daughter for a swim. *My daughter.*

I step out of the shower and wrap a towel around my waist. Liv is lying on the bed, fast asleep. I sit on the edge of the bed. My fingertips brush down her cheek, moving the hair away from her face. The connection is like a bolt of lightning through my body and my cock wakes up again.

"Damn it," I mutter under my breath.

She wakes up, startled at my closeness. Her eyes peruse my body as her fingers close in a fist, keeping her from touching me.

"You've seen it before. No big deal." My words are bitter.

"Stop being an asshole." I deserve that.

She rolls to the other side of the bed and stands up. "You look a lot better today. I'm going to get your meal, herbs, and more water. I'll be right back."

"I have a right to be angry."

"You do. Remember, you haven't walked in my shoes." Her shoulders fall as she shuts the door behind her.

Weakness takes over, and I lie on the bed. We've been traveling different paths of pain for different reasons. We need to find a middle ground for Poppy's sake.

I've been alone for so long, only having to worry about myself, and now I have an insta-family. It's one thing to look forward to a family in the future and another to be dropped in the middle of it.

Light streaks from the hallway as a man's silhouette enters my room. I would recognize his body frame anywhere. Mac walks over to the drapes and rips them open.

"Hey, what the hell are you doing?" I protest.

"You need the light to illuminate your dark soul."

"Fuck you. Maybe I like the darkness."

He ignores me. "You are one of the most insightful people I know, except when it comes to someone you think has done you wrong. She has been worried sick about you and hasn't left your side since you've been here."

"Do you know—"

"Yes, I know. Poppy's your daughter. She told us before we got to you."

"That's fucking fantastic. She tells you before she tells me."

"Declan, put yourself in her shoes. She never saw you again after you disappeared and didn't know how to find you. You were a big player back then, so a roll in the hay and you splitting wasn't out of character. Even if she found you, she probably thought you wouldn't be willing to bring up a child."

"What?! Of course, I would want Poppy in my life."

"You're saying that as you are now, not like you were back then. You've been through some heavy shit. While you've been globe-trotting and working on your recovery program, she's been bringing up Poppy on her own, thinking she would never see you again. Imagine her surprise when you showed up out of nowhere."

"Okay, so that's one point for you." He doesn't know the half of it. I'll save my horror story for later.

"That's ten points for me, and if you don't get your shit together, I'm going to kick your ass as soon as you're better. Listen to what she has to say."

"God, it's good to be home. Some things never change. What's up with Z?"

He shrugs. "She's not talking. She is one tough woman. I'll let you get some rest."

"Good talk. Thanks."

"Anytime."

"When did you get to be so wise?"

"Finding a strong woman who has your back will do that for you. Also, having a child changes how you see everything." Mac's face lights up. "Get some rest."

I don't shut the drapes. Maybe I need to let the light in and shed the Dark Lord for good. Poppy is my reason to live my best life. I lie back and let the darkness take me, wishing for light and sweet dreams.

## Chapter Fifty

Olivia

I CREATE space between Declan and me by entering his room only to give him his meals and herbs. I admire his resilience. He seems to get stronger with each meal and herbal dose. Katoo says he doesn't need the night feedings anymore, giving me a chance to sleep in my bed with Poppy.

She asks about Declan several times to make sure he's okay and when she can see him. Children are intuitive creatures. She's bonded with someone who shares her blood, among other traits.

After a bedtime story involving a princess and a prince, she falls asleep, and I'm not far behind, with Ozzie snoring at the foot of the bed. I won't burst her bubble that happy endings with princes don't exist, which brings my thoughts back to her prince.

I can't help but worry about where things are going to go with Declan. If he got some of his memories back, I imagine he may remember our night together five years ago and maybe has put two and two together about Poppy.

Dreamless sleep takes me, and I wake to an empty bed. I throw on some sweats and go in search of my daughter, our daughter. This will take some getting used to. I'm reluctant to share her with someone else. I've had her to myself for so many years.

I search the entire house, including the kitchen, where the team has gathered for coffee, tea, and breakfast. They say they haven't seen her, and I panic. Everyone searches for her inside and out. Ozzie looks up from chewing on his bone.

I crouch down next to him and rub behind his ears. "Hey, buddy, where's Poppy?"

He stands up, walks to the stairs, and looks at me like I'm supposed to follow him. He runs up the stairs to Declan's room and scratches at the door. I tell him to stay and crack open the door.

Declan is sprawled out with his arms to the side. A small bundle huddles next to him with red hair peeking out from the sheets. He wakes up and puts his finger to his lips to be quiet. He's wearing sweats with no shirt.

He comes into the hall and pulls the door closed to a crack. Ozzie jumps on him and whines. They greet each other as old friends. Declan has infiltrated every part of my life.

I cross my arms in front of me. "We've been looking everywhere for her."

"She snuck into bed with me last night and said I shouldn't be alone while I'm getting better. She said Mommy never leaves her alone when she's sick. I could not kick her out. Besides, she was determined to stay. Her determination reminds me of someone."

Poppy can be stubborn without budging. I nod in agreement and see a crack in his facade. I tell Ozzie to go get his bone. This moment is for the two of us.

Declan's face reveals nothing. "We need to talk."

I walk to the top of the stairs and tell the guys I found her.

He guides me to my bedroom, shuts the door, and locks it. We're not going anywhere until we resolve what's between us. He sits on the edge of the bed.

"This has taken a lot out of me, but nothing compared to when Z told me I have a daughter. I'm going to hand it over to you so you can explain why you never told me. I shouldn't have found out from the Queen of Poison. Oh, and by the way, Mac informed me I need to, in your words, stop being an asshole."

"How in the world did she know?" I'm stunned.

"She said she keeps a close watch on her employees."

I have screwed this up royally. He shouldn't have found out from her. "First, I tried to tell you before we went up to the eighth floor, but you sounded like you already knew, which I thought was odd." I play with the ends of my hair.

"You took your sweet time letting me know I have a four-year-old daughter. I heard you and your mom talking, and I thought you were going to tell me more about my past, which could wait. You're not off the hook." He sits with his back against the headboard and folds his hands in his lap.

"We had one night together five years ago."

He wiggles his brows. "I remember after she gave me the drug. I thought it was a dream at first, but then I remembered it the next morning and the accident. It was quite a night, including a broken condom."

"I didn't know. I'm sorry something so great was followed by something so awful. To say that night changed my life forever would be an understatement." Here goes nothing. "The connection we had for one night was like nothing I had ever encountered and never came across again, but the next day, you were gone. I expected it with your track record. I didn't know I was pregnant for another eight weeks. There was no way to find you. It's as if you didn't exist. Believe me, I tried to find you. She has your name, Craig."

He scrubs his face with his hands. "You couldn't find me because my last name is Creighton, not Craig. I was undercover. At least you know why I disappeared. It still doesn't explain why you didn't tell me as soon as I returned."

"What did you want me to do, throw myself in your arms and thank you for coming back?" I rest the back of my hand on my forehead. "Oh, Declan, thank God you're here. Everything will be all right now." I put my hands on my hips. "I didn't know if you were going to stay or go or who you had become. You weren't supposed to meet Poppy the way you did. You don't have a right to judge me. I'm a single mom trying to bring up a daughter in a crazy world without a father."

"Well…" he begins.

"Don't interrupt me. I'm on a roll. I'm in love with you, the man you are now. We've both changed so much. Maybe we needed to go our separate ways to come together. I want you in my life and Poppy's life. I'm sorry you had to find out this way, but I had no control over it."

He slides down to the end of the bed. "Come here."

I stand in between his legs. He pulls up my shirt and pulls down my sweats around the middle of my hips. His finger traces my stretch marks.

"We made a life that night, and I wasn't here for either of you. I wanted to see both of you grow and feel her kick and move in your belly. I wanted to be a part of her first steps, first words, and first giggle. I'm never going to get that back. Along with a lot of other stuff." He peppers my stomach with kisses.

Tears run down my face. This man is going to be the end of me, but what a sweet ending.

He looks up at me. "How are we going to tell her?"

"She already adores you. It won't be a stretch for her to accept you as her father."

"I don't mean that. How are we going to tell her I'm her king and not a prince?"

I throw my head back and laugh, but he's dead serious. I think he might be right.

"When's her birthday?"

"July twenty-second."

"Mark your calendar because we're having the biggest birthday party ever."

Our heads turn at the knock on the door as the handle rattles.

"Mommy, Mommy, I can't find Prince Declan." She sobs, "He can't be gone again."

Declan grabs the door, unlocks the bolt, and whips it open. He kneels and opens his arms to her.

"I'm right here, sweetheart." He rubs her back.

She lays her head on his shoulder and doesn't acknowledge me. "That's good because you need to make me your special pancakes."

"You're right. I do." He looks at me for guidance on our next steps.

"Poppy, Declan and I need to talk to you about something. Why don't you go sit on the bed?"

"But, Mommy, I had to go to Prince Declan's room. He needed someone to help make him feel better, like you do for me." Her bottom lip quivers.

"You did the right thing. You are the perfect person to make him feel better." I glance over at Declan. "We need to talk to you about something else."

Declan and I sit near the headboard as Poppy sits at the foot of the bed.

"You've been asking me about your father a lot lately, and I told you I didn't know where he was. The good news is I found him."

Her eyes get wide, and she's on her knees. "You did? Where is he?"

"He's right here. Your father is Declan."

She crosses her arms. "That's not funny."

I pull her into my lap. "I'm not being funny. It's true. I had to be sure he was the real Prince Declan."

Declan tries to convince her. "We have a lot in common. We both speak many languages, and you have red hair like your aunt Kendall did when she was little. I'm so happy to be your father. I'm the luckiest man in the world. But, Poppy, there's some bad news."

She nods and folds her hands together under her chin.

"I'm not a prince. I'm a king."

"Am I still a princess?" Her head pops up.

"Yes, and Mommy is a queen." He tickles her as she squirms out of my lap and giggles. She crawls into his lap, and her tiny hand covers his poppy tattoo.

"Mommy said her favorite flowers are poppies. I guess they're your favorite too."

Declan looks over at me, knowing why I named her Poppy. "They are, but now you're my favorite poppy." He kisses the top of her head with the most tenderness I've ever seen.

"King Declan, can you make me pancakes? I'm hungry." She stands up and kisses him on the cheek. "I'm happy you're my daddy." She jumps off the bed and runs out of the room.

Declan pulls me into his lap. "Queen Creighton. It has a

nice ring to it. What do you say you go back to the States with me? I'm also going to need another one of those. This time, I'm going for a prince."

## Chapter Fifty-One

Declan

"You need to slow down, cowboy. Poppy took the news a little too well. There will be fallout later, we'll have to deal with it together. She might throw in anger and resentment for good measure along the way. Bringing up a child is not rainbows and horseshoes." Liv lists the finer points of being a parent. She is almost five years ahead of me in real parenting experience.

"How is an almost five-year-old supposed to take that kind of news? I would imagine it's overwhelming. I thought she did quite well with me going from prince to king, though." I grin.

I flip her on her back and hold her arms above her head. She squirms underneath me, which makes my hard-on turn to steel.

"We have some catching up to do." I push my knees between her legs and grind down so she knows exactly how my strength has come back.

"Ordinarily, I would be on board with counting the ways

you can make me come. However, your daughter is waiting for pancakes." She smiles.

Her words sink into my chest, past my breastbone, and make a beeline for my heart. "Say it again."

"Pancakes." She giggles.

"Say it, or I'll wrestle you, and this time, it won't be so easy to explain it to Poppy," I tease.

"Your daughter."

"I'm not going to need time to get used to having a daughter." I kiss her forehead, making my way down her face and neck.

"Aristotle," she whispers as her breath catches on her words.

"What?" I question, even though I know exactly what she's talking about.

"Love is composed of a single soul inhabiting two bodies."

Her legs grab my waist as she thrusts upward, which feels great, as she turns me onto my back.

She double-fists pumps. "I win!"

The single soul we created is the best thing that's happened to me since Liv. I kiss her with passion and commitment. I want to be here for both of them. Our tongues play with each other and fight for control. She might have won the quote game, but I won her and Poppy.

The door flies open, and Poppy steps in. "Mommy, Daddy, you need to hurry. I'm hungry."

"She called me Daddy." I'm giddy with joy. "Looks like we'll be spending a lot of money on food. My little girl is hungry all the time."

Liv nods. I throw her to the side. "I'm coming right now, princess."

"I see how this is going to go. Just remember who holds your happy ending."

I smile over my shoulder and slowly make it down the stairs. Liv is right behind me in case I need her.

Mac, Campbell, Beck, Sean, and Dean sit around the island drinking their tea or coffee.

Campbell looks up. "We tried to tell her we could make her breakfast, but she insisted her Daddy make her special pancakes. Mac and I introduced ourselves as her uncles. It didn't hold much excitement for her."

My grin is so big it hurts my cheeks. "That's right. The princess has one king, and you are the paupers."

"There's one true king here, and I think we all know who that is," Beck pipes in from the other side of the island. He's not wrong. He was in line to be king of a tribe in Zambia but gave it up to his sister. "Besides, I'm sure I can throw her higher in the air than you."

"Oh, really?" He's thrown down the gauntlet.

Liv steps up. "No, thank you. No one will be throwing her in the air. I thought I was going to have heart failure the other day. Let's eat for now."

I make pancakes for Poppy and then need to sit down. Fatigue sets in quicker than I'm used to. Bouncing back requires more time as I age.

Campbell takes over for me at the stove, and Poppy eats until she's ready to explode.

Neil calls me into the dining room for a debriefing. Part of me doesn't want to hear about Z or the drug or anything having to do with this mission. I want to talk to Liv about our plans.

"How are you feeling?" His question is unexpected. He's usually just business.

"I'm getting there, but this took a lot out of me. Navigating the past with the present was mind-boggling. Z's drug works in the opposite way. I regained some of my memories from five years ago. She is curbing the side effects with other drugs to make it seem like she's minimized their effect. Z revealed there is a mole inside MI6 who was involved in my 'accident'. We need to find the mole and stay under the radar."

He nods as if he has some insider information on the mole. "This is a very tight-knit unit. No one else at MI6 knows we're working on this op. As you may remember, she didn't get the cancer-causing drug off the ground either, thank God. I can't say I'm sorry about her current situation. No one will hear from her, not even Deep 8. I worry that we're on their radar. They must be putting two and two together. By the way, we exchanged artillery with gunmen at your cabin. It needs some repairs." He sits back in his chair and twirls his teacup. This is the most relaxed I've ever seen him.

"You had a shootout without me? How disappointing. I always love to get fired up with weapons."

"You had enough on your plate. We've got our next lead on Deep 8, and this one is a real winner. I'll brief the team when we get back to New York. There are some new players in this game. I'm not sure how the team is going to react."

I focus on my coffee cup, preparing myself for what I want to say.

"I need a favor."

"Anything," he says without hesitation.

"I need to change the name on Poppy's birth certificate from Craig to Creighton."

"Already done."

"What are you talking about? How?" I'm flabbergasted.

"Margot suspected Liv was pregnant with your child. After she was born, I ran a DNA test and then changed the name on her birth certificate. Your first question is going to be why didn't I tell you? My answer is that you were in no condition to handle a child. Besides, this is between you and Liv. Both of you would get there eventually."

On some level, he's right. The last five years have been scrambled. Nothing has jelled, and my life was a mess. Timing is everything, and there was no way I would have been ready for any of this. My head is in a different space, one that sees the future with eyes wide open.

"I'm too tired to fight with you, and you're probably right. Fate has her way with everyone. I won't let you down when it comes to their well-being and safety."

"I never doubted you. It's time for me to think about my future and get out of the business. Maybe after this next assignment. Sean has offered me a spot on the team, but I'm not sure I want to take it."

His words ring true with me. I don't see myself leaving the security firm yet. I have more to do and an appetite for wanting to take Deep 8 down to the ground. First, I have to convince Liv that she and I should be together, in the same place.

# Epilogue

### Declan

WE STAY at the cabin for a few more days until I am stronger. I can't wait to make love to Liv again. This time will feel different, closer, more intimate. In the words of Dean Karnazes, "You have to go through hell to get to heaven." I've been there one too many times. My punch card is full. This time, I'm holding onto heaven.

Liv comes out of the bathroom in a blue silk robe. The robe slides off her shoulders, revealing my gift of her gorgeous body adorn in pink lace lingerie. She's almost to the edge of the bed when Poppy bounces in our room with her two furballs in tow. My plans to get frisky with her tonight are blown to hell. I smile at the irony of my life.

Liv gets under the covers, holds my face in her hands, and says, "Welcome to parenthood."

"I wouldn't want it any other way." I smile.

Poppy jumps in our bed, kisses each of us, and falls asleep. Ozzie and Prince make themselves comfortable at the foot of the bed. I will never be able to resist having my daughter close to me as I watch her sleep.

I nudge Liv's arm and point to the door. We slide out of bed and tiptoe downstairs. The kitchen is our designated area for important conversations coupled with great coffee.

I sit on the stool and pull her in between my legs. My hands snake under her robe as I caress the curves of her body. I nip her earlobe and pepper her neck with tender kisses.

"We need to talk about our plans for the future."

"I can't focus when you're distracting me," she says in a husky voice, doing nothing to abate my hard-on.

"Agents have to focus under physical assault."

She steps back. "That was a one and done."

"I guess you didn't get the memo. I got rid of the one-and-done philosophy. It wasn't good for morale or my forever plans."

She gives me the smile I'm hanging my hopes on.

"I have a proposal. We both need jobs. If we go to the States, I can continue to work for MBK, and you can find a job in pharma somewhere in New York or New Jersey. They are loaded with pharmaceutical companies, big and small, and would jump at the chance to hire you. You won't have to worry about your contract because Bio2Chem is getting shut down." I take her hands in mine. "Poppy will get one of the finest educations in the world, and we can be together as a family."

She has a ghost of a smile on her lips. "What about my mom?"

"It looks like Neil is going to keep her busy here on the farm. They are very cozy." I wiggle my brows. "I'm keeping my cabin so we can come back and visit whenever you want. Cologne was my nightmare, but I found the most beautiful parts of my life lived here, which I didn't even know about, thanks to you and Poppy."

She kisses me. "I think you have put some thought into this, and it's a solid plan. Things might be rough for Poppy. This is the only home she's ever known."

"We have a resilient little girl. I think she'll do fine with our help."

She has a worried look on her face. "I'm going to have to pack up our stuff, so I'll meet you in New York City."

"Nope. I asked Sean if I could stay here and help you. I want all our firsts together. We're a team now, including Ozzie and Prince. We need to get a bigger place for all of us."

"Team Creighton."

"That's King Creighton, how quickly you forget." I get a smack on the shoulder.

I grab her ass and pull her to me, ravaging her mouth as my hands go back to roaming over familiar territory that will never get old. She moans, which revs me into high gear, but I put the brakes on for my surprise.

"I hate to wreck the mood, but we need to celebrate with my special decaf. Tonight, I'm going to show you how to make it. Can you get the grounds down from the cabinet?"

She reaches up and grabs the glass jar from the top shelf.

"I need you to open it and put one scoop into the French press." I want to smile, but I'm afraid I'll give it away. Margot helped me pull this off.

She reaches into the container and pulls out a black velvet box. "What's this?" Her cheeks turn rosy, and her lips curve up on one side.

"I have no idea. Why don't you open it and find out?"

She opens the box and gasps.

I kneel on both knees and grab her around the waist. "You are my sun in the morning and my stars at night. I don't just need you, but I want you and Poppy in my life. I never thought about forever with anyone because it meant I had to let someone know the real me, scars and all. My freedom was at stake, but freedom comes from the inside with emotions I've never felt until I met the two of you. Yes, I was stupid and immature years ago, but I'm a different person because of you. Will you be my queen?"

Tears stream down her face as she pushes the box toward me with shaky hands. I slip the princess cut diamond with aquamarine baguettes on her finger. The diamond had to be princess cut, and the aquamarine reminds me of her eyes. I stand up and hold her to me.

She wipes her tears away. "I knew I would never love anyone as much as I love you. We had a rocky start fighting the attraction. The best part is that Poppy gets to be with her father. You are an amazing man."

"I love you because the entire universe conspired to help me find you."

"Are you giving me a quote?"

"Yep."

She shakes her head. "I don't know who said it."

"Paulo Coelho, the author of *The Alchemist*. I win."

"We both win."

### Campbell

We're back in New York City, being briefed by Neil about our next assignment. Each mission uncovers another clue about Deep 8.

No one knows who they are or what their end goal is for their new world order. Hell, we can't even tie the pieces together.

"The U.S. government at the highest level has asked for

our help. We have more contact and have more insight into Deep 8's inner workings than anyone else in the world." Neil's words are tentative.

Mac speaks up, "Can you confirm who is the highest level of the U.S. government we will be dealing with?"

Neil shifts in his chair. "POTUS, The President of the United States. He put together a task force called PAXOPS, PAX for short, the Roman god of peace. This team will have direct contact with the president's Chief of Staff as well as the Secretary of State and Secretary of Defense. This group will go dark; no one outside the unit will know about the operation, and we'll add SPECOPS as needed from inside the U.S. military."

We're given time to digest what is being asked of us. The group around the table includes Mac, Declan, Sean, Beck, Dean, Pippa, and me. Somewhere along the way, we're going to need major backup. Mac looks at Sean and Dean, who in turn share a look with the rest of us that asks, "Do we want to do this?"

"Hell yeah, we're in," Sean speaks for the group.

The rest of us smile, looking forward to crushing evil. Deep 8 has done damage, and some of us are out for revenge.

Neil nods. "So far, we have a new mineral they can't get to and a drug that isn't fully developed. We shut down their diamond operation in Zambia, but every time we cut off one tentacle, another one grows. The mission we're about to—"

The emergency ringer goes off on my phone as well as Mac's and Declan's. Few people have this ringtone. Quinn Donovan, an old childhood friend, is one of them. I haven't seen or heard from her in years, so this phone call sets me on edge. Mac nods for me to answer.

"Quinn, what's going on?" I bring her up on a video call.

She fades to black and then comes back up. "Cam, can you hear me?"

Neil motions for me to put the call up on the Promethean board so everyone can see what's going on.

"Yeah, we can hear you. You're in and out."

"Liam has been working on a high-level government operation, but he's gone missing." Her screen freezes. Liam is Quinn's older brother.

When she's live again, she looks around as if waiting for someone to come and get her. I don't recognize her location.

"I'm in… looking… underground…. AI…. nukes…. America." We're getting every other word, and nothing makes sense. Her face freezes again.

My heart rate kicks up, and sweat beads on my forehead. "You're breaking up. I don't know what you're trying to say."

"Find Liam. He holds the key. It… too late… me. My computer…. treehouse."

We watch as two men come into the frame wearing silver masks over their faces, resembling androids. They put a bag over her head, snatch her up under her arms, and turn off the camera.

"Quinn!" I stand up and yell as if it will change what happens to her.

"I have it recorded so we can analyze it later." I hear Neil say, but I don't acknowledge him.

I look to my brothers for some clarity, but they have none as pain crosses their faces.

Neil twirls his thumbs. "Looks like you have your next assignment. This time, it's going to take the entire team."

"You knew this was coming." I raise my voice to pin him for an answer.

"Yes and no. We have a nuclear problem, but we don't

know who the players are yet. Dr. Liam Donovan is at the center of it, but Quinn is working on the other end of it. They sent a special ops team to get her out, but they didn't make it in time. Her brother disappeared about a week ago without a trace. This op gets top priority because their research is vital to global security. We'll meet with the president and his team at oh eight hundred tomorrow and be out by the afternoon. Campbell, I'm making you the point man, considering how close you are with her brother."

I'm in panic mode. My hearing shuts off, and my mind travels back to the time when I first met Liam. We were six years old and inseparable from then on. He introduced me to his sister Quinn, a three-year-old in pigtails.

As we got older, she always wanted to hang out with us when we were conducting some sort of science experiment. Her insights for improvement to help our results indicated her intelligence was superior.

The three of us grew close over the years, and I consider them family. Now, I'm left with the thought I may never see them again. Whoever took them better brace themselves because we are coming for them.

The room gets quiet, and eyes are on me. The expressions on everyone's faces reveal sadness but also anger.

I stand up and slam my fist on the table. "If Deep 8 is behind this, I hope they know who they're dealing with because this is war. Revenge will look like a walk in the park."

---

*The greatest danger is the one you don't see coming.*

CAN Campbell get to Quinn in time or has a nuclear war been set in motion? Want to know more about MBK's adventures and Deep 8's conspiracy? Grab your copy of RISK in the Deep 8 series now!

# FREE BOOK

I love staying in touch with my readers.
Sign up for my newsletter for updates, giveaways, and other
exclusives, and receive **Silent Night** for **FREE** at

https://bit.ly/FREEKenzie

**She must save her brother. He only sees her betrayal. Will
they find love or fall prey to a deadly rescue plan?**

Silent Night introduces you to the entire MBK Global
Security team. If you like page-turning action, steamy scenes,
and heart-breaking betrayals, then you'll love this story.

## Please consider leaving a review.

If you enjoyed **BURN,** I would love it if you let your friends know so they can experience the action-packed and suspense filled story of Declan and Olivia.

Reviews are so precious to writers. Writing a review helps other readers find my books and is helpful when deciding what to read next.
If you have a minute, please leave a review. Thank you in advance for taking the time to help others find BURN.

## Also by Kenzie Macallan

### The MBK Global Security

### Truths

### (Mac & Marbella's story)

Mara is hiding a terrible secret. He's on a dangerous mission. Can Mac protect the love of his life from a ruthless killer?

### Secrets- a novella

She wants him to leave. He's investigating his brother. When the Russians close in, will they make it or head for heartbreak?

### Edges

### (Dean & Leigha's story)

Leigha is under threat. Dean is undercover. Will deadly family secrets ruin the romance of a lifetime?

### Masks

### (Michael & Raquelle's story)

Raquelle is investigating him. Misha is accused of fraud. Will a sinister conspiracy ruin their shot at unforgettable love?

## Deep 8 series

### Wild

### (Sean & Jess's story)

Jess leaped into a war zone to get the story. Sean will endure hell to bring her home. Sparks fly, but will romance die on the wrong side of a bullet?

### King

### (Beck & Pippa's story)

Pippa is a hacker turned agent. Beck will become king of a diamond empire. Can two unlikely lovers survive a sinister conspiracy?

### Risk

### (Campbell & Quinn's story)

She created a game-changing nuclear weapon. He must keep her safe from a powerful enemy. As embers ignite between them, will their passion lead to an explosive meltdown?

### Torn

### (Roger and Harlow's story)

Harlow is undercover to find her father's killer. Roger must find his father before Deep 8 kills him for the software that will change the world.

# About the Author

Kenzie Macallan is an author who skillfully weaves intricate action-adventure romances as art imitates life. Not really, but her vivid imagination often finds solace within the pages of her books. Having explored the diverse landscapes of Africa, Greece, Switzerland, Holland, France, England, and Scotland, her travels have ignited a relentless wellspring of storytelling.

This fuels her artistic endeavors, from painting captivating portraits to capturing moments through her camera, all while nurturing her green thumb in the garden. While culinary mastery may elude her, she loves to bake, much to the gratitude of her husband.

Kenzie's true passion lies in transporting readers to captivating realms, where flawed yet endearing heroes emerge, intelligent and resilient women take center stage, and unexpected endings leave them in awe. With each new adventure, Kenzie eagerly anticipates the opportunity to further enchant her readers and embark on a shared journey of discovery.

She loves to hear from her fans.
Join her newsletter for cover reveals, new books, deals, and giveaways.
Website: www.kenziemacallan.com

# Acknowledgments

I want to thank my husband who has to pull me away from my computer when I've been at it too long. He always gives me his unwavering support. We seemed to have found the right balance even when you interrupt me with TikTok videos. You're amazing!

A huge thank you goes out to the readers who took a chance on me and read this book. If you left a review, I'm forever grateful because they are like diamonds, so hard to find and yet shine brightly. Your support is greatly appreciated. You make this journey worthwhile.

Karen, my editor, I can't do this without you. You find my gaps and mishaps and I get to go back and fill them in. Let's keep this series rolling on the right track.

Thank you to Tiffany Black for this sexy cover. You get the vibe everytime.